WESTERN KELTON
Kelton, Elmer.
The smiling country

THE
SMILING
COUNTRY

Other Books by Elmer Kelton

Barbed Wire
*Bitter Trail**
Shadow of a Star
*Buffalo Wagons**
*Hot Iron**
*The Texas Rifles**
Donovan
*The Pumpkin Rollers**
*Cloudy in the West**

*Available from Forge Books

Elmer Kelton

THE

SMILING

COUNTRY

A Tom Doherty Associates Book

New York

This is a work of fiction. All the characters and events
portrayed in this novel are either fictitious or are used
fictitiously.

THE SMILING COUNTRY

Copyright © 1998 by Elmer Kelton

All rights reserved, including the right to reproduce this
book, or portions thereof, in any form.

This book is printed on acid-free paper.

A Forge Book
Published by Tom Doherty Associates, Inc.
175 Fifth Avenue
New York, NY 10010

Forge® is a registered trademark of Tom Doherty
Associates, Inc.

Library of Congress Cataloging-in-Publication Data

Kelton, Elmer.
    The smiling country   /   Elmer Kelton.—1st ed.
       p.   cm.
    "A Tom Doherty Associates book."
    ISBN 0-312-86471-X (acid-free paper)
    I. Title.
PS3563.A2932S55   1998
813'.54—dc21   98-13571
                                 CIP

Printed in the United States of America

0 9 8 7 6 5 4

To Kindra, Kelby, Tyler, Kourtney,
and Kyle

THE
SMILING
COUNTRY

CHAPTER

1

Hewey Calloway did not know how old he was without stopping to figure, and that distracted his attention from matters of real importance. In his opinion anyone who wasted time worrying about his age had more leisure than was good for him. He had not acknowledged a birthday since he had turned thirty a dozen years ago—or was it fifteen?

In horse years, Biscuit was older than his rider, but the brown gelding was equally indifferent to the passage of time. Any minor concessions to his age were offset by steadiness and a light-reined response to any task Hewey called upon him to perform. He could outguess a cow in nine of ten confrontations and outrun her the other time.

Hewey could not say nearly so much about the green-broke pony on which Skip Harkness picked his way along the rocky mountainside above Limpia Creek. Since Hewey and the freckle-faced kid had left the corrals and chuck wagon camp down on the yucca flat, the colt had stepped high and kept its ears working nervously while it watched for a booger. Any booger would do. It had already pitched twice, once spooking at a jackrabbit skittering through the underbrush, then taking fright at the cry of a disturbed hawk that sought to scare the horsemen away from its nest high in a tree. The two outbursts had been little challenge, for Skip was young and wiry and laughed at every jump.

Hewey respected anyone efficient at his trade, but he worried about this button's long-range prospects. A kid from a blackland farm back in East Texas, Skip had cowboyed a couple of years and learned just enough to be dangerous to himself and everybody around him. Small triumphs tempted him to kick trouble in the ribs when it could just as well have been left asleep. Instead of pulling up on the hackamore rein to stop the pony from pitching on treacherous sloping ground, Skip had encouraged it to buck harder by spurring high in its shoulders and back in the flank. The colt pitched until its sorrel hide glistened with sweat.

Hewey could not bring himself to criticize, for he used to show off too, not all that long ago. He still gloried in a challenge, but he saw no future in suicide. He said, "I've seen broncs that'd throw you so high the hawks'd have to look up to see you."

"Ain't been a bronc throwed me since I was sixteen."

Hewey guessed Skip to be eighteen, no more than nineteen at the outside, with his heart in the right place but his head on backward. "Biscuit would've busted you good when he was a colt. He flattened me several times."

"Was that before or after the War between the States?"

The kid was thumbing Hewey in the ribs about his age and Biscuit's. This was 1910.

"Wasn't nothin' I could do then that I can't still do. I can ride more miles, find more cows and rope more calves . . ."

He quit talking, for Skip's satisfied grin said he had thrown out the bait and Hewey had swallowed it, hook and all. Hewey never understood why some buttons barely weaned from mother's milk took such pleasure in warting their betters. His nephews would never do such a thing, not Cotton or Tommy. They showed respect, even when he knew they disagreed with him. He wished he had one of them here now instead of this reckless kid with more brass than good sense. They could teach Skip something about manners.

If he put his mind to it he could almost feel sorry for the young-ster, born too late to see Texas before the grasping hand of civi-lization reached out and spoiled it. Hewey had ridden across more country than Skip was likely ever to see. He had driven cattle to the Kansas railroad and had broken broncs from the Rio Grande to the Canadian line. He had shipped out to Cuba under Teddy Roosevelt. He had traveled horseback across much of the West before it was parceled out by barbed-wire fences and ribboned with roads for the automobile. Skip would never have that opportunity or even real-ize what he had missed. Hewey Calloway had done it all, yet here he was, still in the prime of life.

He would admit, when he looked into a mirror, that his hair and his whiskers showed about as much gray as brown, but that was a sign of maturity and reliability. If his joints sometimes ached when he threw the blankets aside of a morning, most of the pain faded once he got the muscles working and the blood flowing freely. He was sure he was a better hand now than he had ever been. He would never ask, but he was probably drawing down five or ten dollars a month more than Skip or the other weanlings on this outfit. At least he should be. He could ride anything they could and rope rings around them.

If a genie were to pop out of a whiskey bottle and offer him three wishes, Hewey would give one or two of them back. There wasn't much he would change, beyond tearing down the fences and ditch-ing all the automobiles. Anybody who couldn't get where he was going on horseback or in a wagon was in too much of a hurry.

The kid offered, "You want to ride my bronc a little while, just to keep your hand in?"

"There's no fight left in him now. You've already spurred it out of him." A real hand didn't let some button sweat the rough edges from a bronc and then turn it over to him as if he were too old to do it himself. Hewey *could* still do it himself, any time he wanted to. And he often wanted to, for he still enjoyed a good contest between man and horse.

The J Bar crew was rounding up two-year-old steers to ship to Kansas for summering on Flint Hills grass, but the wagon boss had sent Hewey and Skip to look for a bunch-quitting bull that had fled from yesterday's drive. It had evaded three years' worth of roundups, the branding iron and knife, and had left a long scar across the chest of one unlucky cow pony that had not moved out of its way. The bull had a reputation for being easy to find but hard to catch. The few pursuers it had not outrun, it had outfought, so most local cowboys accorded it an averted gaze. It ranged in one of the narrow, brushy canyons that time and rainfall had carved through the Davis Mountains. Grazing mostly in the dark of the night, it drank from the small and hidden *tinajas,* depressions that eons of runoff water had scoured from flat rock.

The solitary maverick responded to its mother's wily Longhorn blood, which overpowered the gentler influence of its Hereford sire. Old Man Morgan Jenkins was trying to breed the Longhorn blood out of his herd, and this bull was putting its outlaw stamp on too many calves to suit him. Such brush-popping fugitives furnished entertainment to cowboys who loved the chase, like Hewey and Skip, but they were a financial albatross to ranchers and their bankers.

Hewey was bothered a little when Skip was the first to spot their quarry. He knew his own eyes were still sharp enough; he figured Skip just happened to be looking in the right direction at the right time.

Hewey stepped to the ground and tightened Biscuit's cinch so the bull's strength and weight would not pull his saddle down on one side. Skip took no such precaution, and Hewey was not given to offering advice that had not been asked for. If the kid was half as smart as he thought he was, he shouldn't have to be told.

Skip had a way of turning routine into a contest. "Reckon that old horse of yours can catch him?"

"Biscuit'll kick gravel in your eyes."

Skip did not give him the chance. He spurred the bronc and took the lead. Hewey was tempted to overtake and pass him, just to demonstrate that he could, but he decided the trail the bull followed in its hasty retreat was too narrow and treacherous to accommodate two fools. One was enough.

Hewey took his time, loosing the horn string that held his rope. His sun-browned hands were leather-tough, scarred by rope burns and mesquite thorns, the knuckles large except for one knocked down years ago in an encounter much like this one.

The fugitive bull outran Skip into a heavy brush thicket. Skip followed him partway, then stopped in confusion. As Hewey caught up, Skip said, "Can't see him anyplace. Looks like he sprouted wings and flew."

"Outsmarted you is what he did." Hewey listened intently for the sound of popping branches but heard none. "He's laid down in some thick brush where you can't see him. Let's go root him out." He motioned for Skip to take the left side of the draw. Hewey moved up the right, weaving around the mesquite and catclaw.

Though he was watching closely, the bull almost took him unawares. He heard a snort; then a black apparition exploded out of a tangle of mesquite, head down and sharp horns coming straight at Biscuit. The horse whirled so quickly that Hewey had to grab the saddle horn to keep his seat. The bull made a thrust at Biscuit's haunches as it passed, but the horse was an old hand at avoiding such calamities.

Skip shouted, "I've got him." He spurred by while Hewey was

trying to collect his wits and get his breath back. The bronc crow-hopped as Skip shook out the coils. Its only experience with a rope had been on the receiving end, frightening and painful.

Dread burned in Hewey as he saw that Skip had the near end of the rope secured to his saddle horn instead of taking a couple of dallies that he could turn loose in a hurry. There were many places more pleasant to be than sitting on a nine-hundred-pound bronc tied to an ill-tempered bull that weighed sixteen hundred pounds and was looking for something to kill.

Boy, Hewey thought, *you're fixing to learn not to suck eggs.*

The chase was fast and rough, the bull shattering brush, its cloven hooves scattering small rocks in their wake. It probably would have gotten away had it not lost its footing on a bare, slanting slab of rock and slid on its belly. It arose quickly, but its speed was hindered by a limp. Foamy saliva streamed from its mouth. When it became weary enough and provoked enough, it would turn to fight. Then it could be roped, though retrieving that rope might cost bull, horses and men some blood, hide and hair.

Hewey had once seen a tiger in a circus. The sound welling from deep in the Longhorn's throat reminded him of the great cat's roar. The bull wheeled and lowered its head.

Skip shouted, "You stay back out of the way. I can handle him."

Like Richmond handled Grant, Hewey thought.

Skip's rope hissed like a snake as he sailed his loop over the horns. The bronc tried to buck just as the bull hit the end of the line. The impact jerked both animals off their feet. Skip gave a surprised shout and hit the ground on his back. The bronc regained its feet and ran in panic. As the rope again stretched taut, it snapped at the saddle horn, popping like a whip. The horse galloped away, holding its head high and wringing its tail.

The loop was still around the bull's horns, the frazzled end of the rope lying on the ground. Skip jumped to his feet, instinctively grabbed it, then dropped it as the bull lowered its head again and charged. The boy sprinted toward a catclaw bush not much taller than he was. "Hewey! Do somethin'!"

It was high time this scatterbrained kid learned that the way of the braggart was strewn with shame and regret. "You told me to stay out of the way."

"Hewey!"

The bull stepped on the trailing rope and broke its stride long enough for Skip to reach the other side of the catclaw. He looked desperately for his bronc, but it was still running. It might as well be ten miles away for all the good it could do him. The bull made a run around the bush after the boy, hooves clattering on the hard ground. Skip managed to stay two paces ahead, circling.

Hewey suggested dryly, "Why don't you climb the tree?"

The catclaw was well named, for its branches were armed with needle-pointed thorns shaped like claws. Perhaps a cat might climb that bush, but Skip never could, not even with a sharp-horned bull providing incentive.

The bull stopped and began to paw dirt back over its shoulder, a sign it had barely begun to fight. Skip crouched on the opposite side of the tree, ready to run to the left or the right as circumstances might require. "You just goin' to sit there and laugh?"

Hewey leaned on his saddle horn. "Been a long time since I saw a circus. You might be able to run faster if you took your boots off."

The bull feinted to the left, then the right, but Skip kept the bush between them. Stymied, the animal stopped and pawed dirt again.

Hewey said, "I wish the boys at the wagon could watch you handle this bull. I've got half a mind to go back and get them."

Sweat cut trails through the dust on Skip's flushed young face. It was hard to see which was strongest, anger or fear. "Time you got back there wouldn't be nothin' left to see, just a puddle of blood and a little bit of hair."

Hewey decided the lesson had gone on long enough. He eased Biscuit toward the bull, which shifted its attention from Skip and charged at the horse. Hewey kept Biscuit far enough ahead to avoid the horns. At a safe distance from Skip he cut around and brought Biscuit up behind the bull. His loop sailed down around the long horns. He left enough slack that the bull stepped into the loop with its right foot. Hewey quickly drew the rope tight, pulling the foot up against the head. The animal faltered, lost its balance and fell heavily, raising a puff of dust. It lay struggling, unable to rise with its leg immobilized against its muzzle.

Skip complained, "You took long enough." His voice cracked, perhaps from outrage, perhaps from a remnant of fright, most likely from both. The red in his face exaggerated the freckles.

"Wanted him to wear himself down a little." Hewey untied a short length of rawhide rope coiled on the back of his saddle and pitched it to Skip. "Tie him."

Skip struggled to bring the other three legs together, accidentally backing into the catclaw bush in his efforts to stay clear of the threshing head and dangerous horns. The clutching thorns ripped the back of his shirt.

Hewey dismounted and untied a short dehorning saw he had brought for good purpose. "First thing we'd better do is to tip his horns so he won't gore any more horses."

Skip knelt on the bull's head to keep the animal still while Hewey sawed off the outer several inches of horn. He gripped the muzzle and raised the head to let Hewey work on the other side. The bull snorted mucus in Skip's face.

Hewey ran a finger over the rough edge after the sharp tip was gone. "He could still bust your ribs with that. But he wouldn't poke a hole in you that the Lord never intended."

Skip's emotions began to subside. "I thought you were fixin' to let him put a new hole in my butt."

"I just wanted him to educate you a little. I'll bet you're a lot smarter than you were twenty minutes ago."

If Skip felt any appreciation, he kept it well concealed.

Hewey said, "I'll let you and that bull sulk together while I go catch your horse."

Skip's bronc gave up running after catching a forefoot in the looped hackamore rein. At first it resisted Hewey's efforts to free it from entanglement, and it stepped on Hewey's toes before it calmed down. "Broncs and farm-raised buttons," Hewey muttered. "You deserve one another."

Skip's face had lost its angry color by the time Hewey led the bronc back. The boy said, "At least Old Man Jenkins ought to be tickled. We got him his bull."

Hewey watched the animal fight against the restraint of the rawhide that bound its feet. "Mr. Jenkins didn't send us out here to *not* get him."

A ranch owner paid little attention when cowboys did the work he expected of them. He paid close attention when they didn't. That you could and would do the job was taken for granted when you went on the payroll. Excuses were worth only about a nickel a carload, and good reasons about a dime. Hewey rarely offered either.

Skip asked, "Now that we've caught him, what're they fixin' to do with him?"

"Take away his bullhood and send him to Kansas with the steers. He's a throwback to the old days."

"Like you?"

Putting the spurs to me again. He learns awful slow. "Them old Longhorns had a lot of good qualities."

"They were mostly leg and horn, and the meat was so tough you couldn't cut it with a cleaver."

"Nature bred them to survive in a tough country. They could grub out a livin' where nothin' else but a horned toad could stay, and you couldn't hardly kill one with an ax."

"Looks to me like you're kin to them, a little. All you old cowpunchers are."

"Maybe that's why I hate to see the last Longhorns go. It's like buryin' old friends."

Skip studied the helpless form lying on the ground, straining against the rawhide that bound its feet. "If that's the way you feel about it, we could turn him loose and tell the wagon boss we never did find him."

Hewey suddenly appreciated the kid a little better. "I hate to tell a lie." He pondered the ramifications, then knelt to untie the knot in the *peal.* "Better hit the saddle. He's liable to be on the prod when he gets up."

The bull realized its feet were no longer secured. It kicked free of the loosened rawhide and rose shakily, hind end first. It pawed dirt, bellowing its anger to the world. Then it turned and trotted off, tossing its head.

Hewey said, "Looks like he's gettin' away." He followed the fugitive but did not let his horse out of a walk, so that the bull quickly outdistanced him. "Biscuit's tired. We'll never overtake that outlaw like this." He turned back to pick up the fallen rawhide. "No need in tellin' a lie, exactly. We'll just say we had him but he got loose. The horses were too give out to catch him again."

Skip grinned.

Hewey said, "You ought to never deceive the man you work for. Except when you need to."

They watched the bull disappear into a thicket three hundred yards away, crackling brush and bellowing its indignation. Other cowboys might eventually catch him, or he might live out his life in these hidden canyons, his wild spirit undiminished. In either case he would be less of a hazard to men and horses because his horns had been blunted.

Hewey said with satisfaction, "There'll be at least one more calf crop carryin' that Longhorn blood."

"It'll take real hands to run them down."

"Wild cattle and wild horses are the makin' of a good cowboy. You don't learn much handlin' gentle milk stock."

"I just wish we could've thrown him into a bunch and seen him challenge some of them other bulls. Ain't nothin' I'd rather watch than two big stout bulls fightin' one another."

"You've got a streak of mean in you."

Hewey and Skip turned away, heading back toward the chuck wagon camp. His scare past and anger drained, Skip reverted to his more typical high spirits. "Gave us some fun for a while, didn't he?"

"Me and you would call it fun. Some people call it work."

"My old daddy throwed a fit when I left home for a ridin' job. Said I'd never amount to a damn, takin' up the saddle instead of the plow. But I wouldn't want to be anything except a cowboy."

Hewey said, "My brother Walter got him a homestead and took up farmin', but them lace-up shoes never fit my feet."

"Only thing is, there's always a boss like Old Man Jenkins or Bige Saunders watchin' what you do."

"They don't own you. You're free to saddle up and go any time you want to. It's easier to take a few orders when you know you've got an out."

"Ever been tempted to do somethin' besides cowboy?"

"Not much. You've got to make choices. You choose one thing, you give up another. You can't have it all."

The cowboy occupation offered many pleasures, though there were days when Hewey wondered if they were worth the bruises, lacerations and general soreness that often supplemented his meager wages. He believed being a cowboy was a privilege reserved to a chosen few. He did not know how the Lord had come to pick him, for his willful nature caused him to stray from the gospel path now and again. But he was not one to question his maker's judgment. He was grateful to be among the chosen.

He looked off to the distant blue mountains and fell quiet, withdrawing into the bitter and the sweet of old memories. There were times when he felt like talking and no one could shut him up. Other times he had nothing to say.

Skip kept his jaw working, making profound observations based on the accumulated wisdom of his eighteen or nineteen years and trying to prod Hewey out of his silence. But Hewey barely heard. In his mind he was at home in Upton County with Walter and Eve and their two boys. And he was remembering a teacher whose name conjured up images of wildflower fields. They called her Spring.

The chuck wagon and its accompanying "hoodlum" wagon were camped beside an old set of rugged corrals constructed of heavy tree branches stacked between double posts and tied in place with rawhide. The corrals were a remnant of the 1880s, as Hewey knew himself to be when he bothered to give the matter any thought. Approaching camp, he saw horses circling in a run, raising a cloud of dust inside the largest pen.

Several cowboys, a mix of Mexican and Anglo, stood outside the rough fence, watching as Aparicio Rodriguez swung a rawhide reata and dropped its loop around a long-maned neck. The bite of leather made the caught horse pitch and squeal in protest. Aparicio began speaking in a soft Spanish and slowly working his way up the rope. Soon the bronc quieted down, its ears pointed toward the wiry vaquero.

Hewey would acknowledge that Aparicio was the best hand on the ranch, except for himself. He smiled much but talked little except to horses.

Skip said eagerly, "Looks like they brought in that new set of broncs."

Hewey grunted. Cow work in this rough mountain country was challenging enough just on its own account. The challenge was compounded by having to do it while breaking a set of raw ponies that knew nothing except bite, kick and pitch. But that was what the ranch paid him thirty dollars a month for.

Old Man Jenkins was reputed to be worth a million dollars. Hewey was taking it away from him at the rate of a dollar a day. A million days, a million dollars.

Skip said, "It's a wonder the old man don't dock us for the entertainment we get out of ridin' them broncs."

"I saw how much entertainment you were gettin', runnin' around that bush ahead of them horns."

Skip's face became troubled. "You don't have to tell the boys about it, do you? They'll hooraw me for a month."

Cowboys could be merciless to a braggart. They would do whatever it took to bring him down, then laugh at him until he ate crow or quit the outfit.

"Just promise me I won't have to listen to any more chin music about what all you can do."

"You sayin' I'm boastful?"

"If brag was whiskey, you could open a saloon."

Skip took it in fair grace. "I'll try to remember."

He might try, but Hewey knew he would backslide. It was not in Skip's nature to hide his light beneath a bushel.

Hewey recognized Old Man Jenkins sitting on a tarp-covered bedroll near the chuck wagon. Morgan Jenkins was a rancher of the 1880s school, as much a relic now as the Longhorn. More than six feet tall, he had probably weighed two hundred pounds of pure muscle and bone in his prime. Now, well into his seventies, he weighed a bit more, and his shoulders were bent a little. But in moments of stress Hewey had seen him straighten his back and become once again the formidable figure he had been. It was said of him that once he had single-handedly trailed and confronted four horse thieves, shooting one and escorting the other three to jail.

In contrast to his physical size, he was given to economy in his gestures as well as in his expenditures. Where others might holler and wave both arms, Jenkins beckoned with the index finger of an arthritis-knotted hand. Hewey sensed that the come-along was meant for him.

"Think you can unsaddle that bronc by yourself?" he asked Skip.

The youngster already seemed to have forgotten Hewey's cautionary words about boastfulness. "I could do it with one hand tied behind my back."

I ought to have let that bull chase him a little longer, Hewey thought.

He tied Biscuit to a corral post and spent a minute surveying the new broncs that still milled around nervously, looking for a booger strong enough to make them break out of the pen and run. He was fixing to have his work cut out for him the next couple of weeks, but nobody ever said life had to be dull. As a matter of fact, he looked forward to pitting his skill as a bronc stomper against the wild rebellion of the young horses.

He turned and walked toward the wagon so Jenkins wouldn't have to tire himself out crooking that finger again. He stopped at Blas Villegas's chuck box and dug a tin cup out of a drawer, filling it from a coffeepot suspended over a pit of glowing coals. Blas raked the coals with a pothook. "Don' burn yourself, Hooey. She's plenty hot."

"Fine. I'd sooner drink dishwater than cold coffee."

Blas had been a vaquero much of his life, but one bronc too many had left him with a shattered knee and a crooked leg that would never straighten again. He had turned to that refuge of many a crippled cowboy, cooking at a wagon.

Jenkins did not get up from his seat on the bedroll or waste a lot of breath in his greeting. "Hewey."

"Mr. Jenkins." The *mister* was more in deference to age than to the old man's money. Hewey stood in awe of no one's bankroll. In fact, he felt sympathy for Jenkins because the rancher's age and infirmities prevented him from making a hand on horseback anymore. In Hewey's eyes nothing was sadder-looking than an old cowboy too stove-up to ride.

Jenkins gestured for Hewey to sit on a nearby bedroll. Hewey waited for him to initiate the conversation. When the old man did not, Hewey asked, "You bring them broncs with you?"

He knew better, for he could see Jenkins's open touring car parked a respectful distance from the wagon. But the idle question broke the silence. The driver had the hood up, messing around with something on the engine. Hewey had no idea what; he had never had any truck with automobiles. To him they were the ruination of the country. For a long time he had hoped they were a passing fancy and everyone would get back to the horse as God intended. Now it appeared they would bankrupt the nation first; then maybe the fad would die the death it deserved.

As for that driver in his duster and goggles, he seemed as out of place in a cow camp as a monkey in church. Hewey thought anybody who went around holding his nose that high was in danger of drowning if he ever got caught in a rain. The man seemed to have an exalted opinion of himself because he knew how to drive a car, but he probably couldn't drive a Jersey cow down a sheep-fenced lane. Hewey had to feel a little sorry for him.

Jenkins said, "Them broncs ain't none of your concern. I got a proposition for you."

The rancher had red-rimmed eyes that indicated he liked whiskey more than he should. It probably gave him comfort from his arthritis and other miseries that went with having celebrated so many birthdays. Hewey had heard he could put away a prodigious amount under the right provocation, though he could not remember that Jenkins had ever offered him a drink.

Jenkins had made his start in the freewheeling maverick-catching times after the Civil War, when an ambitious young man with a fast horse and a quick loop could build toward a fortune by burning his own brand on unclaimed cattle. The period had been relatively short, for those who made theirs first declared further mavericking illegal, kicking down the ladder by which they had climbed so Johnny-come-latelies could not follow.

Hewey had arrived too late to take advantage of the opportunity, though accumulation of worldly goods had never been of much concern to him anyway. Property he could not tie to his saddle and carry with him to the next job was a burden, not an asset.

"Hewey, I just bought the Circle W outfit, a hundred sections down yonder under the rimrock."

Hewey was not surprised, for Jenkins was never comfortable knowing he didn't own everything within a day's trip from his headquarters. Since he had acquired that car, the miles he could travel in a day had stretched a right smart.

Jenkins said, "I want you to run it for me."

Now Hewey *was* surprised. "Me, run an outfit? I've never done nothin' like that."

"It's time you did. Look at you, six years older than God and still workin' for cowboy wages. It's time you taken a grip on yourself and tried to amount to somethin'."

"I ain't that old, and I've always made you a hand."

"True enough, but I can hire more *young* hands than I need. All I have to do is honk that horn in Alpine, and a dozen come runnin' down the street draggin' a saddle and a bedroll. But somebody who's had experience enough to run an outfit . . . that's a horse of a different complexion."

Hewey struggled for words he thought Jenkins might understand. "It's a lot of responsibility. I've never liked bein' responsible for anything or anybody except myself."

"I never could understand a man that didn't want to better his lot in life."

"I'm satisfied with myself the way I am. Ain't much I'd want to change."

"Nature's changin' you whether you like it or not. Them creases in your face keep gettin' deeper, and your gitalong don't get along like it used to."

"I can still move fast enough to get out of the way."

"From all them years of work, have you saved up any money?"

"A hundred dollars, maybe. But I've had ten thousand dollars' worth of fun."

"A hundred dollars! That ain't even enough to bury you in any style."

"I wasn't figurin' on that happenin' for a long time yet."

Jenkins's frown furrowed his face like a prune. "Ain't often I give a man a chance to go from forty dollars a month to seventy-five."

"You're only payin' me thirty."

"Sixty-five, then. All the more reason you ought to consider the opportunity."

Never had Hewey felt comfortable giving orders, so he had given very few in his life. He had always liked best just being one of the boys, doing whatever the job called for with easy competence and without pressure. If the work became tiresome or the boss got under his skin he would draw his time, saddle up and ride away without regrets. For a good hand, there was always another job down the road.

That was what he would do now if Jenkins tried to twist his arm too much. Lately he had been looking off toward the north a lot anyhow. He had already worked two years for the J Bar, longer than he was used to spending in one place. It had been a long time since he had cowboyed in the Guadalupes, and he had studied on going back. It was a smiling country, like Upton County, where Walter and Eve and the boys had their homestead. For that matter, just about everywhere Hewey had worked had been a smiling country.

Jenkins knew cowboys, for he was still one at heart. He knew when to stop pushing. "I won't try to make you do somethin' that's against your religion. I'll just have to find me somebody that's got ambition. I'd do better with a family man anyway." His eyes narrowed. "You ain't never found a woman that gave you a marryin' urge?"

Hewey stared into his half-empty cup. "I did once."

"What happened?"

Remembered pain softened Hewey's voice. "We both smartened up before it was too late, and I left."

Jenkins thought about it. "You ever wonder if you did the right thing?"

"Doesn't everybody?"

Jenkins shifted his gaze to the touring car and its driver, who was clamping the hood shut. "Looks like he's finished monkeyin' around with that engine. Wish sometimes I still used a horse and buggy. Didn't need to hire no fifty-dollar driver for that."

Fifty dollars! Hewey was just drawing thirty, and he was a top hand. But he wouldn't trade places, not for a hundred.

He said, "I wouldn't swap one bronc in that pen yonder for a dozen of them stink wagons."

Jenkins frowned. "Them broncs are for the young hands to break. I don't want you ridin' any of them."

Hewey almost spilled the coffee that remained in his cup. "I've already broke twenty-five or thirty broncs for you, and I ain't ruined one yet."

"I ain't worried about you ruinin' them, I'm afraid one of them is liable to ruin *you*. I know your age, Hewey, even if you don't. I don't want you on my conscience." Jenkins dropped his coffee cup in Blas's washtub and walked toward his car. He hollered at the driver, "You got that contraption fixed?"

The driver wiped his greasy hands on a cloth. "She'll run like a young filly on a spring day, Mr. Jenkins."

Hewey snorted. He would bet that driver wouldn't know a young filly from an old stud. And he was being paid fifty dollars a month!

The car started with a backfire that set all the broncs to circling again in the corral. Jenkins shouted back, "You stay off of them green ponies, Hewey."

Hewey did not respond, for he did not want to make a promise he would not keep. He watched the automobile kick up a trail of dust across the pasture until he was satisfied that Jenkins would not think of something he had forgotten and come back.

What the old man did not know would not hurt him.

Hewey walked to Biscuit and untied the rope from his saddle. He said, "Skip, let's take a close look at them broncs."

CHAPTER

2

Blas Villegas took the chuck wagon ahead to the railroad pens while Hewey and the other hands followed with the herd. Hewey rode point, ahead of the dominant steers that had taken it upon themselves to move into the lead. Afar, Hewey could see the smoking locomotive, and he wondered how Biscuit was going to take to it. Biscuit was a ranch horse, not used to the commotion that went with being in a big town like Alpine.

Hewey had been riding a couple of the new broncs, but he thought it advisable to use Biscuit for the last stage of the drive because Old Man Jenkins would almost certainly be waiting at the pens. He would remember, even if Hewey had chosen to forget, his admonition that the broncs be left to the younger hands. Hewey did not want to risk raising the rancher's blood pressure; that could be dangerous for a man of his age.

He noticed a truck bumping its dusty way toward the herd, following the ruts of a rough wagon road that led from town. To him, a truck in cow country still looked badly out of place.

The driver honked his horn and spooked Biscuit. Skip Harkness's bronc began to pitch. One stirrup flopped free, and the surprised kid saved himself only by grabbing the saddle horn. Hewey thought the truck driver was probably Old Man Jenkins's high-toned car jockey, badly in need of a stern lesson in cow-camp etiquette. As the truck pulled to a stop, Hewey reined toward it, rehearsing the lecture in his mind until he saw that the man behind the steering wheel was a stranger.

A passenger stepped out on the right-hand side. Hewey blinked in surprise, for he recognized the tall, thin figure of his brother, wearing denim overalls, a farmer's brogan shoes and a floppy felt hat that offered only limited protection to a face used hard by the elements.

"Walter," Hewey shouted. Biscuit sidestepped, wary of the clanking motor until the driver cut it off. When the noise stopped, the horse moved closer but remained like a coiled spring, ready to jump away at the least provocation. Walter turned to offer a big, rough hand to the woman who had been sitting in the middle. She stepped to the ground and dusted herself the best she could. She wore a slat bonnet that almost covered her face, but Hewey knew she was his sister-in-law.

He had been about to dismount, but he decided to remain in the saddle until he determined which direction the wind blew. With Eve Calloway, he never could be sure whether it would be a warm, pleasant one from the south or a cold one from the north. She could change quicker than West Texas weather. Their last parting had been amicable, but he remembered others that were frosty as a February morning.

Walter walked slowly toward Hewey, careful lest he cause the nervous Biscuit further fright. "Big brother," he said, "when're you goin' to give up tryin' to be twenty years old? You need to quit ridin' these skittish broncs."

"When I'm a hundred and six."

"You'll never get that old. Some fool horse'll kill you first."

"Many a good one has tried. But anyway, it's been years since Biscuit was a bronc." Hewey gripped his brother's calloused hand, which felt like dry rawhide. He tipped his hat to Eve. She said only, "Hewey."

At least she did not seem angry. Hewey decided to step down from the saddle. He ventured, "You're lookin' good, Eve."

She wasn't, really. She had always tended to be on the skinny side, but her long, plain gray cotton dress hung loose as if she hadn't been eating lately. She was moving along toward forty and showed every year of it. The lines in her face indicated deep worry as she stepped close to give Hewey a perfunctory peck on the cheek. He held his hands up awkwardly, never knowing for sure if he should hug her or not. He decided against it.

"Hewey," she asked quickly, "where's Tommy?"

He blinked in confusion. "Tommy? Where's he supposed to be?"

"At home, but he's not. We figured he'd be here with you."

Hewey looked in surprise at Eve, then Walter, then Eve again. "I ain't seen him. Or heard from him either." He had not seen his two nephews since the last time he had been to Upton County. That had been three . . . no, four years ago, or pretty near. It was hard to keep track of time, busy as he had been.

Anxiety pinched Walter's eyes. "He left home. Took a little dun horse Alvin Lawdermilk gave him, and he rode off without sayin' anything. We thought it was likely he came up this way lookin' for you."

"If he did, he hasn't found me." Hewey began to share their concern. "I understood why Cotton wanted to leave home when he came of age. He had his sights set on other things besides the hoe and the plow. But Tommy was a farm boy at heart. I thought he'd be content to stay there all of his life."

Walter shoved his hands into his pockets and stared at the ground. "We thought so too, but lately he's taken an itch to see other places, do other things. Eve says he's a lot like you."

Hewey gave his sister-in-law a sideward glance, knowing she would not have meant it to be complimentary. When anything threatened the stability of home and family, Eve found it easy to blame Hewey's wayward influence. Much of the blame was justified.

He detected a hint of that blame as Eve said, "I don't reckon you intentionally enticed him, but Tommy's always looked up to you. I just hoped he wouldn't pick up your roamin' ways."

Hewey replied, "You've made it plain many a time that you'd be a sight happier if I gave up ridin' and taken to the plow."

"We'd all be glad if you did, but we decided a long time ago to quit tryin' to change you. You'll be Hewey Calloway as long as you live."

"I've tried bein' somebody else, and it never worked." He had taken Walter's place one summer when Walter's leg was broken. For a while he had forced himself to become a farmer and bring in Walter's crops, but he had hated every day of it.

He saw disappointment in Eve's blue eyes before she turned and touched a handkerchief to them. He wished Tommy *had* shown up here so Walter and Eve could take him home and stop worrying. Now Hewey had something to worry about, too.

He wanted to change the subject. "How about the farm? You-all makin' it all right?"

Walter said, "We stay ahead of Old C. C. Tarpley and his bank, if that's what you mean. Fact is, C.C.'s softened up considerable. His health has been failin'."

Eve said, "He may be startin' to worry about whether they'll let him into heaven or not."

"I'd say he's got a right smart to worry about." Hewey looked toward the steers. The herd had moved past him while he was talking to Walter and Eve. "Chuck wagon's camped on the far side of the shippin' pens. We'll be havin' dinner after we've penned the cattle."

Walter said, "Can't stay. One of Blue Hannigan's truck drivers had a load of freight to deliver to Alpine, and we caught a ride with him. He's got to be back in Upton City tonight."

Hewey was surprised again. "That's Blue Hannigan's truck? He's always done his freightin' with mules and wagons."

"He's bought two trucks since you saw him last. Says a man has got to keep up with the times or they'll roll over him and leave him layin' in the road."

"They've rolled over me, all right. Just about flattened me out. But I can't feature Blue Hannigan drivin' a truck. I always figured he was half mule."

He had never had a better friend in the world than Blue Hannigan unless it was Snort Yarnell and the late Grady Welch. They were kindred spirits, cowboys to the core, even though Blue had eventually married and turned to freighting to make a better living. Grady had died beneath the hooves of a two-bit bronc.

He said, "If Tommy shows up, I'll send him home."

The lines deepened in Walter's face as he put his arm around his wife's shoulder. He seemed to read something in her sad eyes that Hewey could not see. "No, let him stay if he's set on it. Maybe he'll work it out of his system. But let us know, and watch out for him, won't you? Don't let him get himself hurt or into any trouble."

"I'll do what I can." Hewey tried to hide his reluctance. He had turned down Old Man Jenkins's offer of a good-paying job because it would give him responsibility he did not want. Now, like it or not, he would be considered responsible for his nephew.

Walter gripped his hand. "Obliged, Hewey. Come see us when you can."

Eve gave Hewey a silent hug. The tears in her eyes told him why she did not trust herself to try to speak. She turned away, letting Walter give her a boost up into the truck.

Hewey called, "Walter, just a minute." He had to work up nerve to ask the question. "How's Miss Spring Renfro?"

"She's still teachin' school over at the Lawdermilks'."

"Has she . . . has she gotten herself married yet?"

"She's been waitin' for the right man to come along, I guess. We all thought you were him, once."

"So did I, once." Hewey looked away, clearing his throat. "Tell Cotton hello for me, next time he's home."

"And if we see Spring Renfro?"

Hewey could only shake his head. He did not know what to tell her.

The locomotive backed the empty cattle cars along the spur track to the shipping pens as Hewey and the rest of the crew brought up the J Bar steer herd. Old Man Jenkins's touring car was parked to one side, out of the path of the cattle. The driver leaned against the automobile, goggles pulled up over the broad-billed cap he wore. Jenkins was opening the gate to the largest pen. He could have delegated that job to his driver, but Hewey guessed the old man wanted to see it done right, as if there were any *wrong* way to open a gate.

Hewey rode up a little ahead of the herd and stationed himself just past the opening so the steers would not pass it by. He hazed the leaders in, then backed away so those that followed would not shy aside. Most of these cattle did not often see men on horseback, and those few occasions were usually associated with unpleasantness of one kind or another.

The pens were dry and dusty, for the hooves of earlier herds had already stirred the bare ground after a long winter of relative inactivity. Skip Harkness rode up on the bronc that had come near throwing him off when the truck's horn sounded.

Hewey said, "Caught you asleep, didn't he? You've got to learn to stay awake every minute when you're sittin' on a bronc."

Defensively Skip declared, "He never even come close."

Hewey wondered why he felt duty-bound to nursemaid every green farm kid who wandered onto the J Bar. They should be the foreman's responsibility, not his, but somehow most of them seemed to gravitate toward Hewey. The gringo kids anyway. The young Mexicans drew toward Aparacio Rodriguez, who, at thirty, give or take a little, was sort of a big-brother figure to them.

Watching Skip, wishing the boy were a little smarter and a lot less sure of his invincibility, Hewey thought of his nephew Tommy. *Where the hell has that kid got off to? He could be anyplace from here to El Paso.*

A trainman signaled the engineer to back the wooden cattle cars slowly until the one nearest the coal car was evenly aligned with the slanted loading chute. The foreman, Bige Saunders, rode to where Old Man Jenkins waited on an elevated walkway beside the chute. There they could look down upon the steers and count them as they ascended into the cars.

Hewey tied Biscuit to an outside fence and beckoned with a jerk of his head for Skip to follow him. The boy dismounted carefully, for the hissing of the steam locomotive made his bronc step sideways, its ears nervously pointed forward and its eyes rolling.

Climbing over fences to reach the loading chute, Hewey and Skip pried the car door open and slid a platform forward to bridge between the end of the chute and the sand-covered floor of the car. Hewey jumped on it to be sure it was set solidly. A collapse under the weight of the steers would be a small calamity. He motioned for Skip to help him swing the side gates forward and complete a closed corridor that would prevent cattle from jumping to freedom between the chute and the car.

Jenkins shouted for the cowboys to bring the steers on. Hewey picked up a long pole propped against the fence and took a place on the elevated walkway where he could lean over and prod any animals reluctant to pass through the door into the darkness of the car. *This is why they call us cowpunchers,* he thought.

Jenkins and Saunders both counted the cattle as they ascended, Jenkins calling a halt when the proper number had passed to fill the car without overcrowding it. Hewey turned back the extra animals and put his shoulder against the car door, sliding it into place and closing the latch.

The trainmen had not helped with the loading. Hewey could not blame them for standing back, for the railroad did not count that among their duties. But he wished he could see Jenkins's car driver lending a hand. For a man paid fifty dollars a month, he didn't seem to be doing much. Remaining well out of the dust, he stood by the automobile as if afraid it might decide to run off like a horse left untied.

Following signals made by one of the trainmen, the engineer moved the train forward to spot the next empty car into place, aligning the door with the chute.

Skip asked, "Is the grass really greener where these steers are goin'?"

"They'll think they've died and gone to heaven. Them Kansas Flint Hills look like a wheat field when it rains."

"You've seen that country?"

"Spent a season up there once, takin' care of summer cattle for a feller who lived down at Uvalde."

"Is there anyplace you *ain't* been?"

"Never been to California yet, or Nevada or Utah, but me and Biscuit'll visit all of them before we're done."

"Think the two of you have still got time enough?"

"Time don't mean much to Biscuit. He wouldn't know a calendar from the United States Constitution."

As the loading progressed, Hewey counted the empty cars and realized there were a couple more than were needed to carry all the Jenkins steers. The trainmen called a halt, claiming some sort of difficulty with the locomotive that had to be fixed before work could continue. Sitting on the fence, rolling a cigarette, Hewey noticed a string of horses pushed by four cowboys approaching the loading pens. He recognized one of the riders and walked down to open the gate to a pen that had been emptied of cattle.

"Howdy, Hewey," a lean and lanky puncher shouted jovially as the horses rushed past him into the corral. The sun caught a glint of gold where a front tooth should have been.

"Snort Yarnell!" Hewey shouted back. "Somebody told me you was dead. Guess you just smelled like it."

Snort reined up and looked at the Jenkins outfit's horses, tied along the outside fence. His gold tooth gleamed in a broad grin. "When did you J Bar punchers start ridin' burros?"

"About the same time you Slash R waddies commenced ridin' camels." Hewey shut the gate as the last of the loose horses passed through. "Or are those goats you just brought in?"

Snort dismounted and thrust his big hand forward. Hewey took it. Each man tried to squeeze hard enough to make the other holler, but it came out a draw. Hewey slapped Snort on the shoulder, raising a puff of dust from the cowboy's blue work shirt. "I didn't think you could get any uglier, but damned if you ain't managed."

"Ain't much a man can't do if he makes up his mind to it."

Snort was accompanied by three eager young cowhands, none of whom looked to be out of their teens. His loud talk and boisterous manner attracted a youthful following wherever he went. Most of the kids would eventually outgrow him and pull away as maturity overtook their playful spirits and they realized Snort would remain an adolescent forever except in years.

He knew how to have a good time, though. Hewey could hardly remember when he had not known Snort and welcomed his company, for a little while at a time.

Snort peered through the fence at the remnant of steers in the next pen. "I'm surprised you're still workin' for Old Man Jenkins. He's tighter than the bark on a tree."

"Old Blas cooks good, that's the main thing. If I had more money, I'd just spend it. What you doin' with the horses?"

"Fixin' to load them on that train and ship them to Fort Worth for the horse and mule auction."

"Scrubby-lookin' bunch. Looks to me like they got burro blood in them."

"You think so? I wisht you'd look at that black yonder, the one with the white stockin' foot. Throwed every cowboy on the Slash R payroll. Even me, and I'm the best bronc rider this country ever seen."

Hewey was not impressed. The black horse stood hipshot, its head down as if asleep. "He's got feet the size of a number two washtub. The Slash R must have a bunch of sheepherders workin' out there."

Hewey should have been warned by the calculating gleam that came into Snort's eyes. Snort licked a tongue across that gold tooth and spat a brown stream of tobacco. "I guess you think some J Bar hand can ride him."

"I'll bet any hand on the place can ride him except maybe Old Blas. He could too if he wasn't crippled up."

"You got some money to go where your mouth is at?"

"I will have when we get the cattle loaded. Mr. Jenkins is due to pay us."

"I'll take credit. Bet you thirty dollars, but I'll pick the J Bar hand to do the ridin'."

By this time the two men were surrounded by cowboys, including the three who had come with Snort and most of the J Bar hands. Skip Harkness declared, "Let me ride him, Hewey. I'll turn his hide inside out."

Hewey shook his head. Skip was not half as good as he thought he was. "That'll be up to Snort. It's his choice who makes the ride."

Snort's youthful companions offered side bets, and some of the J Bar cowboys took them up, betting five, ten, fifteen dollars apiece. Old man Jenkins and Bige Saunders noticed the commotion and came down to see what was causing it. Jenkins frowned at the hands' eagerness to bet. "I never did approve of gamblin' unless it's on cattle." He took a long look at the black horse in question. "But it don't appear to me like there's any gamblin' to this. If these Slash R boys want to contribute to you-all's fortunes, I don't see any harm in it."

He did not put up any of his own money, nor did Saunders. Hewey figured they were too old to have any sporting blood left. He said, "All right, Snort. Pick your man."

Snort let his gaze drift over the J Bar hands, quickly dismissing Aparicio Rodriguez because the good-natured vaquero had a reputation all over the Davis Mountains country as being *puro jinete,* a bronc rider of exceptional ability. He lingered a little longer on Skip than the others, and Hewey feared he was about to choose the kid.

Snort took his time, coming back finally to Hewey. Hewey smiled, knowing he was by all odds the best rider in the outfit, by his own estimation better even than Aparicio. He could ride that black and darn his socks at the same time. But Snort turned and walked to the fence. He pointed at Jenkins's driver, who stood on the outside looking in, his goggles turned up over the top of his cap. "I pick *him,"* he said.

Hewey sputtered. "But he's not a hand. He just jockeys that automobile."

"He works for Jenkins, don't he? He's on the J Bar payroll, ain't he?"

Hewey looked to Jenkins for support, but the old rancher offered him no help. Hewey protested, "That don't count. He ain't paid to ride."

"You're the one agreed to the deal. Either he rides or you forfeit the bet." The gold tooth gleamed. Hewey thought Snort looked like a fox eating watermelon.

Hewey, for his part, felt like a coyote with both forefeet in a trap, being rinkydooed by a sly old sport like Snort Yarnell. It wasn't that he would mind seeing the driver get thrown halfway to the moon, but Jenkins might fire the whole outfit if he was left without the services of his chauffeur. The old man probably couldn't even crank the motor, much less handle the wheel.

Disgusted with himself, Hewey said, "Looks to me like we've got no choice but to forfeit."

The driver took off his duster and laid it across the fence. "You ain't lost yet."

Hewey gaped. "You would try to ride that bronc?"

"Why not?"

"You couldn't ride a kid's stick horse. You'd be about as much use as teats on a boar hog."

"What've you got to lose?"

"Mr. Jenkins stands to lose a driver."

"Then maybe you'd have to learn to operate an automobile yourself." He climbed into the corral and began unlacing his high-topped boots. "Your feet look to be about the same size as mine. Lend me your boots and spurs."

"What for? You won't make it past the first jump." But Hewey could see that the man was serious. He sat in the sand and removed his boots, leaving the spurs on them. He pulled off his socks to keep from getting them full of dirt. Not for a hundred dollars would he put on the dude's lace-up boots. He would look almost as ridiculous as the driver did with that combination of jodhpur britches and cowboy boots.

The chauffeur had to pull hard to get his feet into Hewey's boots, and his pained expression indicated that they pinched his toes. "All right, who's goin' to catch that horse?"

Hewey looked at Jenkins, hoping the old man would put a stop to this, but the rancher only muttered something about fools and their money and stomped off to see if the trainmen were making any progress fixing their locomotive.

Bige Saunders warned, "If you-all get Mr. Jenkins's driver killed, the old man won't be fit to live with." He trailed after Jenkins.

Doesn't want to watch the massacre, Hewey thought glumly. He had rather be somewhere else himself.

Snort's companions seemed only too happy to catch up the black horse. The animal appeared unperturbed. It stood calmly while the hackamore was slipped over its head and the saddle girted down tightly. Snort turned to the driver, his voice condescending. "Ready any time you are, Marmaduke."

"The name's not Marmaduke. Friends call me Peeler."

"Peeler?"

"Like in *bronc peeler.*" The driver handed his cap and goggles to Skip Harkness. "Try not to let these get dirty."

One of Snort's friends held the black's ears, though the horse looked as if it might be asleep. Peeler gripped the hackamore rein, a handful of mane and the saddle horn as he swung up. It occurred to Hewey that Peeler was doing this properly. He had probably watched somebody sometime.

The cowboy released the ears and stepped back out of the way. For a moment the horse seemed not to notice. Then with a loud bawl and a breaking of wind, it made a violent leap forward and came down solidly on all four feet. Hewey imagined he could feel the ground tremble under the impact. It should have been enough to bust the rider's teeth, but Peeler was still in the saddle as the horse made its second jump.

Hewey stared in amazement. The rider seemed to anticipate the bronc's moves and meet them halfway. Very little daylight appeared between him and the saddle, and never for long. Pitching, twisting, spinning half around, the horse failed to shake him. Its long jumps dwindled into crow hops as it tired, and finally it ran in slowing circles around the corral. Peeler drew on the hackamore rein and brought the bronc to a stop, stepping off to the ground.

He handed the rein to Snort Yarnell. "Thought you said this pony could buck."

Snort made a resigned smile. "Thought they said you was just an auto jockey."

"I am, but I wasn't always." Peeler sat in the sand and began struggling with Hewey's boots.

Snort turned to Hewey. "Looks like you-all ran a ringer in on us."

"Like you done with that sleepy-lookin' black? Anyway, you chose him. I tried to get you to pick somebody else."

Snort laughed. "That's when I ought to've known you had somethin' up your sleeve. You're a licensed and certified liar, Hewey Calloway, the only one I know that can hold a candle to me. So we'll pay up like men and try to get you the next time."

The locomotive's whistle blew. Old Man Jenkins waved his hat over his head, meaning they had all better get back to work if they wanted to have a job tomorrow.

Hewey put on his socks, then his boots. He shook hands with

Peeler. "I've never been mistaken but two or three times in my life. Reckon this was one of them. You're entitled to share my winnin's."

"Forget it. This helped remind me why I learned to drive an automobile."

Hewey sat at a table in a corner of the saloon, staring down at a blank sheet of paper. The J Bar cowboys and the Slash R hands were spread out along the bar, Anglo and Mexican all mixed together. Racial lines were easily blurred by a little whiskey. Snort Yarnell motioned. "Come on, Hewey, you're fallin' behind."

"I'll catch up. Got to write this letter first."

He was momentarily distracted by an elderly swamper, dragging a stiff leg as he swept up glass from a bottle that had rolled off a table and broken on the floor. He was another old cowboy too broken up to ride anymore and reduced to a demeaning job to earn his grub and sleep in the dry. *Hell of a way for a good man to end up,* Hewey thought.

He touched the sharp end of the stub pencil to his tongue and began a slow and halting effort.

Alpine, Texas
May 21 1910

Dear Walter & Eve—
I take pencil in hand to tell you I have not seen Tommy. I have just come into a little extra mony and am sendin it to you to put against your dett on the farm, like I have done before. Dont worry, I dont need it. If Tommy shows up I will let you no.

Yours very truly.
Hewey Calloway
P. S. — If you see Miss Spring Renfro

He could not think how to end the last sentence and tried to erase it, but it would not all come off the paper. He addressed an envelope to Walter and Eve Calloway, Upton City, Texas, and tucked the letter into it with fifty dollars in paper money. He licked the envelope, sealed it and handed it to the bald-headed bartender along with a quarter. "I don't have a penny stamp, but I'd be obliged if you'd put one on this and see that it gets to the post office. Keep the change."

"You're a generous man, Hewey Calloway. It'll be the starvin' of you someday. You ready for another drink?"

"Ready and rarin'."

He had had several already, but not enough to make him overlook the risk of falling over the edge, splurging the wages Old Man Jenkins had paid him and the bet he had won from Snort, most of which he was sending to Walter and Eve.

Jenkins had been in the saloon earlier and had enjoyed a drink at cowboy expense. After he left, Snort had demanded, "Don't he ever buy any himself?"

Hewey replied, "How do you think he got rich?"

Now Snort had his arm around Peeler's shoulder. "Where in the hell did a car jockey ever learn that kind of ridin'?"

Almost everybody in the room had bought Peeler a drink. His cap and goggles lay on the floor where he had dropped them without realizing it. Hewey picked them up and placed them on the bar so nobody would step on them. Peeler said thickly, "I was raised in Callahan County, helpin' my old daddy break horses and mules. Rode awhile with Booger Red Privett's bronc show 'til I got tired of them outlaws bustin' my back. Figured herdin' an automobile ought to be easier than stompin' broncs."

"Pays better, too," Hewey put in. He had never been apt at figures, but he knew the difference between thirty dollars a month and fifty.

An out-of-tune piano stood in a back corner. A kid from the Slash R was playing it in a heavy-handed and discordant way. Nobody seemed disposed to criticize his musicianship.

Hewey did not know where the girls came from, but three appeared, dancing with the cowboys. One of them took Hewey in her arms and did a reel with him, though the kid at the piano was playing a waltz. Hewey's head was spinning by the time they finished. He collapsed into a chair, leaned back too far and fell heavily. He struggled to free himself from the overturned chair but hung a spur in one of its braces. He floundered like a turtle on its back.

He saw someone hovering over him and heard a youthful voice. "Need a little help, Uncle Hewey?"

Hewey blinked, trying to bring the face into focus as it swayed back and forth like a pendulum. It was somehow familiar, yet he could not see clearly enough to identify the features.

"It's me, Uncle Hewey. Tommy."

"Tommy?" The voice was his nephew's, though it sounded deeper and more mature than he remembered. Hewey said, "Don't you know a saloon ain't no place for a self-respectin' Calloway?"

He did not expect the strength his nephew showed as Tommy took his hand and helped him to his feet. Hewey kicked his spur loose from the chair, which fell back with a clatter, almost tripping Skip Harkness and the young woman he was dancing with. They did not seem to notice.

Hewey leaned against the table for balance and scolded, "Your mama'd be awful disappointed to find a boy like you in a place like this."

Tommy said, "She'd be disappointed in both of us. And I ain't a boy anymore. You just ain't seen me in a long time."

Tommy still seemed to sway from side to side. "Hold still," Hewey told him, "so I can get a good look at you."

Tommy righted the chair and held it steady. Hewey seated himself, careful not to knock the chair over again. Funny, he thought, how much a kid could change when you weren't watching. Tommy appeared broader in the shoulders and a foot taller than Hewey remembered. He looked much like his older brother, Cotton. Hewey could see a lot of his father in Tommy's features and some of his mother in the eyes. "You're not a man yet, though, not quite. Why ain't you at home, in school?"

"I finished all the schoolin' there was two years ago. I decided to come lookin' for you."

"How'd you find me?"

"Just asked around. Anywhere you've been, they remember Hewey Calloway."

Hewey tried to sound severe. "You ought to be helpin' your daddy right now. Plantin' time, ain't it?"

"Me and Daddy ain't gee-hawed too good lately. I want to learn to be a cowboy like you."

"You're too late. They ain't makin' no more cowboys like me, hardly. The times have gone off and left us."

"You always said I was a natural hand. I've been breakin' horses and mules for Alvin Lawdermilk the last couple of years when Daddy could spare me."

"Then why don't you stay home and work for Alvin?"

"I've learned all there is to learn around Upton City. I want to see different country, different people."

"People are pretty much the same wherever you find them, most of them good, a few not worth hangin' with an old rope."

"I thought maybe you could get me a job where you're workin'."

"Old Man Jenkins runs a pretty tough outfit."

"I can make him a hand if he's got any openin's."

Hewey knew that a couple of the J Bar cowboys had ridden the caboose when the train pulled out, committed to seeing after the steers when they reached the Flint Hills. They would not be back

until fall, and maybe not then if they stumbled onto some good-
looking Kansas girls bent on getting married. Hewey had known it
to happen.

He said, "We'll talk about it in the mornin'. Maybe you'll see
things a little plainer in the light of day."

Tommy smiled. "I'll bet *you* will."

The bartender came over, eyeing Tommy with suspicion. "Hewey,
this boy don't look like he's shavin' regular yet. They got a town
ordinance . . ." He had been nervous all evening because many of
the hands from both ranches looked under age.

"We was fixin' to leave." Hewey pointed his chin toward Snort
Yarnell. "You-all let too much riffraff in here anyhow."

Snort took that as a compliment and saluted Hewey with a
whiskey toast.

> *"Here's to the boys that labor and sweat,*
> *And thirty a month is all they get."*

The Jenkins driver had a death grip on the edge of the bar, his
eyes wide and glassy. Hewey hoped the old man didn't need to go
anywhere tomorrow.

Hewey beckoned to Tommy and walked outside, where a dun
horse was tied to a post. A couple of rolled blankets were tied behind the cantle, and a war bag of miscellaneous belongings hung
from the saddle horn on the left side, opposite a coiled rope. Tommy
asked, "Where we goin'?"

"Biscuit's in the wagon yard. Chuck wagon's camped at the shippin' pens. You had any supper?" It was an idle question, for Blas
would have crawled into his blankets hours ago, and his cookfire
would be down to a few lingering coals at best.

"Ain't hungry. I shared supper with a sheepherder out east of
town."

"Mutton, I'll bet." Hewey could eat almost anything if he had to, but he could stay happy for months on end without eating any mutton.

"It ain't bad atall. Daddy's bought him a little bunch of sheep. Looks like they're goin' to be moneymakers."

"Don't you let them J Bar cowboys hear you say that. Or worse, Snort and that bunch from the Slash R. It'd be a chaps offense." That was a form of punishment in which a cowboy had to bend over and let somebody lash his backside with a pair of leather chaps. It was performed more in the spirit of fun than in seriousness, but it did nothing to enhance dignity.

Tommy led his dun horse to the wagon yard and waited while Hewey retrieved Biscuit. He had a little trouble getting the saddle on the brown and afterward stirred a couple of dogs into a barking fit. Hewey wondered why he always seemed to have that effect on dogs. He had never harmed one in his life, but they never quite trusted him. Horses, on the other hand, usually came around to his way of thinking after he had ridden them awhile.

He saw the flickering light from a lantern Blas had set atop the chuck box to guide the cowboys back to camp when their night of celebration was over. He said, "Stake your horse out here and be right quiet. Last thing you want to do is wake up the cook. He'd burn the breakfast biscuits sure as hell."

Hewey found his own bed. Knowing he was likely to be somewhat impaired on his return, he had had the foresight to roll it out before he left camp for the night's entertainment.

Tommy spread his blankets. Hewey noted that he had no tarp to repel rain. It did not rain often in these mountains, but on those rare occasions the downpours could be heavy. If Tommy stayed, Hewey would have to see about getting him a tarp to cover his bedroll.

Tommy was likely to come up short in other ways too. Breaking horses and mules for Alvin Lawdermilk at home was a far cry from working on a big outfit like the J Bar in the Davis Mountains. Without even trying, he could think of twenty easy ways a green kid could get himself skinned and bloodied. Hewey would have to watch over him like a mother hen. Best thing was to try to talk him into going home. That would take the responsibility from Hewey's shoulders, and he avoided responsibility like he avoided measles and chicken pox.

He drifted off to sleep rehearsing the speech he would lay on Tommy to hasten his return to the farm.

Next morning he could not remember a word of it.

CHAPTER

3

Hewey was not ready to quit his blankets when Blas clanged his pothook against an iron rod and hollered the hands up for break-fast. He had been half asleep, half awake, his nose assaulted by sharp smoke from the cook's fire and his ears by Blas's reckless banging of lids against the pots and Dutch ovens. Hewey did not know why his head hurt so badly and his stomach was so sour. He remembered eating a couple of boiled eggs from a bowl on top of the bar last night. One of them must have been bad.

He had not bothered to remove his clothes before going to bed. He put on his hat, then his boots with their pair of sporty gal-leg spurs that had a shank shaped like a woman's leg, complete with garter and high-heeled shoe. Loud talk told him Snort Yarnell and the other Slash R cowboys were coming into camp. As a neighborly gesture Bige Saunders had invited them to share breakfast because they had brought no chuck wagon to town.

Hewey hurried to his feet, not wanting Snort to catch him in his blankets this late in the morning. The sun was almost ready to come up. Snort was always looking for something to hooraw a man about. The better he liked someone, the louder the hoorawing.

Snort shouted, "Hey, Hewey, you up?"

"Been up for an hour. Already had my coffee."

Snort seemed in much too good a humor for the night to have been so short. He could drain a barrel of whiskey and still wake up at daylight, ready to go. Hewey wondered sometimes if Snort was all human.

Snort recognized Tommy and made a big fuss over him. "I heard you say you're lookin' for a cowpunchin' job. If old Bige don't hire you, come over to the Slash R. I'll take you under my wing and show you things you never heard of."

Hewey said dryly, "His mama'd be tickled to hear that." He felt a bit guilty, realizing that as an old family friend Snort had visited the Calloway homestead periodically and had seen Tommy since Hewey had.

Cold sober now, Hewey felt the weight of responsibility even heavier than last night as he introduced Tommy to Bige Saunders. Because Bige was foreman, it was his place to hire and fire, though Old Man Jenkins was likely to whisper in his ear on occasion. Bige was a man of fifty years and a solid hundred and seventy-five pounds, his shoulders broader than Hewey's, broad enough to carry the weight of a boss's responsibilities.

"So you're Hewey's nephew," he said, contemplating Tommy in the first light of dawn. "Can't say you favor him, though I'd mark that as an asset. Had any experience workin' stock?"

Tommy explained that the Calloways raised cattle in a modest way as well as crops. He did not mention the sheep.

Hewey hoped Bige would decide Tommy was too young and in-experienced. There was a lot of difference between growing up on a stock farm and being an honest-to-God cowboy. He put in, "Up against a big outfit like the J Bar, that little old place of my brother's ain't big enough to make a decent horse trap."

Hopefully Tommy described his experience in breaking horses and mules for Alvin Lawdermilk.

Bige said, "I knew Alvin way back yonder. He still favor the whiskey like he used to?"

"Not anymore. He's taken the pledge."

That didn't sound like Alvin, Hewey thought. He had probably just said so to satisfy the preacher, Brother Averill.

Bige favored a little toddy himself once in a while, but Hewey had never seen him take one when there was a job to see after. Old Man Jenkins could not have found a more responsible foreman and wagon boss if he had hunted all over hell and half of Texas. Hewey thought it ought to be clear to Bige that Tommy was not ready for a job like this, but the favorable gleam in Bige's eyes indicated that Hewey was going to be saddled with the worry of looking after Tommy whether he liked it or not.

Bige said, "Goin' wage around here for a green hand is twenty-five a month, chuck and all the ground you need to roll out your beddin'."

Tommy had never earned twenty-five dollars a month. Alvin Lawdermilk would likely have paid him thirty or thirty-five had he been able to work full-time, but Tommy's responsibilities on the family stock farm had prevented that. His father probably needed him at home a lot more than Bige or Old Man Jenkins needed him here. Still, Hewey could understand the boy's need for independence. He had been a lot younger than Tommy when he had set out on his own.

Bige shook Tommy's hand. "Well, son, with your uncle Hewey's help I expect you'll be makin' us a top hand in no time. Two men went to Kansas with the cattle, so I'll pick you a string of horses out of theirs."

Tommy pumped Bige's hand and grinned with delight.

Hewey's stomach went a little more sour. Damn those boiled eggs!

Before they left town, Hewey insisted that Tommy write his parents a letter and let them know where he was. He watched Tommy to be sure the job was done and the letter posted.

Hewey said, "Any time you get to feelin' homesick, just let me know."

Tommy did not take the hint. He inhaled a long breath of fresh mountain air, his blue eyes shining with pleasure. "I think I'm really goin' to like it here."

Hewey could see that he would have the boy on his hands for a while if Walter and Eve didn't come and take him home.

Snort and the Slash R cowboys drifted away, back to the ranch they worked for. Hewey had half expected Snort to draw his time and set off for someplace new. He had already stayed at the Slash R longer than anywhere Hewey could remember. Perhaps Snort was getting old and looking for a place to light. For that matter, Hewey's tenure at the J Bar had stretched well beyond his usual limit. But in his case he was not getting old; he was just getting easier to suit.

Tommy watched Blas lift up and latch the chuck box lid, preparing the wagon to move. The boy asked eagerly, "Where do you reckon we're goin'?"

"Back to the ranch. We've got calves to brand and a new bunch of broncs to break."

"Broncs? That sounds like fun."

Hewey glanced toward Skip Harkness. That was what Skip would say, too. *I'll have to watch this boy pretty close,* he thought.

Hewey was still riding Biscuit so Mr. Jenkins would not worry about him forking broncs. The first gate they reached, he would turn Biscuit into the remuda and catch out one of the broncs he had been breaking.

As was typical of ranches so near the Rio Grande, the J Bar crew had more Mexican vaqueros than Anglo cowboys. Border conflicts were not altogether a thing of the past—they still happened on occasion—so the tendency was for members of the two groups to draw toward their own kind when the work did not push them all together. Last night's celebration in the saloon had let the fences down for a little while.

Part of the problem was a language barrier. Hewey had worked along the border and picked up just enough Spanish to get by on, though Mexican children who heard him often covered their mouths to hide their amusement. Most of the vaqueros spoke little English and frequently called upon Blas or Aparicio to interpret. Hewey doubted that Tommy knew much Spanish, if any at all. He would probably starve in Mexico; he would not know how to ask for food or water.

Before the outfit was two miles from Alpine and the remuda strung out toward the broken country, Tommy and Skip Harkness had struck up a friendship. They rode side by side. Hewey was too far back to hear more than fragments of their conversation, but he could see that they laughed a lot and gestured with their hands, exchanging shady jokes they probably thought were new. Hewey had heard them years ago.

He understood why the two would hit it off. They were within a year or so of the same age, and they had in common that both had been brought up to be farmers but had left home to taste the cowboy life. Hewey wished Tommy would pair up with someone who exhibited more judgment—like him, for instance. Hanging around with Skip, Tommy might be exposed to all kinds of foolish notions. It was not Hewey's business to tell Tommy who his friends ought to be, though he might give the boy a subtle hint, like telling him that Skip had the brains God gave a ground squirrel.

He thought of his own long friendship with Snort Yarnell. Snort had never appeared to worry about consequences; he simply did what he wanted when he wanted and to whomever he wanted. He had gotten Hewey into many a ticklish jackpot, but so far none had been fatal. Most had seemed funny later, looked back on from the safe vantage point of time, funny and totally foolish.

Loose horses tended to move faster than the wagons, so Hewey had to ride out in front and slow them down after a while to prevent them from overtaking Blas. The driver of the hoodlum wagon laid back the first wire gate they came to because Blas's crippled leg made it inconvenient for him to climb up and down. The gate was left open for the horses to follow. Hewey signaled for Tommy to close it after the remuda had passed. Skip and Tommy both held back, giving chase to a jackrabbit and trying unsuccessfully to rope it. Hewey could hear their laughter a hundred yards away.

They returned in a long trot. Hewey demanded, "Did it take both of you?"

"Tight gate." Tommy grinned.

"I don't know what you'd've done with that rabbit if you'd caught it. Try a badger sometime."

He had done that himself once and had found the badger coming up the rope to meet him and in no mood for compromise. Catching a badger was not terribly difficult. Getting the rope back could be hazardous.

Next time he saw a badger he would point it out to the boys. The experience would broaden their education.

No one had bothered to put up signposts along the way, for the wagon road to the J Bar was not a public thoroughfare. Anyone who did not know his way had no business following it anyhow. Blas needed no signposts, or even a road. There was probably not a wagon rut or cow trail in these mountains which the old vaquero had not traveled at some time or other, and few ranches on which he had not worked.

Folks claimed he had helped the army track holdout Apaches thirty or forty years ago, though he never made claims or even answered questions about those times beyond a nod or a negative shaking of his gray head. Perhaps he was ashamed of something there, for both sides had done terrible things to one another. Or perhaps it was simply so far in the past that it no longer held interest for him.

Hewey had a keen eye for horses. In a short while he had surveyed the penful of new broncs, deciding which would be likely to make dependable working horses and which would never be even decent bait for the Mexican panthers that prowled their way up from the Big Bend of the Rio Grande. Horses were much like men in that most found a level at which they functioned comfortably, a few like Biscuit would prove outstanding, and a few never would be worth the price of the cartridge needed to put them out of everybody's misery.

It was customary that the foreman assign a "mount" of broncs as each hand's individual responsibility. Bige Saunders preferred that each man take turns, picking one at a time to avoid any appearance of favoritism. He did not make the Mexican hands take second best after the Anglos; he treated everyone the same.

Aparicio was roping out the broncs one by one. Hewey had his eye on a likely-looking sorrel. He pointed to it and said, "Catch me that one, *por favor.*"

Saunders waved Aparicio off. "Hewey, seems like you neglected to tell me that Mr. Jenkins said you wasn't to ride any more broncs."

Hewey tried to look innocent. "He said that? I must've forgot."

"Forgetfulness overtakes us all when we get older. You've celebrated too many birthdays, Hewey. You've got to quit ridin' these broncs before one of them cleans your plow for once and for all."

"I'm just now comin' into my prime."

It occurred to Hewey that he would probably have to quit the J Bar one day soon and find a job on some ranch where they didn't discriminate against a man simply because he had had more experience than most. But he couldn't leave just yet because Tommy would want to go with him, and he hadn't been on the payroll long enough to earn his first paycheck.

Saunders looked at Tommy. "Which one do you want?"

Tommy said, "That sorrel."

Hewey said, "You've got good judgment. Alvin Lawdermilk must've taught you a right smart."

"I picked him because you did."

"Then you *do* have good judgment."

Skip Harkness made his first choice on the basis of the wildest-looking, the most likely to offer him a rousing fight. By that measure, he selected well. He picked a long-tailed bay whose conformation indicated a strain of mustang and whose rolling eyes suggested war.

Skip said, "I believe he'll give me plenty of fun."

Hewey responded, "I believe he'll kill you."

Most of the broncs bore rope burns across their noses, indicating they had already fought through a session or two with the hackamore, being staked to a heavy log or wagon wheel until they learned the hard way that the rope was boss. The marks would heal, but the lesson would remain with all except a few unreachables. Supposedly the broncs had been saddled and ridden—or ridden at—a time or two by the outfit that raised them, but horse dealers could be notoriously cavalier with the facts. Hewey contended that most had missed a calling in politics.

Ideally, breaking broncs was a task best done in winter when cowboys had more free time on their hands, but Jenkins believed the best training for a cow horse was working with cattle, and Hewey could not argue the point. When the broncs were well broken and had learned something about following a cow, Jenkins would resell them at a profit and bring in a new batch of raw ponies. A believer in the adage that idle hands are the devil's workshop, he had a strong commitment to protecting his employees' moral fiber.

Hewey advised Skip, "If I was you, I'd work up to that bay sort of gradual. I'd ride them other two first and get myself in shape."

"I'd rather start with the roughest one while I'm fresh. After him, the others'll be like pets."

Warmed-over advice was as stale as warmed-over coffee, so Hewey seldom made the same suggestion twice. "If I was you, then, I'd take time to write a letter home. It might be the last one your poor old mother ever gets."

Tommy eyed the boy with misgivings. "I think Uncle Hewey's right, Skip. That pony looks like a bad one."

"That's the way I like them."

From the moment the loop circled its neck, the bay bronc went into a stomping, squealing fury. It plunged against the rope, dragging Skip and Tommy halfway across the corral, their boot heels firmly dug into the dirt, raising dust like a dry fog behind them. When it reached the fence, it whirled and quartered back the other way. The impact when it hit the end of the line sent Skip sprawling on his face, but Tommy braced the rope around his hip and hung on. The bronc reared and pawed.

Hewey hollered, "Watch him, Tommy. He'll stomp you." He started out to help, then decided to hold back. The boys had to learn.

Skip pushed to his feet, picking up his fallen hat and dusting himself with it. A hint of fear insinuated itself into his eyes, or perhaps it was an awakening wisdom. "He may be a little tougher than I figured."

Tommy said, "It'd do him a world of good to drag a log around for two or three days before you try to get on him."

"If you say so. I guess he'll keep."

You're getting smarter all the time, Hewey thought. Perhaps Tommy was a good influence on Skip instead of Skip being a bad influence on Tommy.

They had to put a loop around the bay's forefeet and throw him down to put a hackamore on him. Hewey tried to leave it to the boys but finally could hold back no longer and pitched in to help. He tied a length of heavy rope to the hackamore as a rein, dallied it to his saddle horn and led the bronc out onto the flat, where several long logs lay scattered over a beaten-out stretch of ground covered only by a thin stand of short burro grass. Tommy started to tie the rope to a log that had once been part of a cottonwood trunk.

Hewey said, "It's Skip's horse. Let him tie the rope."

The log was heavy enough that the bay would have difficulty in dragging it, yet it would yield enough to minimize the risk of injury. The colt made a running start and was jerked up short at the end of the rope. It fell backward onto its rump, kicking, then scrambling to its feet. The log had moved six inches.

Tommy said, "Time he's drug that thing around for a few days he'll be a heap better educated."

Hewey said, "Time Skip's tried to ride that knothead a couple of times, *he'll* be a heap better educated, too."

Skip said, "I'll have him eatin' out of my hand."

Hewey grunted. "Or maybe just eatin' your hand."

Tommy's sorrel fought the rope, but he put up less fight than Skip's long-tailed bay. Tommy handled him with quiet ease. Hewey warmed with pride.

The hands rode their new broncs in the evenings after they finished the day's rounding up and branding. The location was central enough to a large part of the ranch that camp did not have to be moved for several days while the nearby pastures were being worked. The fresh colts were left staked through the day while the cowboys rode out on their regular business. By the time the wagon had to shift to another camp, most of the broncs would be more tractable. They might progress far enough to be ridden on roundup, earning their keep.

Though Tommy's sorrel and most of the others quickly adapted to their new situation, Skip's bay seemed no gentler after spending two days tied to the log, led away only for feed and water. When approached, it rolled its eyes and challenged the end of the rope. The impact jerked it around unceremoniously but did not alter its behavior.

Hewey warned, "That horse is plumb mean, and maybe half idiot to boot."

He saw dread in Skip's eyes. Sooner or later the boy had to either climb into the saddle or back down in front of everybody. He would not back down. Hewey doubted that any man in the crew would. None of the Mexican hands would want to retreat in front of the gringos, and none of the gringos would want to look diminished in the eyes of the Mexicans. The rivalry was friendly enough, but it was real. The battle of the Alamo had not been laid entirely to rest.

The third evening Skip could no longer put off the confrontation. He looked out across the flat where some of the young broncs were still tied. All had been ridden except his. He said, "I reckon it's time he learns who's boss."

Hewey thought Skip's voice sounded hollow. "I don't know that he's ready to get religion yet."

"I can handle him."

What Skip couldn't handle, Hewey thought, was the feeling that the rest of the crew might consider him afraid. "If you're bound and determined . . . Come on, Tommy, let's give him a hand."

Hewey wrapped the end of the hackamore rein around his saddle horn and led the bronc into the corral. It resisted all the way, setting its legs, hopping, twisting, tugging back on the rope as Biscuit stubbornly dragged it forward.

Hewey secured the bronc to a snubbing post in the center of the pen and backed Biscuit away to avoid being kicked by the flailing hooves. Bige Saunders stood near the fence, frowning. Hewey rode back to him.

"Bige, I don't believe that boy can handle this one."

"He seems to think so." Skip was carrying his blanket toward the thrashing bronc. Tommy followed with the saddle.

"He's too game to quit on his own, but you could tell him to. You could say that pony needs to be staked out some more."

"He's already had three days. I don't think three *weeks* would make much difference."

"Then tell Skip you've decided to let somebody with more experience ride him first. Me maybe, or Aparicio. That'd give the kid a respectable way out."

"It'd shame him. Skip picked that pony. He'll have to ride him, or try to."

The bay fought so frantically that Skip was unable to keep the blanket on long enough for Tommy to follow it with the saddle. Hewey got a rope on one foot and tied it up so the bronc could not paw or kick without falling. After several tries, he and Skip and Tommy, all working together, got the saddle on and cinched down. The pony humped its back so much that it reminded Hewey of a camel.

Hewey threw his right arm around the bronc's neck and grabbed both ears. "All right, get on him." He would bite down on an ear if necessary, but he had rather not get all that hair in his teeth. It always left a gritty taste that kept him spitting until he could wash it down with coffee.

Skip swung into the saddle. The pony tried to jump but went down on its rump. Tommy untied the rope that bound a foot.

Skip's voice was shaky. "All right, turn him loose."

Hewey relinquished his hold on the ears and jumped back. The bronc lashed a hind foot at him as it went by. The hoof just missed

Hewey's ear. Out by the fence, Aparicio Rodriguez laughed. Cowboys almost always laughed at a near thing, especially when it happened to someone else. The trait was common to Anglo and Mexican alike.

Hewey had not seen many range broncs pitch harder than this one. He thought it could hold its own against professional buckers in the 101 Ranch Wild West Show. Skip's hat sailed off and was pounded into a shapeless lump beneath the hooves. He grunted each time the pony hit the ground. Every jump lifted Skip a little higher from his seat. He gave up trying to make a show of it and gripped the saddle horn. Pride gave way to the instinct for survival.

Though Skip was making a good fight, he was wearing down while the bronc seemed only to gain strength and determination. Daylight between the kid and the saddle grew broader with every jump. One stirrup flopped free, then the other. As Skip left the saddle, Hewey rushed forward, waving his hat and shouting, trying to spook the horse out of kicking range. But the bay managed to strike the kid with one hind foot while Skip was still in the air. Free of the rider, it pitched on across the corral, squealing its rage, the stirrups bouncing. The back of the kid's head hit the ground.

Hewey rushed to Skip's side, Tommy and Saunders and Aparicio close behind. The young cowboy lay limp and unresponsive. No one was laughing now.

Saunders said, "He's knocked out cold." He motioned for a couple of the young hands to lift Skip and carry him out of the corral so the still-excited bronc could not run over him.

Hewey and Aparicio trapped the horse in a corner, and Tommy grabbed the hackamore rein.

Hewey yelled, "Boy, what you fixin' to do?"

Tommy said, "Ride him. Worst thing we can do is let him get away with it. He needs to be rode, and right now."

Hewey argued, "If your mother could see you she'd kill both of us."

Aparicio offered to take over the ride, but Tommy said, "You take ahold of his ears." The boy gripped the horn with his right hand, the rein and a handful of dark mane in his left. He swung into the saddle and pulled his hat down tight. "Ready," he said.

The first long jump lifted him several inches from the saddle. He regained his balance and gripped firmly with his knees. Watching, Hewey could almost feel the jarring impact of each landing. But Tommy rode the bronc until it quit pitching and began circling the corral in a run, its hide dripping sweat. It drew its breath in great sobbing drafts.

At length the pony quit running and stood still, trembling in confusion and fatigue. Tommy swung down quickly and stepped away so it could not kick him if it took a notion to. It was too weary to try.

Hewey felt weary too from witnessing his nephew's performance.

Bige Saunders walked up to Tommy. "Good ride, but you look kind of gray around the gills."

"Just winded, is all. Is Skip still out?"

"He's tryin' to rally, but he doesn't know whether he's in Cape Cod or Hickory Bend."

"He made a game try. Let's don't tell him I finished his ride."

Saunders grunted. "I don't imagine that bay'll buck as hard the next time Skip tries. You took the starch out of him."

Hewey said, "It took the starch out of me, watchin' him. I told you, Bige, us Calloways know how to ride."

Bige frowned. "I hope you know how to quit, and when."

As Bige walked away, Hewey put his arm around Tommy's shoulder. "Young'un, I never taught you to ride like that."

"I learned by ridin' broncs for Alvin Lawdermilk. I wanted to be just like you, Uncle Hewey."

"Like me?" He thought of Eve and what she would say. "God help us all!"

When the branding was finished, Tommy asked Hewey what they were likely to do next. Hewey said, "First thing you need to learn is that you don't ask questions. You watch the boss. If he saddles his best drive horse, you catch your best drive horse. If he saddles his best cuttin' horse, you're fixin' to work the herd, so you catch up the one that's quickest and quietest around the cattle."

"But Bige didn't saddle a horse at all. He left a while ago on the chuck wagon, headin' for town."

"In a case like that, you just keep workin' on your broncs and wait for them to tell you what to do."

Bige returned with a big load of flour, coffee and other camp necessities, which caused Hewey to wonder some, but pride still would not let him ask questions. With the branding finished, he saw no need to restock the chuck wagon. When Bige was ready, he would tell them what he wanted them to know.

That happened in the bunkhouse dining room at supper. Bige said, "Mr. Jenkins'll be here after a while in his automobile. First thing in the mornin', him and me are goin' down under the rimrock to the Circle W outfit that he just bought. Hewey, I'd appreciate it if you and the boys would bring the horses and follow the wagons. We'll be countin' the Circle W cattle."

Bige was the kind of boss who issued orders as if he were asking a favor, not giving a command.

Hewey replied as if he were consenting to the favor out of the goodness of his heart and not as a condition of employment. "We'll be tickled to do that. You reckon Blas knows the way?"

"Blas knows every cow trail from the Guadalupes to the Rio Grande. All you need to do is follow him. I'd be obliged if you'd keep an eye on everything, Hewey."

There they were again, giving him a sort of straw-boss responsibility he had not asked for. But how could he refuse a favor so politely requested? "Why, sure."

He had never been to the Circle W and had only a general notion how far it was from J Bar headquarters. It made no real difference whether the trip was short or long; making it was simply part of the job he was being paid for, and trailing horses was always pleasurable. He relied on Blas to set the pace and the route.

As they went along, the going became rougher, the trail steeper and rockier, so the chuck wagon and hoodlum wagon could not make good time. It was a challenge to keep the remuda from overtaking and passing them. Blas camped the first night beside a clear-running narrow creek where an old set of brush corrals would hold the horses. The grass was green, so Hewey suggested that the hands loose-herd them and let them graze awhile, though the traveling had been slow enough to allow considerable grazing through the day.

He was glad for the stop. He wondered why he felt tired. The shipping, then the branding, had kept him going at a steady clip for weeks, but that had never seemed to bother him much in the past. He speculated that it was the responsibility of watching out for Tommy, seeing to it that he did not let Skip Harkness lead him off into some kind of foolishness that might get him hurt or fired. In some ways, Skip reminded him of a young Snort Yarnell.

Hard work had never bothered Hewey, but responsibility had always been a smothering burden.

While the horses were grazing, he found a pair of markings on a boulder twice the size of Blas's wagon. One was a name and a date and the words "10th CAV" scratched into the rock, like a tombstone without a grave. The other was a faded black painting of a strange oblong figure with a square head and stick arms, a spear in one hand.

Tommy and Skip rode up to look at the markings with him. Tommy pointed to the painted one. "What you reckon that's supposed to represent, Uncle Hewey?"

"Some kind of medicine man maybe, or some kind of a god. There used to be Apaches here, and before them I expect there was others."

"There's probably a story behind it, and behind that other one, too. Tenth Cavalry. Those were buffalo soldiers, weren't they?"

"I think so. That was before my time. There was all kinds of people passed through here in the years gone by—Indians, Mexicans, white men . . . all of them gone."

Many stories went untold in these mountains, secrets hidden beyond the haze of uncountable years, old victories now forgotten, old crimes long buried. Sometimes Hewey's skin prickled as he imagined he could hear ancient spirits whispering to him in languages he could not understand, trying to tell him something no one but God knew anymore.

It was a grand country, on its face at least, but through those stories he *had* heard, he was aware that it had known darkness, too. Some of the people who had passed this way had been victors, some of them victims, some seeking peace and some on their way to war. They had left little trace of themselves beyond random markings on the stones. Men probably lay buried where he now rode, but he had no way of knowing. Whoever they had been, however long or short their stay, whatever triumphs and tragedies they had experienced here, the stones were silent and the wind had long since taken their tracks away.

One day Hewey would also be gone, and he had not even carved his name on a mountainside so that someone in the future would know he had once been here. It was a disturbing thought, one he did not allow to burden him for long. Tomorrow could take care of itself. This was today. Today had always been more important to Hewey than either yesterday, which could not be changed, or tomorrow, which he could only guess at.

Skip said, "I'm goin' to scratch my name on there, too."

Hewey said, "You oughtn't to. It'd be like markin' up somebody's tombstone."

"A hundred years from now that may be the only trace left of me."

Tommy shook his head. "I'm figurin' on still bein' around a hundred years from now."

Hewey said, "And me with you."

Skip argued, "A hundred years from now you'd be a hundred and fifty years old . . . maybe a hundred and seventy-five."

"That," said Hewey, "is when I may decide to give up ridin'."

He was gratified when Skip rode away without adding his name to the inscriptions on the rock.

Hewey inspected the old corrals and shored up a couple of weak places where horses might slip through and escape in the night. After the remuda was safely penned, he staked Biscuit outside on grass at the end of a long rope so the brown could graze freely. He patted the horse's neck and talked as if the animal could understand whatever he said. Working alone much of his life, he had picked up the habit of talking to his horse when he had no fellow humans to talk to.

He heard Skip Harkness's voice behind him. "I'd like to be around the day he answers you back. I'll bet you jump two feet high."

Hewey felt a twinge of embarrassment along with faint resentment. This had been a private conversation. He sensed that Skip was trying to impress Tommy with his wit, for he still could not resist showing off a little. Reformation came slowly to some. "At least he doesn't talk a lot of nonsense, like some cowpuncher kids I've known."

"Too bad he *can't* talk. I'll bet he could tell some funny stories on you."

"He'd have the good sense to keep his mouth shut. Some people could learn a lot from a horse."

Blas clanged a pothook against a steel rod, calling the hands to supper. That gave Hewey a welcome excuse to end the conversation, which was not going anywhere. Walking ahead of the others, he heard Tommy talking quietly to Skip. "You oughtn't to tease Uncle Hewey. He's just gettin' sort of old, is all."

Must think I'm losing my hearing, too, Hewey thought. The words stung a bit, but he supposed from Tommy's viewpoint he was a little long in the tooth. He was more than twice his nephew's age.

He lifted his bedroll down from the hoodlum wagon so he could sit on it while he ate. Tommy joined him, his own bedroll too small to provide much of a seat. Under pressure of time, Hewey had forgotten his intention of buying Tommy a protective tarp before they left Alpine. It probably wasn't going to rain anyway. It didn't often. There was not room enough left for Skip on the bedroll, so he sat on the ground and leaned back against the end of the roll for support.

The new adventure was good for Tommy's appetite. He had heaped his plate high with beef and beans and two tall sourdough biscuits. He said, "I don't know when I ever tasted better."

Skip commented, "Blas cooks good, but it gets monotonous after a while: biscuits and beef and beans, beans and beef and biscuits."

Hewey said, "It's hard to have variety when the kitchen keeps movin'. Anyway, try batchin' for a while and you'll appreciate a good cook."

A high canyon wall just west of camp blocked the setting sun so that dusk came early and stretched out awhile. With darkness and the first bright stars came a light chill, though not enough to cause

Hewey to dig into his war bag for a denim jacket. He heard a horse squeal, and hooves shuffled in the corral as one of the more dominant animals bullied a timid one. Night birds called to one another from the trees. Wood crackled as it burned down into glowing coals in Blas's fire pit.

On the other side of camp, one of the Mexicans plucked at a guitar, and Aparicio Rodriguez's voice rose in a plaintive song of unrequited love and welcome death. It seemed to Hewey that most Mexican songs were melancholy at heart. Many cowboy songs as well told sad stories of dying on the range far from home, or of long-ago loves who had been left behind.

The music carried Hewey back to another time, to a summer's courtship of Spring Renfro. He asked Tommy, "Since you finished your schoolin', do you ever see Miss Renfro anymore?"

"Every time I've been over to the Lawdermilks'. She's always there."

"Has she changed any?"

"Got a little older, I guess." From the vantage point of a boy in his teens she had been old to start with, having been in her thirties when she became his teacher.

"I mean, is she still pretty?"

"I never thought of her that way. Old maids ain't supposed to be pretty, are they?"

"She's not an old maid yet. From where I sit, she's still young."

"From where you sit, I guess just about everybody looks young."

Skip Harkness was a bad influence on the boy, Hewey thought.

Tommy looked up at the stars. His voice was tinged with awe. "Ain't it beautiful out here, Uncle Hewey? I never saw the like of these mountains."

Hewey nodded. "It *is* a smilin' country."

"I can see why you never could be happy with anything but a ridin' job. It never was this pretty on the farm."

"Your mama and daddy would argue with you about that. It's not just what you see that makes somethin' pretty; it's findin' what you *want* to see."

"This is what I wanted to see, all right."

Hewey suspected it would take a while to talk Tommy into going home . . . if he even could.

CHAPTER

4

The Circle W pleased Hewey on first sight. Most new places did, then gradually lost their luster through familiarity. One point which appealed to him was that the previous owner seemed to have shared Hewey's aversion to barbed wire. Except for a couple of horse traps, most of the ranch's hundred square miles were in one large pasture fenced only around its perimeter. It reminded him of the open-range days of recent memory, when hide-ripping wire was scarcer than rain.

Most ranchers claimed that smaller pastures were easier to work, but Hewey saw no reason why everything should be easy. A little physical exertion was good for the soul. He made an exception for opening gates.

As he had heard the story in town, Augie Wilson had put the ranch together in the late 1880s and early '90s for the eventual benefit of his two sons. Unfortunately, one had died of dysentery serving under Teddy Roosevelt in Cuba. Hewey could relate to that, for the same ailment had caused him to miss the charge up San Juan Hill. He had never so much as shot at a Spaniard. Hindsight had made him grateful for that. The Spaniards were said to have blown up the *Maine,* but none of them had done him any personal injury. Still, there was a void in his life. He wished he could have enjoyed the excitement of charging up that hill with Teddy. What a bully show it would have been!

The other Wilson son had been a sticky-fingered sort who developed a bad habit of burning his brand on other people's calves, earning him a one-way trip to the Huntsville penitentiary. Having no family member to help her run the ranch or to leave it to, Wilson's widow had chosen to sell it and spend her declining years in the comfort of Fort Davis town.

Wilson's dislike for barbed wire had been equaled by his love for the Longhorn, so the scattering of cows that retreated ahead of the horses showed the original wild Texas strain. Hewey suspected Old Man Jenkins would not wait long to bring in Hereford or Durham sires, consigning the Longhorn bulls to a packinghouse—as many as his cowboys could catch, anyway. In three or four generations, most of the old blood would be bred out. That was the trend in this new century: throw away whatever was old and traditional, grasp whatever was regarded as modern . . . fast automobiles, fast trains, electric lights that required no matches and no blowing out.

He had even seen a flying machine set down on a flat stretch of ground outside of Alpine. It looked like a cross between a kite and a prickly-pear burner. If God had intended a man to get that high in the air, He would have put feathers on him.

Tommy seemed favorably impressed by the lack of fences because he'd had to shut so many wire gates on the way here after the horses had gone through. Some were so tight that Skip had to join forces with him to fasten them. Hewey could have done it, but he figured the boys needed the education. A seasoned cowboy knew to stay on horseback and let somebody else do most of the footwork.

Tommy said in admiration, "It's a wonderful-lookin' country."

True, its scenery was more spectacular than Upton County's. A high gray rimrock towered over the western side of the long valley like a great stone wall built to keep the barbarians out, or perhaps to keep them in, depending upon how you chose to look at it. Some of the mountains ranged from six thousand feet in altitude to more than eight, and the valley that made up most of the ranch was probably close to four, easily a thousand to fifteen hundred feet higher than the Calloway homestead. It was a high-lonesome country, sure enough.

One good thing about the altitude in Hewey's view: this region was too high for growing crops. It ought to remain safe from the plow.

A man could freeze the buttons off his shirt here on winter mornings, though that towering wall probably provided shelter against the west and northwest winds. It had been Apache country even to the time of Hewey's boyhood. He wondered how Indians had made it through January and February in nothing more than breechclout and leggings.

He need not dwell on that because he would probably move on before next winter. For now, the spring sun was pleasantly warm. Grass was turning green at its base, poised to receive the rains that usually began here in June, except in those years when they forgot to come at all. Given decent moisture, it was a great country for cattle in the summer and fall. It was fair enough through winter if the landowner avoided overgrazing and saved back enough summer forage. Spring, usually dry, could be long and challenging, but ranchers hung on to the hope that June would bring rain. Hewey could see a thunderhead building over the rimrock, probably setting the stage for an afternoon drenching.

Tommy would wish he had a tarp to shed water from his bedroll. Well, next time he would know. Life was one hard-learned lesson after another.

Letting the remuda set its own easy pace, Hewey noticed a roadrunner trotting to one side. "Smart little bird," he told Tommy. "He's lettin' the horses scare up dinner for him."

A tiny lizard, frightened into movement by the passage of the remuda, scurried away from the noise and into the path of a far deadlier hazard. In a startling dash the roadrunner overtook it, spreading its tail to brake to a quick stop. It threw up its head, and the lizard disappeared down its throat.

Skip declared, "Poor little devil didn't have a chance."

Hewey said, "It would've had better luck if it'd been too big to swallow whole. That *paisano* bird might've just grabbed it by the tail, the tail would've broke loose, and the rest of the lizard would've gotten away. They can grow a new tail, you know."

Skip was incredulous. "That story's too big to swallow whole, too."

"It's a fact. Why, I've heard the Mexicans tell about *paisanos* that raised herds of lizards like me and you would raise a herd of cattle. They wouldn't eat anything but the tails, and pretty soon the tails would grow back. Them birds didn't have to waste time huntin'. They just laid around gettin' fat and watchin' their herd grow new tails over and over, the way sheep grow a new clip of wool every time you shear them."

Tommy suppressed a grin; he had heard his uncle spin windies before. Hewey took pleasure in the quizzical expression on Skip's freckled face as the young cowboy floundered between scorn and reluctant belief. It did a green kid good to guess a little, reminding him that he didn't know everything.

Skip said, "There ain't no bird that smart." But he still wavered.

Hewey shrugged. "I never seen it for myself, of course. I'm just tellin' you what's been told to me."

Tommy observed Skip's confusion as long as he could before he let his grin break free. "Uncle Hewey, you're still the best liar I ever listened to. Better than Snort Yarnell."

Hewey smiled. Even backhanded praise was welcome, coming from his nephew.

The farther Hewey rode onto this ranch the better he liked the look of it. He appreciated that many of the cattle hoisted their tails and took to the breaks in a sturdy lope at first sight of horses and riders. That demonstrated a healthy Texas independence. Most of the calves had been left unbranded because of the probability that their ownership would change.

The long rock wall and the distant blue mountains framed the broad valley like a picture, topped by a crystal-clear sky. Wildflowers in bloom lent their colors to the green of the rising grass, and Hewey breathed deeply of their perfume.

So what if he had to patch the knees of his britches when he got settled, or dig a few thorns from his hide? A lot of folks in town would spend good money to see such as this, and he was being paid thirty dollars a month for the privilege.

For the last part of the drive Hewey freed the half-broken bronc he had been riding and saddled Biscuit, for he knew Old Man Jenkins would be watching the procession roll into ranch headquarters.

As the cottonwood trees and the ranch buildings came into view, Skip said, "Tommy, I'll bet the corral gate is shut. I'll race you to see who opens it."

"On that spavined nag? My bronc can run rings around him."

Hewey warned, "Mr. Jenkins'll teach you boys some words you never heard before. You was hired to drive horses, not to race them."

Skip argued, "A little race never hurt nobody."

"Don't come cryin' to me if you find yourself sittin' on a street corner in Alpine with your pocket empty and your stomach talkin' to you."

He remembered, though he would not tell these boys, that he and Snort Yarnell had run many a horse race together and sometimes had lost everything but their shirts. First the boys should learn the way things ought to be. They would learn soon enough the way things actually were.

The headquarters reminded Hewey of something out of his boyhood, as if little new had been added in thirty or forty years. Though a stream ran nearby, a windmill tower stood tall to catch the wind coming up the valley or down from the rimrock to turn the wooden Eclipse fan, insurance against drought that might dry up the surface water. Whoever had first settled the place must have imported Mexican artisans, for most of the buildings were of adobe. The main house was constructed low and flat, as was an even longer structure Hewey judged to be a bunkhouse and kitchen for the hands. The main barn was of weathered wood, a stranger to paint. The corrals were of the same brush construction as most of the camps on Jenkins's J Bar, though the swinging gates were built of sawmill lumber. A couple of small sheds had adobe outer walls and were open in front.

It seemed right and proper that as much as possible be built of materials which existed in nature and close at hand. Thick adobe walls held the heat out in summer and in during winter. Hewey had been in frame houses where cold wind whistled between the boards and he could not haul enough wood to keep the place warm. He had slept outside in July and August rather than lie beneath a sheet-iron roof that trapped enough heat to keep supper biscuits warm all night.

Adobe suited him fine. He would enjoy this place for however long he stayed.

The boys' race ended prematurely, and the two came back, their horses breathing hard. Skip was looking over his shoulder. Tommy said, "Mr. Jenkins and Bige Saunders have already got the gate open."

Hewey smiled. The boys dreaded a lecture from either boss about the evils of running their horses unnecessarily. Half the basic training for a cowboy was in learning what *not* to do.

They put the horses through the gate, and Bige pushed it shut behind them. Jenkins walked up, broad shoulders hunched like he had rheumatism. Hewey could believe it, him riding all this way over the rough road in that car. Jenkins eyed Hewey's mount critically, perhaps with a little suspicion. "You were ridin' Biscuit when I last seen you, and you're ridin' him now. You sure you ain't pushin' him too hard?"

"He hardly knows he's been rode."

Blas and his swamper had pulled the chuck wagon and hoodlum wagon up close to the long adobe building and were carrying the groceries inside. At least Blas would get to cook indoors for a few days, though Hewey doubted it made much difference to him. The old vaquero enjoyed being outside except when the weather was bad. During his long years, he had probably slept more nights under the sky than under a roof. Even so, it would do his bones good not to have to be out in the rain or the chill night wind.

A couple of strangers approached from the main house. One had the look of an old cowboy. The other bore all the earmarks of a money changer. Jenkins introduced the cowboy first, probably feeling more in common with him than with the other man. "Hewey Calloway, this is Oscar Levitt. He's Mrs. Wilson's brother, here to see after her interests while we count the cattle. Mr. Petrie here, he's her lawyer. Says he don't know straight up about a cow, but he knows inside and out about transfers and deeds. He's here to keep me and Mr. Levitt honest."

"Pleased to meet you fellers," Hewey said, shaking hands with each in turn. Levitt's hands were rough as old cowhide, but his eyes were direct and honest. Petrie's hands were slick as kidskin, and his gaze barely touched Hewey's face before he turned his attention elsewhere. Hewey wondered why Jenkins even bothered to introduce Levitt and Petrie to him, for he was just a working hand here. He supposed the old man was hoping to butter him up and make him reconsider the foreman's job. Hewey thought he would enjoy staying on this place awhile, but he didn't want the weight of being a boss to interfere with his sleep.

Bige said, "Mr. Levitt's got a ranch of his own in the Guadalupes. He brought some of his crew to help with roundin' up and countin' the cows."

Hewey felt a pleasant glow at the thought of a roundup in this valley. It was the kind of work he had always liked best, for most of it was done a-horseback. He could see Jenkins's touring car parked in the shade of a big cottonwood near the main house. Peeler lay on his back, his feet extending out from beneath the running board. It seemed he was forever having to fix something on that contraption. Pity, Hewey thought, that a good horseman should waste his time messing around with an automobile. What if he *was* getting an extra twenty dollars a month? There had to be something wrong with an able-bodied man who would willingly pass up a riding job.

Because most of the ranch was unfenced, the roundup was conducted in the old-fashioned style of the open range. The cowboys rode a daily circle several miles in diameter and picked up all the cattle they came across. Each drive overlapped the previous day's to catch unworked stock that might have drifted into the cleaned area.

If Augie Wilson had disliked barbed wire, he had had no prejudice against building corrals at strategic intervals to facilitate working his cattle without having to push them the long miles to headquarters. The size and location of each drive was calculated to bring herds to one of these sets of corrals.

A day's gather might run from a hundred to three hundred cows, given the animals' natural instinct to graze in clusters rather than disperse evenly over the entire range. As the riders pushed their individual gathers into a larger herd, a cloud of dust hovered over it, twisting and turning in constantly changing patterns like the drifting cumulus clouds overhead. Cows and calves separated in the move set up a din of anxious bawling as each mother sought reunion with her offspring and each calf frantically searched for the proper udder to relieve its hunger. Calves that could not find their own mothers might try to steal milk from another cow and, more often than not, were kicked or hooked away in a hostile manner. Maternal instincts had their limits.

Congregating cattle in bunches almost always resulted in head-butting, horn-gouging contests between bulls routed from their own individual domains and thrown together into open competition for whatever females might currently be in heat. These fights could be long and savage, for Longhorn bulls were aggressive, ready for war against any male they considered a challenge to their dominance. Hewey had long observed that one major problem in trying to upgrade a herd by the introduction of more productive beef blood was that Hereford or Durham bulls were a poor match for the Longhorns in combat. Any Longhorns allowed to remain in the herd would claim most of the females and fight the other bulls away.

The Longhorns did not bluff. They went into a fight ready and willing to kill any opponent that did not turn tail and run.

Hewey had always found it interesting to watch these jarring contests of will, trying to guess which bull would come out victorious. Usually, but not always, it was the largest and oldest, the most experienced, though there came a point in life when the older bull's strength and reflexes began to fail, and it was forced to yield to the younger and more vigorous. Whipped down, the older bull would eventually have to break free and run lest the younger one pierce its vitals with a sharp horn. These whipped males usually found a place at the edge of the herd, away from the others, and continued muttering empty threats to vent their frustration.

Skip Harkness took particular enjoyment in watching these bawling, bellowing battles, taking sides with one or the other of the combatants. "Hey, Hewey, bet you a dollar Old Spot yonder makes that black one run like a scalded cat."

"You better give them bulls some room. They'd knock over a locomotive if it got in their way while they're fightin'."

The most dangerous place to be was in the path of the loser when he decided to quit the battle, for usually he was in a blind panic to escape an opponent's horns. Hewey had seen them knock down full-grown cows and trample calves to death in their haste.

The daily procedure was for both Bige Saunders and Oscar Levitt to count the cattle, Bige representing the buyer and Levitt watching out for his sister's interests. Because both were experienced cattlemen, their counts never differed by more than one or two head. Only cows and bulls were tallied; the calves were thrown in with the deal. Once the day's count was finished and any differences reconciled, the cattle would be driven through a narrow chute where Hewey would use a pocketknife to bob off the long hair at the ends of their tails so they would not be counted a second time if they got caught up in another gather. As the last of the day's cows trailed out of the chute, the ground was littered with short tufts of hair, easily lifted by any breeze that swept through. The square-ended tails looked awkward, but the hair would grow out again after a while.

It came as no surprise that Jenkins ordered the Longhorn bulls to be separated from the herd and driven into a holding trap. When the counting was done, he would ship them to a Fort Worth packinghouse and replace them with whiteface bulls.

Driving them to the trap was like a foretaste of glory for Skip Harkness because every mile was punctuated by fights as the animals struggled to establish an order of dominance. The strongest might have to combat half a dozen before he proved himself the cock of the walk. Then, bloody but triumphant, he would assume his place at the head of the line. The others would fall in behind him, more or less in the order of the ranking they had won or lost in battle.

People who preached disparagingly about the violence of man in comparison to the tranquility of the animal kingdom had never watched cattle sort out the intricacies of their social structure.

When the fighting died down and the trip became dull, Skip contrived to throw together a couple of bulls that had already demonstrated their combative natures but had not yet fought each other. More often than not he was able to stir up a rousing fight.

Halfway through the roundup, Skip precipitated one of these contests as a small herd of bulls neared the ranch headquarters and the gate to the holding trap.

"Hewey," the farm boy said, "you pick your bull. I'll bet you a dollar on the other one."

Hewey declined. "Better save your money."

Skip turned to Tommy. "How about you?"

"I ain't got a dollar to spare. Bet you a quarter, though."

Hewey thought about reminding Tommy that his mother regarded gambling as the devil's snare, but there were some lessons a boy had to learn for himself. One of the young vaqueros declared, "I bet you too, Skip." Tommy and the vaquero went into whispering consultation and chose a red bull with white spots that had whipped every challenger so far.

Skip said, "My money's on the lineback. Help me throw the two of them together, Tommy."

Hewey warned, "Tommy, give them bulls plenty of room. They can hurt you."

Tommy heeded Hewey's advice, but Skip rode in among the bulls and pushed the red one up to the lead position, where the lineback, drooling, lumbered along in an ill humor, angry noises rumbling from its throat. It did not take long for the lineback to take umbrage and ram a horn against the interloper's ribs. The red bull bellowed in anger, pawed dirt and rushed the lineback. The two butted heads with a thud like a clap of thunder, then scrambled for footing while their horns locked together. One pushed as the other gave way, then stumbled and went off balance, giving ground while its opponent pushed. The rest of the bulls seemed to ignore the pair except in yielding them space.

Hewey said, "Skip, this is a fool's game. If one of them gets crippled or killed and Mr. Jenkins finds out you set up the fight . . ."

Skip said, "They'd fight anyway. They didn't need me to get them started."

The fight began going against the lineback. The pleasure in Skip's face gave way to disappointment. He moved in closer and shouted encouragement to his champion. "Get in there! You can whip him!"

Hewey yelled, "Skip, get the hell out of the way!"

The warning was too late. The lineback abruptly wheeled and broke into a dead run to escape the red bull, blind to anything in its path. And in its path was Skip Harkness.

Struck before it could react, Skip's bay bronc was bowled over by the bull's strength and weight. Skip had time only for a grunt of surprise before the lowered head slammed into him, driving a horn deep into his stomach. The lineback flung the youngster aside as if he were a rag doll.

Hewey could only murmur, "My God!"

Tommy shouted, "Skip! Look out!" But the damage was already done. The red bull trampled Skip as it raced in close pursuit of its opponent. Skip lay on his back, trembling in shock. His shirt reddened around a large hole ripped through its front.

Hewey leaped from the saddle and hit the ground running, Tommy close behind.

Tommy cried, "Skip, are you all right?"

It was obvious he was not. Hewey brushed Tommy aside and ripped the shirt open, popping buttons. A hole in Skip's belly bubbled blood. Hewey's stomach turned over in fleeting nausea. Tommy turned away, trying not to gag.

The bay bronc rose unsteadily to its feet and staggered off, shaking itself like a dog coming out of water. It did not seem injured. Hewey saw no blood except Skip's.

In Spanish, Aparicio upbraided the vaquero who had participated in the bet. Hewey said, "That won't do any good now. Lope to the house and bring a wagon. Better still, send Mr. Jenkins's car if that driver is around."

Aparicio looked down at Skip, confirming all his fears, and spurred off in a long lope. Hewey pulled a handkerchief from his pocket. It was not clean, but this was no time to worry about niceties. He wadded it and shoved it partway into the wound, hoping to stanch the flow of blood. He wished he had a handful of flour from Blas's kitchen.

Tears trailed down Tommy's paled cheeks. "We've got to do somethin'."

"Ain't much we can do here except try to keep him from bleedin' to death." Hewey pressed down upon the handkerchief. He did not like Skip's ashen look or the way he trembled.

Tommy insisted, "Is he goin' to die?"

Hewey feared he was, but he did not want to betray that feeling to his nephew. Best to keep him hoping so long as there *was* any hope. There would be time enough later for grief. "Tommy, I wisht you and the boys would go on and put these bulls in the trap before they scatter. I'll stay here 'til Aparicio gets back."

Tommy's voice broke. "I oughtn't've bet with him. If he dies, it's my fault."

"You're not doin' him any good standin' here cryin'. There's a job to get done. And I don't want to hear any more about whose fault it is."

Reluctantly Tommy mounted. The Mexican hands who had gathered around Skip backed away and joined him after two made the sign of the cross. Hewey heard them discussing Skip's poor chances and was glad Tommy understood little Spanish.

Skip groaned. Hewey gently squeezed his shoulder. "You just hang and rattle, kid. Help'll be comin'."

Under his breath, he whispered a prayer for mercy on a foolish boy.

Pity and anger clashed, the anger because Skip had recklessly put himself into this predicament. It bothered Hewey's conscience that such a feeling should come upon him at a moment like this, but damn it, he had tried to teach the boys better, Skip and Tommy both. Part of the anger was at himself for not being a better teacher. Skip should not have been his responsibility, but somehow he was. Just by being around and being older, Hewey had owed him guidance that would have avoided a wreck like this.

He would acknowledge that his own life had been reckless. Too many times he had yielded to the urges of the moment without regard for what might follow. Too often he had followed impulse rather than reason, bringing grief to himself and to others around him. He could not really blame this youngster all that much. To some extent, recklessness was a trait common in the cowboy trade. It took a reckless man to get on a bronc that had every intention of throwing him off and stomping him into the ground. It took a reckless man to put a loop around a pair of sharp horns that with the least turn of bad luck could end up goring him.

He gripped Skip's hand and felt his eyes burn. "You're a good boy. Don't you be turnin' your horses back to the outfit."

Skip's hand went limp.

Hewey heard an engine. The Jenkins touring car raced across the valley toward him, bouncing over ruts and clumps of bunchgrass. It braked to a stop in a swirl of dust. Leaving the motor running, Peeler jumped from behind the steering wheel. Old Man Jenkins was slower getting out, but he moved with more alacrity than Hewey would have expected for a large man of his years.

Jenkins said, "We'll take him to town in the car. It's a lot faster than a wagon."

Skip's features were relaxed, the pain gone. Hewey covered the cowboy's face with his hat.

He had to try twice before he could bring himself to speak. "There's no use bein' in a hurry now. The kid is gone."

CHAPTER

5

Hewey and Tommy stood together on the station platform, hats in their hands, watching two station workers slide the wooden box into the baggage car to begin its long trip back to Skip Harkness's home in East Texas. Tommy sniffled a couple of times, and something got in Hewey's eye . . . dust blown up from beneath the train more than likely. A local minister had just finished offering a prayer, generously praising the many good qualities of a young cowboy he had never known. Old Man Jenkins hunched beside the baggage wagon, supervising the loading of the coffin as if he feared the railroad people did not know how to handle the responsibility.

"That was a good lad," he told the baggage man, "and he worked for me. He deserves to be treated kindly and with respect. You can't put a value on a good lad."

You can if he's a cowboy, Hewey thought. *Twenty-five dollars a month, thirty if he's a top hand, fifty if he can drive an automobile.* Jenkins had barely known Skip's name when he was alive, but he was generous now that Skip was dead, paying the cost of sending the youngster home to be buried among his own. He was a rancher of the old tradition, feeling more kinship with the cowboys who worked for him than with the bankers who tended his wealth.

Blas Villegas and Aparicio Rodriguez stood beside Hewey and Tommy, seeing Skip off. Blas crossed himself as a railroad employee slid the door to the baggage car shut. Aparicio followed suit.

The two men were of a different heritage than Skip, but they were kinsmen in their trade and their chosen way of life.

The train slowly began moving eastward, black smoke trailing. Hewey heard Tommy choke, trying to force back a fresh rush of tears.

Hewey said, "It ain't somethin' you ever get used to, seein' your friends die. But the older you get, the more it'll happen, 'til one day you look around and it's you they're sayin' words over."

"He was too young to die, Uncle Hewey."

"And too reckless to keep himself alive." Hewey said no more because he did not want Jenkins to hear. Hewey and the others had avoided telling him that Skip had brought the accident upon himself. Even an *old* man needed a few illusions.

Jenkins headed back to the Circle W in his automobile, Bige Saunders and Blas Villegas riding with him. The cowboys who had come to see Skip off would return on horseback. Tommy untied his dun, then stood beside it with his head down, making no effort to mount. He said, "Uncle Hewey, I don't know if I can go back out there. I'd keep rememberin' what happened."

"You'll remember it no matter where you're at. It's like gettin' back on a horse after he's throwed you off. Best thing is to go out yonder where it took place and look the devil square in the eye."

"But I feel like I caused it. If I hadn't bet with him, he might not've thrown those bulls together."

"He'd've done it whether you bet with him or not, so stop whippin' yourself over the shoulders like some New Mexico *penitente*. He flirted with Lady Luck once too often."

What Tommy needed was to go home, Hewey thought, and remain there where he belonged. "When the roundup is finished, I'll take you back to your folks. But for now, a good cowboy don't quit in the middle of the works and leave the boss shorthanded."

"You sayin' I'm a good cowboy?"

"I don't know many better except me and Aparicio and Snort Yarnell."

It looked for a while as if the work they had done would go for nothing. The cattle count went cleanly enough and without friction, for Jenkins and Oscar Levitt were cattlemen who understood and trusted each other. Because cattle prices had been agreed upon beforehand, lawyer Petrie had no function during the counting except to endorse the numbers as the other two called them.

The big dollars took care of themselves. It was the nickels and dimes that almost blew up the ranch sale, for there Petrie got his hands into the pot up to his elbows. Inventorying and pricing the miscellaneous items led to argument after argument over everything from the wagons and the Wilson family buggy down to the hay in the barn, the value of shovels and pitchforks, and finally the evaluation of a steel crowbar. Petrie thought it ought to be worth fifty cents. Jenkins offered two bits.

Oscar Levitt put an end to the wrangling by slamming a quarter down onto the table and shoving it toward Petrie. "There!" he declared. "I want to be gettin' home."

When the last papers were signed and the check handed over, Jenkins and Levitt watched Petrie's departure with considerable satisfaction. Jenkins declared, "If I ever need to change my brand, I may just burn a line across their ribs and call this the Crowbar Ranch."

Not until the work was done and most of the crew was preparing to return to the J Bar did Hewey tell Jenkins that he was taking Tommy home. "The boy's still grievin' about Skip. He's havin' a tough time stayin' here where it happened."

Jenkins was disappointed, but he understood. "I've buried a lot of friends and kin. It never gets no easier."

"Every time one goes, you're that much closer to bein' left by yourself."

"I been watchin' that nephew of yours. He's got the makin's. Pretty soon he'll be as good as you were in your prime."

"I'm still in my prime."

"We could argue all day about that, but I ain't got the patience. Thing is, I hate to see you-all quit. You could take the boy home to visit his folks a few days and do me a favor at the same time."

"What kind of favor?"

"You know a man named Frank Gervin?"

Hewey would not have thought of the name for twenty dollars. "Fat Gervin, in the Upton City bank? I know him."

"Is he dependable?"

"I guess you could say that. You can always depend on him to do the wrong thing."

Jenkins frowned as he pondered Hewey's appraisal. "My Fort Worth banker got me in touch with him. Gervin sold me a string of broncs."

Hewey's eyebrows lifted. "Sight unseen?"

"If you can't trust a banker, who *can* you trust? Anyway, Gervin says they come from the ranch of a man named Lawdermilk."

"Alvin Lawdermilk. He raises good stock."

"So Bige tells me. You and the boy could take a short vacation, then bring me the horses."

Hewey nodded. "I can't promise you about Tommy; he's liable to stay home." At least Hewey hoped he would. "But I'll bring you your broncs."

Jenkins wrote out checks for Hewey and Tommy. "I still need me a foreman to run this Circle W outfit. Do some thinkin' on it, won't you?"

"I've already thought on it. I just want to be a plain forty-a-month hand."

"Thought I was payin' you thirty."

"After I bring your horses, I'll be expectin' forty."

"You ought to've been a lawyer, pricin' crowbars."

They could have made the trip in two days of hard traveling, but Hewey saw no need to abuse Biscuit or Tommy's dun horse. He took his time, stopping in Fort Davis to buy grub for the trail and to give Tommy time to prowl over what remained of the old army post, from which many sorties had been sent against the Apaches, most of them finding Indians only when Indians wanted to be found.

The only town between there and Upton City would be Fort Stockton. He wanted Tommy to have a chance to see the country. If the boy could be persuaded to remain at home after this stab at independence, it would be well for him to know as much as possible of the world beyond the homestead's outer fences. They climbed out through Wild Rose Pass, where tradition had it that Apaches had ambushed travelers on the old immigrant road, then eased down away from the mountains and across the open desert.

Hewey considered venturing over to Pecos City, where he had had a roaring good time more than once, but that town was out of the way. Sister-in-law Eve would appreciate his bypassing it. Pecos had an exaggerated reputation for violence, a result of shootings in the not-so-distant past and recent confrontations between ranchers and homesteaders over possession of state lands. Not long ago one of the town's more notorious exiles, known as Deacon Jim Miller, had finished his career at the end of a rope in Oklahoma, assisted by a delegation of angry citizens. Eve would say it was not the kind of story a churchgoing boy needed to be told.

They camped a night beside Fort Stockton's Comanche Springs, where cool, sweet water gushed from the ground in a volume that always amazed Hewey. Water was in such short supply across most of West Texas that Nature seemed overly extravagant here. They could have used the likes of this around Upton City. There everybody had to dig or drill for water and could never be certain of finding it. Hewey had seen a driller strike good water, then move fifty feet to one side or the other for a second well and come up dry.

Camped near the spring was a family with an automobile. They had erected a couple of canvas tents and spread their bedrolls inside. The woman of the family and a daughter of ten or so were cooking supper over a campfire.

Tommy said, "I'd think anybody rich enough to afford a car could pay for a hotel room in town."

Hewey thought the automobile an ugly intrusion upon an otherwise pleasant pastoral scene. A wagon and horses or mules would have been more appropriate. "The runnin' of the thing would keep most people broke. You watch, them stink wagons'll have the whole country chuggin' down to the poorhouse. The only folks left outside will be them of us that never had one."

The head of the family invited Hewey and Tommy over to share their supper, but Hewey politely declined. He told Tommy, "Poor feller already has too many mouths to feed . . . a wife, four buttons and an automobile. He'll be lucky to keep a shirt on his back."

The man looked as if he might be a drummer or storekeeper or something of the sort. He certainly did not seem like anybody who could make a hand a-horseback. Pickings could be poor in this part of the country for someone who could not hold a riding job.

Tommy extended a strip of bacon over the coals on a long, sharp stick. He said, "You sure you came just to get those broncs for Mr. Jenkins? Or were you hopin' that once I got home I'd decide to stay there?"

Some boys were too smart for their own good. "I made Mr. Jenkins a promise. Anyway, I thought it'd be nice for you to visit home a few days, and your folks'd be put out with me if I let you ramble around over this country by yourself. You could get snakebit or set upon by horse thieves. Worst of all, you could get taken in by some good-lookin' wheeligo girl and left without a cent to your name."

"Them things ever happen to you?"

"I never got snakebit or robbed by horse thieves."

"I don't have enough money for a girl to pay any attention to me. Mr. Jenkins probably didn't even notice the little bit of pay I drew."

"He noticed. He can tell you to the penny just how much he's got in the bank, and he'd as soon lose blood as to spend it. That's how all them old ranchers got rich . . . Mr. Jenkins, C. C. Tarpley. They never would spend anything 'til it was a case of life and death."

"Daddy always said he respected men who knew how to hold their money together."

"I respect them, too. I just don't want to be like them. Money is made to buy things with."

"I'd like to save enough money to get me a ranch someday like the one Mr. Jenkins just bought."

"You've already got a place, you and your daddy and mama."

"But it was them that put it together. And you. I know you've sent them money, Uncle Hewey. I want to do the same thing they did, but I want to do it myself. When I have my own place I want to know it was my doin', not somebody else's."

"That'll be hard, workin' for cowboy wages."

"Not if I save them. Not if I know where I'm goin' and what I want to do when I get there." His face went solemn. "Me and Skip, we talked a lot. He had the same kind of idea. We even talked about goin' partners so we could get there quicker. He didn't get his chance, but I'm goin' to have mine."

Hewey smiled. "I'll bet you will. If there's anything I can do to help you along the way . . ."

"You can teach me everything you know."

"There's some things your mama wouldn't approve of."

"Even those. I need to know it all."

Maybe they should *have gone to Pecos City,* Hewey thought. But Tommy had plenty of time to learn about the dark side. It would be better if first he knew the sunshine.

Hewey just wished somebody else would do the teaching.

He was tempted to drop in on Upton City before they went to the homestead. The thought of a drink at Dutch Schneider's bar brought his tongue to his lips in imagined pleasure. But Eve's eyes would freeze him all the way to his toes if she knew he had exposed her younger son to that sort of atmosphere. Schneider was a kind and gentle man but socially tainted by the fact that his occupation was dispensing whiskey. It had always struck Hewey odd that women-folks could attach more blame to those who sold it than to those who drank it. Possibly it was because their husbands, fathers and brothers were among the latter.

A long, flat-topped hill in the distance was the first landmark to show that they were approaching the Calloway homestead. They came to the field, where a soft southwest wind rustled sorghum feed nearly waist-high. Hewey said, "Looks like your daddy got the plantin' done without you."

"Probably hired Lester to help him."

"If he did, it was your daddy done most of the work."

Lester the nester boy was locally known for putting on a show of exertion while expending a minimum of effort. He was habitu-ally the last to reach for a pick or shovel, usually after someone else had taken it up. He would manage a rueful look at the missed op-portunity, but he also managed not to break a sweat unless it was in a race to dinner.

Across the field, moving toward them, a man rode a cultivator drawn by a pair of mules. Hewey had to squint. "Looks like your daddy comin' now."

Tommy tensed. Hewey suspected his nephew had been dreading the first confrontation with his parents. He had left home without a by-your-leave.

Walter halted the team at the end of the row and stepped down from the cultivator, wiping sweat from his face onto his sleeve as he walked toward the two horsemen. Every time Hewey saw his younger brother he was struck anew by the realization that the world had lost a good cowboy when Walter decided to become a stock farmer, molding his hands to fit a plow handle instead of bridle reins. He retained none of his cowboy appearance anymore. With his shapeless old hat, his patched and faded overalls and his dirt-encrusted brogans, he looked like what he was, a sunburned, wind-punished, overworked man of the soil, carrying on his gaunt shoulders the kind of heavy responsibility Hewey had always shunned. He was a man of property, certainly, but in Hewey's view property could be more a burden than a blessing.

Hewey said, "I brought back your wanderin' boy." He tried in vain to read his brother's eyes as Walter stared at his son.

Tommy dismounted from the dun horse and took a step toward his father, then stopped, not sure of himself. Hewey held his breath, wondering if the two would speak, if it might even have been a mistake to bring Tommy home.

Walter took two long strides and threw his arms around Tommy, pounding him on the back. "It's mighty good to see you, son." The voice cracked a little.

Hewey expelled the breath he had held in until his lungs ached. He let himself break into a grin.

Walter stepped back to observe his son at arm's length. "Can't see that you've growed any."

"I ain't been gone all that long."

"It seemed like a long time to us."

"How's . . . how's Mama?"

"All right. She'll be a lot better when she sees you." Walter looked at Hewey, who was just now at ease enough to dismount from Biscuit. "When she sees both of you."

I doubt she'll be all that tickled to see me, Hewey thought. Though she might or might not say so, she probably held him responsible for Tommy's leaving in the first place. She regarded Hewey's wanderlust as contagious. Her older son, Cotton, had left home to pursue a dream of finding a place in the new technological world of the automobile. He was working now in a San Angelo garage, repairing cars. Tommy could take automobiles or leave them alone, but he had some of Hewey's restless spirit, an itch to see for himself what lay on the other side of the hill.

Walter looked at the sun, still a couple of hours short of setting. "You-all go on to the house. I need to use up the daylight."

Tommy offered, "I'll take over for you. You can ride Dunny and go in with Uncle Hewey."

Hewey knew Tommy was nervous about the reception awaiting him from his mother, though his father's welcome had been warm. Hewey was uncertain, too.

Walter understood. "No, son, when you've got a dose of medicine to take, best thing is to swallow it the quickest you can." Humor flickered in his eyes. "Besides, if she lights into anybody, it's liable to be your uncle Hewey."

Hewey winced. Walter was teasing, but he might be closer to the truth than he knew.

Walter said, "Tell her I'm liable to be late, so you-all go on and eat supper without me."

Hewey suspected his brother was glad for the excuse not to go in right now. If a storm awaited, he would be better off riding the cultivator, out of earshot.

Hewey dreaded facing Eve without Walter being on hand to give him at least a modicum of moral support. But chances were that if

Walter saw she was in an ill humor he would retreat to the barn anyway and leave Hewey and Tommy to face judgment alone. Years of marriage had taught him the signs.

Looking toward the house and its three big chinaberry trees, which had grown up from saplings he had helped plant many years ago, Hewey touched his spurs gently to Biscuit's sides. His thoughts ran to San Juan Hill. He had missed that battle. He wished he could miss this one.

A little surprised, he said, "Looks like everything's been painted since I was here."

"Last fall," Tommy replied. "Our yearlin's brought more than we expected, so Daddy decided we ought to paint the house and barns before they fell down around us."

The plain box-and-strip house was white, the barn red. They had not painted the windmill tower and cypress fan, though. Surely that would not have required much extra paint. To Hewey, a well-painted windmill added a smart touch to a place, made it look up-and-coming like those on C. C. Tarpley's ranch. Maybe if they had a little paint left over he would do it himself, though ordinarily he tried to avoid work he could not do on horseback.

Aside from the paint job, he could not see that much had changed. The chicken pen had been enlarged a bit, and Walter had added a couple of corrals. It was still a nester outfit at bottom and a stranger to real prosperity, but at least it looked like Walter and Eve were finally on their way up.

Tommy's and Cotton's black dog was old now, but his bark had not diminished. He trotted out from underneath the house and challenged the horses. He had always barked at Hewey, no matter how many times Hewey fed or petted him. The dog often tangled with coyotes that came snooping around the chicken pen at night. Hewey had long hoped he would run up against one with sharper teeth than his own; it would serve the dumb mutt right. But the worst that ever happened to him was an occasional unfortunate spraying by a skunk.

When Tommy stepped down the dog sniffed at him, recognized the scent and went into a wild display of joy. But when Hewey moved close, the animal barked at him.

"If I was you," he told Tommy, "I'd swap that dog for a one-eyed tomcat. You'd have the best of the trade."

They unsaddled the horses and turned them loose in a corral beside the barn. Tommy fetched oats in a bucket and poured them into a trough. Biscuit tried to edge Dunny out of the way so he could have the oats to himself, but Dunny circled the trough and took his share from the opposite side. Biscuit nipped at him, then gave up and tried simply to eat faster.

Sharing was a human concept, not contagious to horses.

Hewey put his saddle on a rack beneath a shed where no horse or mule could gnaw on it. He watched Tommy carefully rack his own saddle and hang his bridle on a hook placed on the wall for that purpose. Tommy knelt down to pet the dog.

Hewey said, "We've stalled about as long as we can."

Tommy looked toward the house with a mixture of hope and dread. "Reckon so. We'd just as well go and see what the medicine tastes like." He started forth, the dog trotting happily beside him.

Hewey saw a vague movement through the screen door and knew Eve had seen them coming. He had rather they would have surprised her, for then she would not have had time to prepare a sermon. He carefully scraped his feet in case he had stepped in something unnoticed at the barn, and held the screen open for Tommy. Ordinarily he would have waited for his nephew to do the honors, but this was no time for such deference.

"Go ahead," he said. "I'm behind you."

"Make sure you're not too far behind me."

Eve stood in the kitchen, to one side of the big Majestic iron stove. Her hands were on her hips, not a good sign in Hewey's opinion. The glare of sunlight through a window behind her obscured her face, so he could not see her expression or what was in her eyes.

Tommy's voice faltered. "I'm home, Mama."

Eve stared at her son for moment that seemed an hour, then enveloped him in her arms. "I'm glad, son, real glad."

Hewey's shoulders slumped in relief. Right now, if he were at Schneider's bar, he could down a double shot of whiskey in one swallow.

Eve held her son at arm's length. "You look like you've grown a foot."

"Daddy didn't think I've changed at all."

"Your daddy probably had the sun in his eyes." Her own eyes blinked a lot. "At least you found your way home."

"Uncle Hewey knew the best way."

"I'm sure he was a world of help."

Hewey was not certain whether she meant it or was being sarcastic. With Eve it was often hard to tell.

She said, "You must be starved half to death, son. I'll start some supper."

"I'm fine, Mama. Me and Uncle Hewey, we've been eatin' mighty good." That was a shameful stretch of the truth. They had eaten little on the trail that could not be boiled in a can or broiled at the end of a stick. But Hewey did not contradict him. This was no time to compromise a reception that had turned out much better than he expected.

Eve turned finally to Hewey. "Thanks for bringin' him home." She smiled at him, which he thought must have taken some doing.

Hewey shrugged. "I was comin' this way anyhow."

"Bet you thought I was goin' to raise Billy Hell with both of you."

"Why, no. We knew everything was goin' to be just fine."

* * *

At the supper table, Walter asked, "You plannin' to stay, Hewey?"

Hewey dropped a third spoon of sugar into his coffee and stirred it. "Maybe a week or so. We got a job to do for Mr. Jenkins."

He explained that he was to pick up twenty broncs Fat Gervin had sold to the J Bar but that Jenkins was in no big hurry about getting them.

Walter stopped a forkful of beans halfway to his mouth. "Never knew Fat to trade in horses. But since C.C.'s health began failin', Fat's taken over just about everything C.C. owns. Reckon he's lookin' to make money everywhere he can."

Hewey snorted. "He wouldn't know a good horse if it bit him on the . . ."—he looked at Eve—"on the neck."

It was generally agreed around Upton City that if Fat Gervin had not married C. C. Tarpley's daughter and thus acquired an inside track toward someday inheriting the old man's money, he would probably be eking out a living swamping for saloons or doing something that offered similarly poor prospects. He had slouched his way to failure at everything else he had tried, including a foredoomed effort at being a cowboy.

Hewey said, "I'll ride over to Upton City tomorrow and ask Fat when he wants to deliver the broncs."

Eve was suddenly concerned. "Walter had better go with you. Every time you and Fat get close to one another, somethin' unpleasant comes of it."

"I don't see what could go wrong. This is strictly a business deal between Fat and Mr. Jenkins. All I'm doin' is carryin' the mail. Anyway, Walter's got his plowin' to do."

Eve frowned. "I just don't want to see you get into a fight with Fat."

"You ain't havin' trouble with the note on this place, are you?"

"No, we're all right now, but you never know when you may need to be on good terms with a banker."

"The only reason Fat's a banker is that C. C. Tarpley says so. But I'll watch myself. I'll bend over backwards to be nice to the son of a bitch. Beggin' your pardon . . ."

Eve pretended she had not heard. A respectable woman was not supposed to be familiar with such an expression, and to acknowledge it would be tacit admission that she was. But Hewey had heard her use it herself on occasions of stress.

He said, "I may circle by Alvin Lawdermilk's place afterwards. That might be where the broncs are at."

Eve looked him square in the eye. "It's still where Spring Renfro is at, too."

Hewey squirmed. "You don't reckon she holds it against me, leavin' the way I did? She told me herself that I ought to go."

"What else could she say? She knew you'd leave anyhow. She just tried to ease your conscience, if you had one."

"It was about the hardest thing I ever done, but it was best for both of us. I wasn't cut out to marry like Walter and turn myself into a farmer. And I couldn't drag her around from one cowpunchin' job to another."

"She would've been happy for you to keep on bein' a cowpuncher so long as you lit in one place and stayed put."

"The milk's a long time spilt, so there's no use in talkin' about it."

"No, there isn't. She's found somebody else."

Hewey looked up sharply. "Who?"

"A nice young fellow . . . widower who went to work as a foreman on Alvin's ranch after Alvin began gettin' stove-up."

"I didn't know Alvin was ailin'."

"Not ailin', exactly, just can't do all the work he used to. It comes to everybody eventually, even to fiddle-footed cowboys."

He knew that was aimed at him. "I'm doin' just fine."

"Sure you are. Those lines in your face are just sun grins. And I

9 9

saw you catch at your side while you were walkin' toward the house."

Hewey did not realize he had done it. The last bronc he had broken had touched off an internal ache that kept coming back, slipping up on him when he did not expect it. But what if he did have a few miscellaneous aches and pains? He had earned every one of them fair and square.

Eve had a way of making him feel guilty even when he was as innocent as a newborn calf. It almost ruined his appetite, for he refilled his plate only once and didn't eat but six biscuits and two helpings of dried-apple cobbler.

He could not see a nickel's worth of change in Upton City, or perhaps a dime. It still fell far short of being a city despite the name. He noticed a couple of new houses, but that did not represent any wild spurt of growth, considering how long he had been gone. The only two-story building was the square stone courthouse topped by a domed cupola, tallest thing in town, taller even than the windmills that stood beside or behind almost every house. Locals liked to tell gullible city folks passing through that there were so many windmills they sucked up all the wind on slow days and left the air dead-still on the downwind side of town.

He looked toward the plain, all-business stone structure of the Tarpley Bank and Trust. He thought about going there first, but instead he angled Biscuit across to Schneider's saloon. A good stiff drink might make the sight of Fat Gervin a little less disagreeable. Once they got past discussion of the weather and wishing it would rain, he could not remember that he and Fat had ever agreed on anything of consequence. The only thing fatter than Gervin's broad butt was his head.

Hewey knew of no one who really liked Fat unless it would be his wife, and sometimes he wondered about her. Once in a while, for a moment or two, Hewey could bring himself to feel sorry for the man, but he would remember some past incident and the sympathy would disappear, leaving no trace.

A truck was parked just past the saloon. Beside it stood a familiar figure with a wrench in his hand, staring in frustration at the engine. Steam boiled into the clear air and disappeared.

Hewey shouted, "Howdy, Blue Hannigan! If it was a horse or a mule, you'd just shoot it."

The freighter looked around, recognition spreading a broad grin across his grease-smeared face. He and Hewey had worked as cowboys together years ago before Hannigan decided to marry and take on the burdens of a respectable family man. He made a show of throwing the wrench at Hewey but held on to it. "Just when I thought the day had turned about as bad as it could get, look who showed up."

Biscuit eyed Hannigan warily, still taking the wrench as a personal threat. Hannigan reached out with the other hand, covered with black grease. Hewey did not hesitate to grasp it, grease and all. He shook vigorously, for old cowboy friends were still the best of all.

Hewey said, "It's God's punishment for you takin' up with the machine age. I never saw a mule steam like that."

"I wish I'd never laid eyes on any machine more complicated than a wheelbarrow, but times change. A truck can travel a whole lot faster than mules and a wagon."

"Not when it's broke down. Maybe a drink would make things look better to you."

"Couldn't make them look no worse. You buyin', or have I got to?"

"I'll set them up. That truck probably keeps you broke, and us cowboys get paid real good."

"That ain't how I remember it." The freighter jerked his head toward the saloon. He drew back the wrench. Hewey thought for a moment he was going to throw it at the engine, but Hannigan pitched it into the bed of the truck. He was not destructive of property, especially his own.

When Hewey's eyes accustomed themselves to the dim interior of the saloon, he saw Dutch Schneider walking toward the bar from the back, where a skinny old man sat hunched over a small table, a bottle and glass in front of him.

Hewey plunked fifty cents on the bar and said, "Dutch, you got anything fit for two hardworkin' men to drink? One, anyway. I ain't sure about Blue."

"Hewey Calloway! So long I have not seen you, it wondered me if they had buried you and I had missed the funeral." Laughing, Schneider walked behind the bar and poured two shot glasses full. "For two good friends, the best in the house."

The genuineness of his welcome warmed Hewey even before he tasted the whiskey. He could not understand why some people in Upton City were always down on Schneider, who had drifted into town years ago from somewhere down in the Hill Country German settlements. He was a quiet, dignified man, much more tolerant than those who criticized him. He attended the local Baptist church on Sundays, though some of the local women whispered that they believed he was a Lutheran, or possibly even worse, a Catholic. But he ran a clean place and sold clean whiskey. That was recommendation enough for Hewey.

Hewey enjoyed the gentle burn as the drink went down, and the glow that followed it. He turned, facing toward the rear of the room. "Tell me that ain't C. C. Tarpley back yonder."

Tarpley had always been slight of build and looked as if he might have to carry rocks in his pockets to keep the wind from blowing him away. Even so, he appeared to have shrunk.

Concern came into Schneider's eyes. "It is indeed Mr. Tarpley.

Often he comes here and sits. He does not drink much, he just sits. I think he waits to die."

Hewey found the concept difficult to accept. "Old C.C. never was sick a day in his life."

Hannigan said quietly, "He's sick now. I ain't sure if it's in his heart or in his head, but either way it's slowly killin' him." He leaned in as if to share a dark secret. "You remember the time Old Man Adcock and C.C. had a hell of a fight in front of the bank? Well, sir, the old man had a note comin' due on that little shop of his a couple of weeks ago and asked for an extension. C.C. said he'd do better than that. He tore up the note. Said he put more value on Adcock's friendship than on the money. No, sir, he sure ain't the C.C. we used to know."

C. C. Tarpley had his faults, but holding grudges was not one of them. He also had his virtues, but generosity was not one of those— at least it hadn't been.

Hewey asked, "What did Fat think, since he's supposed to be runnin' the bank?"

"You could hear him holler halfway across town." Hannigan chuckled, remembering. "I'd best be gettin' back to business. I've got a haul to make if I can bluff that truck into runnin'."

Hewey shook his head. "Job the spurs to it."

"Fat holds the note. I've got half a mind to turn the truck over to him, but he'd probably bust a blood vessel. I'd hate to have his dyin' on my conscience."

After Hannigan left, Hewey studied the racehorse pictures that covered the wall behind the bar. Most bars of this kind were more likely to feature pictures of women in scanty dress or no dress at all. Schneider loved horses like many old bachelors loved women, from afar. Hewey had never seen him on horseback.

He considered another drink but decided against it. Though the bronc deal was made and he had no reason to match wits with Fat

Gervin, he thought it wise to have all his wits about him. Unlike his father-in-law, Fat never turned loose of a grudge, and Hewey in the past had given him grounds enough to stay mad until he was a hundred and six.

Hewey moved back to the table where the old man sat staring off into nothing, his mind far away. "C.C.?"

Tarpley looked up in surprise. "Hewey! Didn't know you was anywhere in the country." He shoved an arthritic hand forward and motioned for Hewey to take a chair.

The voice was thinner than Hewey remembered it. He had always thought C.C. looked old, but now he appeared absolutely aged. "Just got into town."

"I'll buy you a drink."

"Already had one, thanks. I'm fixin' to go see Fat . . . Frank."

When the old man was on decent terms with his son-in-law, he called him Frank. When he was on the outs, he referred to him as Fat, like everybody else.

"What you need to see Frank about? Your brother's got himself in good shape over at the bank."

Hewey explained that he was representing Morgan Jenkins, who had bought a string of broncs from Fat . . . Frank.

Tarpley seemed puzzled. "Now where would Frank get broncs to sell? We don't raise any except what we need for our own usin' at the ranch."

"I reckon he's took up horse tradin'."

"Dangerous business, horse tradin'. It can get you in more trouble than a case of bad whiskey." His eyes were weepy, as if something in the air disagreed with him. "You lookin' for a cow-punchin' job?"

"Already got one, out in the mountains."

"Never did like the mountains. Give me the flats every time. If you fall, it ain't far down."

Hewey was hesitant to ask Tarpley what was troubling him. In the first place, it was none of Hewey's business, and the C.C. he used to know would tell him so in no uncertain terms. In the second place, he probably could not help anyway. C. C. Tarpley had always been too proud to appreciate sympathy. Tougher than whang leather, he had come to the dry Pecos River country while the departing Comanches' tracks were still fresh, cut out a goodly chunk of range for himself and held it against cattle thieves, drought, lawyers, bankers and other hazards of the ranching trade. The one thing he had not been able to beat was the long succession of calendars that changed over his desk year after year.

C.C.'s eyes bored into Hewey until Hewey felt uncomfortable. He had punched cattle for Tarpley in the past and might again if circumstances demanded it, but he would rather not. Like Jenkins, Tarpley was close with a dollar. His idea of liberality was to bring a couple of watermelons to camp a time or two during summer. That was why his canceling of Old Man Adcock's debt seemed so unlikely. He said, "I worry about you, Hewey."

"About me?"

"Life is short. I'm findin' that out for myself. I'm afraid you'll come to the end of yours and not leave anything to show for it."

"I've had a lot of experiences and made a lot of friends."

"But what'll you be leavin' behind?"

"A lot of experiences and a lot of friends."

"That don't count for much on the ledgers down at the bank."

"I don't read ledgers *now*. I sure won't be interested in them after they salt me away."

"Don't make light of it. Death ain't no small thing."

Hewey saw an opening to ask the question. "How come all this worry about dyin'? I don't imagine the angels are in a hurry to receive me or you either one."

"It's comin' whether we're ready or not, and I ain't sure it's the angels that's waitin' for us. I've got a pain in my gut, eatin' away at me. It's tellin' me to get myself ready."

"You been to a doctor?"

"These pill merchants around here? Ain't nothin' they can do when it's your time except sell you patent medicine and drain your purse."

Hewey had had his differences with Tarpley over the years, but he had always liked the old man. Though Tarpley's principal motivation had been personal enrichment, he had helped to build the country in his own perverse way. Hewey had no quarrel with people who wanted to better their own condition. In the process they often bettered the condition of others around them.

Hewey said, "Maybe if you'd go to a doctor somewhere like Kansas City or Chicago they could help you. Even Fort Worth. I always had a good time in Fort Worth."

"I don't mind so much for myself. It's my daughter I worry most about, her married to Frank Gervin. You know and I know, Hewey, he ain't no hand."

Hewey had no argument there. When it came to cattle and horses, Fat Gervin was about as useless as a fifth wheel on a wagon. "I'm afraid I can't be no help to you. Anybody who could make a hand of Fat could probably walk on water."

"Left on his own, he'll likely run through the bank and the ranch both before the grass takes hold over my grave."

Tarpley started to pour whiskey into his glass but set the bottle back down, his attention drifting away. Hewey stood up. "I'm sorry to find you feelin' poorly, C.C. I do wish you'd go someplace and hunt up a good doctor."

Tarpley did not respond. Hewey was not sure the old man even heard him. He walked back to the bar, where Schneider was reading a newspaper. He subscribed to several. Dutch Schneider and Alvin Lawdermilk were the best-read men in the county. They could name just about every king, president and major knave on the international scene.

Hewey said, "I always thought he was too ornery to die."

Schneider looked toward Tarpley. "He still is. I think when the time comes, he will not go."

CHAPTER

6

Hewey stopped just outside the saloon door and looked down the dirt street. Blue Hannigan still tinkered with the truck's engine, using the same bristling language he often employed against recalcitrant mules. Sometimes the mules responded and sometimes they did not. The truck remained indifferent.

Hewey turned toward the bank, resolving to state his business to Fat Gervin and get out as quickly as he could. He tried to regard it as a challenge, like riding a new bronc, for he had always found a certain exhilaration in that sort of contest. But he saw nothing exhilarating about C. C. Tarpley's son-in-law.

When he walked into the bank, he was not surprised to see that Gervin was in. The high ceilings and tall, open windows kept the stone building fairly cool, and Gervin much preferred to spend his time indoors rather than be out on the ranch, where the sun was hot and sweat labor plentiful. His desk was cluttered with paper, indicating work deferred. Fat had always believed in putting off until tomorrow that which did not absolutely have to be done today. The desk was behind a low wooden fence meant to keep the clientele from getting too close to the money.

Taking Hewey to be a potential customer, Gervin stood up, turning on his best come-spend-it-with-us smile. Recognition killed the welcome. Gervin sat down heavily, his chubby cheeks sagging, his face taking on a sour look. "You back already?"

Hewey said, "Already? I been gone four years."

"It don't seem near long enough. I know you didn't come to put money in the bank. You never had twenty dollars at one time in your life."

Gervin never had forgiven Hewey for helping Walter and Eve save their stock farm from foreclosure or for other miscellaneous indignities suffered over the years at Hewey's hands.

Hewey said, "I'm here on business for Mr. Morgan Jenkins." He fished a letter from his shirt pocket and extended it across the desk into Fat's thick hands.

Fat frowned as he read. "Says here you're to receive the horses I sold him and take them back to Alpine. How come him to trust *you* with this much responsibility?"

"I'm the best hand he's got."

Fat snorted. "Must be mighty hard times around Alpine. What did he tell you about the horses?"

"Said they're of Alvin Lawdermilk's raisin'."

"I told him they came from Alvin's place. When do you want to get them?"

"He's not in a hurry. Told me to have a nice visit with the folks before I go back. I'll let you know when I'm ready."

"You do that. Now, I got business to attend to." He started shuffling papers.

He hadn't looked all that busy when Hewey came in, but Hewey had no interest in staying any longer. "Then I'll mosey along. Adios, Fat."

Gervin's voice soured more. "I almost shook off that nickname once. I ain't forgot that you're the one who hung it on me again."

It had happened so long ago, Hewey had almost forgotten. He and Walter had been working on C. C. Tarpley's ranch. Frank Gervin had been on the payroll too, but he could hardly be accused of working. The minute Tarpley was out of sight Gervin would head for the shade, look for something to eat or sweet-talk Tarpley's daughter. Hewey never had figured out what she saw in him. These days she probably wondered, too.

Fat was widely reputed to have a roving eye, though his romantic notions usually came to naught. Whatever seductive charms he might once have had he had used up in winning Tarpley's daughter and carving his initials on the Tarpley inheritance.

Hewey had used the boyhood nickname in an attempt to shame Gervin out of the kitchen and away from the shade, but it had only won him Gervin's enmity. He had no particular regrets about that. A man was known by his enemies as well as by the friends he kept. Around here it was a mark of honor to be disliked by Fat Gervin.

Hewey stepped out into the sunshine, his brief ordeal over. He looked across the street toward a store whose modest sign, almost hidden beneath gingerbread trim, read PHELPS GENERAL MERCANTILE AND SUNDRIES. Though he did not need anything, he would buy some smoking tobacco. The genial Pierson Phelps always treated him like company whether he had spending money or not, but Hewey liked to give him a little business when he could. He had spent four bits with Dutch Schneider. Pierson Phelps deserved no less.

Hewey noticed a wagon and team in front of the store but thought little of it. Farmers and ranchers around Upton City depended upon Phelps for supplies. If they were old-timers, Hewey would enjoy a chance to say howdy. If they were newcomers, he would enjoy a chance to meet them and say welcome. Nobody remained a stranger long around Hewey Calloway.

The gray-haired Phelps came out the front door, carrying a box of groceries. A tall cowboy of forty or so followed with another box, placing it in the bed of the wagon. Phelps brightened as Hewey strode casually toward him. "Look who's here. We see more of Halley's comet than we see of you, Hewey Calloway."

The cowboy seemed to know the name, for he turned abruptly to look. Hewey did not recognize him, however.

Hewey said to Phelps, "You still peddlin' grub? I thought you'd be rich by now and mayor of some big city like Midland or San Angelo, livin' in the lap of luxury."

"I decided my first million wasn't enough. I'll stay 'til I make my second." Phelps turned to the tall cowboy. "Hewey, meet Farley Neal. He's Alvin Lawdermilk's foreman."

Neal gave Hewey a firm and friendly handshake. "I've heard about you."

"Not from Fat Gervin, I hope."

"Yes, but mostly from your friends. You've got a lot of them, seems like."

Hewey tried to remember what he had heard about Alvin's new foreman. "Somebody told me Alvin's stove-up."

"Just enough that he needed somebody to take part of the load off of him. He's wrestled too many rough broncs and too many iron-jawed mules. They've caught up with him."

It wasn't just the horses and mules that had caught up with Alvin, Hewey knew; it was whiskey. "I need to go by and auger with him. Me and Alvin have had some good times together."

"He'll be tickled. He talks about you."

Phelps said, "Come on into the store, Hewey. It's warm out here in the sun."

Hewey stepped up onto the wooden sidewalk and halted in mid-stride. A thin woman in her thirties ventured into the doorway and stopped abruptly, looking at him in surprise. Hewey's jaw dropped. Words ran through his head but would not come off his tongue. He could only stammer.

Spring Renfro seemed equally flustered, a tiny smile so quickly come and so quickly gone he was not sure he had really seen it. Her trembly voice was barely audible. "Hello, Hewey."

"Spring," he managed, then grasped for propriety. "Miss Renfro."

She usually gave people the impression of tallness, though the top of her head would barely reach Hewey's chin. Her thinness exaggerated her height.

Hewey did not know whether to step closer or turn and go. But there was no question of going. His boots seemed nailed to the sidewalk. He could only stare, warmth rushing to his face. He knew he looked like an idiot. For certain, he felt like one.

Her composure regained, she made two short steps toward him and held out her hand. Hesitantly he took it and gave her a weak handshake.

She spoke with reserve, as she might in being introduced to a stranger. "You look well, Hewey."

She looked better than well. To him, she looked wonderful. He wanted to tell her so, but all that came was "Mighty pleased to see you." An idiot could have done better, he thought.

He would have been prepared had he seen her at Alvin Lawdermilk's ranch, where she taught school for children of the Lawdermilk neighbors. He would have expected her there. But here she had taken him unawares and put him into shock.

Often on quiet nights he had thought of her when he sat beside a fire alone or when he rode in the mountains and let his mind dwell upon horseback rides they had taken together during the time he was contemplating marriage. Eventually he had reached a point where the pleasure of old memories outweighed the sense of loss they brought. He had thought he had come to an accommodation years ago with his decision to choose freedom to roam rather than the confining responsibilities of married life.

Now the years fell away in an instant, and his convictions about the rightness of old decisions lay in shambles at his feet. He stood as if hypnotized.

She seemed to wait for him to say something. When he did not, she asked, "Did you meet Farley Neal?"

Hewey nodded, his tongue stuck to the roof of his mouth.

It came to him then, something Eve had told him. She said Spring had found someone, a widower who had become foreman at the Lawdermilks'. He forcibly put down a fleeting resentment. He had given up any claim on Spring Renfro the day he bid her good-bye and rode away seeking adventure with Snort Yarnell. She had every right to happiness wherever she might find it.

He could put away the resentment but not the unexpected pain of seeing her with someone else.

She said, "Mr. Phelps, I believe we still have one box of supplies on the counter."

Hewey broke his silence. "I'll fetch it." That gave him an excuse to move away from her, to collect his wits. Perhaps by the time he came back outside he would be able to wipe that deaf-and-dumb look from his face and say something that would not sound simpleminded. He paused, both hands on the box, and squeezed his eyes shut in an effort to stop their burning. He walked back out into the sunlight, trying not to look into Spring's blue eyes but unable to help himself.

He watched Neal help her up onto the wagon seat and told himself Neal was a lucky man.

Spring looked down at Hewey. Her voice was formal. "Are you home to stay?"

He swallowed, throat dry. "No, just got a little business. Soon as it's done I'll be leavin'."

"Alvin will be disappointed if you don't visit with him before you go."

Neal said, "Glad to've met you, Hewey," and set the team into motion. Hewey could not take his eyes from the wagon until it disappeared beyond the courthouse. Spring did not look back in his direction.

Phelps finally spoke. "Mighty fine woman, Miss Renfro."

Hewey cleared his throat. "As fine as ever was."

"Farley Neal's a good man. They make a handsome couple."

"Where'd he come from?"

"He was foreman a while on C. C. Tarpley's ranch, but Fat Gervin kept tellin' him what to do. He either had to quit or whip Fat, so he left."

"Anybody who can't get along with Fat is all right with me. They fixin' to marry?"

"I've heard nothing definite, but everybody here expects that they will." Phelps squinted one eye. "You thinkin' about putting in a claim on her again?"

Hewey shoved his hands into his pockets. "If I ever had a claim, I gave it up a long time ago. You say Neal's a good man?"

"Reminds me a lot of your brother Walter . . . solid, serious, hardworkin'."

Hewey swallowed again. "Everything I never was. I reckon I'm glad for Spring." He turned away.

Phelps said, "Aren't you comin' in?"

"No, I've got to go back and talk to Fat."

He walked into the bank and made directly for Gervin's desk. Gervin looked up, displeased. "You forget somethin'?"

"No, changed my mind about a long visit. How quick can you have them broncs ready for me?"

Eve did not take the news with good grace. "Leavin'?" she demanded. She put away her sewing and faced Hewey with her hands on her hips. "What do you mean, you're leavin' the day after tomorrow? You said you and Tommy were stayin' a couple of weeks."

Hewey averted his eyes. "Fat's anxious to get rid of them broncs."

It always amazed him the way a woman could sense the truth no matter how good a liar a man thought he was. She said, "You saw Spring Renfro. Now you're afraid if you stay around you won't be able to leave her again."

Denial was useless, so Hewey did the next best thing. He sidestepped. "I didn't say Tommy was goin' with me. I figured once he got home he might decide to stay here." He had hoped so, anyway.

Tommy said, "You can't drive those ponies to Alpine by yourself. Besides, you promised to teach me all I need to know."

"I never promised no such a thing. You said that, not me."

"You didn't say you wouldn't."

"But when Skip got killed, you wanted real bad to get away from that place."

"You made me stay and face it, so I already put the worst of it behind me. I can take it now."

Eve argued, "You don't have to trail after your Uncle Hewey to God knows where. If it's a job you want, you can get one here with Alvin Lawdermilk, or even C. C. Tarpley. At least you'd be close to home."

"But that's what's the matter. I'd be too close. I need to learn to make it on my own without you and Daddy always standin' there to catch me if I fall."

"Won't Uncle Hewey be doin' the same thing?"

"He lets me fall. Says I learn more that way, and it's good for my character."

Hewey said, "If it's fallin' you want, you can do it here at home. Out yonder, them rocks are sharp and hard."

Tommy did not budge. Walter watched and listened, saying nothing. Hewey suspected he sided with his son, for he had not always been the homebound farmer he was now. Walter could understand what drove a boy like Tommy, eager to know the world, though he would await the proper moment before saying so. Hewey could leave, but Walter had to keep on living with Eve.

She turned to Hewey, her eyes stinging. "I wish I knew what would cure that restless streak in you, because it's contagious. You gave it to my oldest son, and now Tommy's caught it."

That was not exactly the straight of it. Cotton had always been intrigued by things mechanical, so the farm could not hold him when he came to his time. He would have left with or without Hewey's influence. Tommy was different. He had always been more comfortable with a life tied to the soil and the seasons, to the grass and the animals, but he wanted a bigger bite of it than the home place could give him. He might indeed have caught some of that from his uncle, who had inherited itchy feet from his own improvident father.

Hewey suggested, "Tommy, why don't you wait 'til you get a couple more years on you? Everything'll still be out there, waitin'."

"You may not still be out there, the kind of life you lead."

Hewey and Tommy left the farm at sunup, cutting across country toward the C. C. Tarpley ranch, where Fat was to have the broncs ready for delivery. Eve's demeanor had been frosty, and Hewey could not blame her. He too wished Tommy would stay home. It was a burdensome thing, being saddled with responsibility for a youngster so closely kin, yet not his own.

Tommy said, "I wish we hadn't had to be in such a hurry. Daddy's lookin' tired. I was goin' to finish that south field for him."

"You could stay here awhile and go back to the ranch later." Maybe if Tommy remained a couple of weeks he would decide not to leave at all.

"I hired out to do a job of work, and I'll stick to it like you've taught me."

They were not long in reaching the outer perimeter of the Tarpley ranch, for it spread across a major portion of the county and lapped over into the next. C.C. had kept adding to it, buying out homesteaders as they finished proving up their claims on state and school lands and became legally entitled to sell. Most had not found this part of the country hospitable to the plow because rainfall was too erratic. C.C. had tried several times to buy Walter out. Walter managed to make a crop of sorts most years, but only because he watered the land with his own sweat. Had he not been grazing a herd of cows and a few brood mares on the place for extra income, he probably would not have survived, and the Tarpley range would have expanded by eight more sections.

Tommy said, "Daddy always talked like C. C. Tarpley was a hard man to work for."

"He just had his own ways, and once you learned what they were, you could get along with him all right. He never liked for a cowboy to see the sunrise through a window, or the sunset either. He wanted you out workin' as long as there was daylight to see by. But he would generally be there with you. Wasn't like some I've worked for, that sent you out and then went back to the house."

"Like Fat Gervin?"

"I can call him Fat because I'm as old as he is, and I don't owe him nothin'. You'd better call him Mr. Gervin, at least 'til your folks have their land all paid out."

"He came near gettin' it once, that time Daddy got his leg broke. If you hadn't stayed and taken Daddy's place . . . Mr. Gervin still holds a grudge against you, I think."

"His grudge goes back a long ways farther than that. When C.C. got mad he'd forget about it in a day or two. But Fat's got a memory like an elephant."

"At least he ain't dangerous. He couldn't whip an old man on crutches."

"That's what *does* make him dangerous. He'll figure some way to come at you from behind and hit you when you're not lookin'. Give me an honest fightin' man every time. If you can't whip him, you may be able to outrun him."

The Tarpley headquarters was imposing, its centerpiece a large two-story white frame house standing on a slight knoll, surrounded by tall chinaberry trees. Their upper reaches extended higher than the roof. Chinaberries also formed a circle around a nearby surface tank, nurtured by its constant supply of water. Hewey recalled that the tank was stocked with catfish, supposedly for C.C.'s own use, though he never seemed to have time to wet a hook. Fat Gervin fished there when he was certain his father-in-law was miles away.

C.C. would be content to live in an adobe bunkhouse or even a dugout, but the late Mrs. Tarpley had insisted upon having a house in town and one on the ranch, with accommodations appropriate to their station in life. C.C. had an eye toward accumulation of land, cattle and capital. His wife had an eye toward architecture and landscaping.

The ranch house had been hers to furnish and maintain as she wished, but the rest of the place was C.C.'s personal domain. A broad layout of corrals, barns and sheds had been built to his utilitarian specifications. All in all, it was a pretty place, but Hewey could not remember that he had seen it often in the full light of day. He had usually left before the sun was up and did not return until night was settling in. C.C. got his money's worth whether he was buying land or labor.

Hewey saw horses in a large corral and reined Biscuit in that direction. A cowboy arose from a seat on the step that led up into the largest barn. He hailed them and slouched out partway to meet the incoming riders. Something about the way he moved reminded Hewey of Fat, though this man would have to put on fifty or seventy-five pounds to match Gervin's weight.

"Howdy." The cowboy had a loosely rolled cigarette dangling from his lower lip and talked around it rather than take it from his mouth. His shirttail was hanging out. "I suppose you'd be Hewey Calloway?"

"I was the last time I checked. Where's Fat?"

The cowboy nodded toward the large white house. "Mr. and Mrs. Gervin are up yonder. He said for me to turn them ponies yonder over to Hewey Calloway. You got anything to show that you're really him?"

Hewey felt a little annoyed that the cowboy doubted him. Everybody this side of San Angelo knew who he was, or ought to. This puncher must have come from someplace farther east, automatically a mark against him. "Call Fat. He'll know me."

The cowboy's frown said he had rather not. "If you say you're Hewey Calloway, I reckon I'll have to take your word for it." He pointed his thumb toward the barn. "The broncs are yonderway. I suppose you're in a hurry to get them started?"

Hewey looked up. The sun was moving toward noon, and he knew Tommy would be hungry. Boys always were. At most ranches they would be invited to stay for dinner. Even a Yankee-owned outfit would offer that much hospitality, and C. C. Tarpley was no Yankee. Hewey waited for the cowboy to say something, then did it himself. "We'll line them out right after dinner."

The cowboy remembered his manners, sort of. "Yeah, I reckon you would like to eat first. We'll see if the cook can rustle up a little somethin'." He did not look like somebody C.C. would keep on the payroll for long. He was probably a Fat Gervin protégé, Hewey thought. Old C.C. *must* be sick to turn loose of things this way.

He remembered the cook, a dour little fellow who seemed as devoted to thrift as C.C. himself when it came to buying groceries for the bunkhouse kitchen. He had gone to work for the ranch after Walter and Eve had left to take up their homestead. Before, Eve had operated the bunkhouse kitchen. It was often expected of a ranch foreman's wife that she cook for the hands without extra pay beyond her husband's salary. That was one reason she held to their homeplace with such a determined grip, for there she never had to cook for anyone again except her own if she did not want to.

The food was about as Hewey remembered it and reminded him of one major reason he had left C.C.'s employ. Without canned tomatoes the cook would have been at a total loss. They seemed to be in everything except the biscuits. For dessert he offered another biscuit and watery blackstrap molasses of a cheap brand so poor that Pierson Phelps refused to handle it in his store. C.C. got it from Midland. No wonder the cook looked as if he would not weigh a hundred pounds soaking wet.

"Mighty fine dinner," Hewey lied, turning to Tommy and the cowboy. Hewey could not remember the cowboy's name, or if it had even been offered. It didn't matter. Some people were meant to be forgotten as quickly as possible. "Let's be seein' about them broncs."

He realized before he reached the corral that something was awfully wrong. He climbed up on the plank fence, looking down among the horses in disbelief. He had never seen a sorrier-looking bunch of scrubs in his life.

"These ain't what Mr. Jenkins bought," he declared, turning to challenge the cowboy. "They're supposed to be from Alvin Lawdermilk's, and Alvin wouldn't give a day's grass to such as this."

The cowboy shrugged, all innocence and puzzlement. "I wouldn't know nothin' about that. All I know is that Mr. Gervin said these are the ones you're supposed to take."

"Like hell they are! They wouldn't make good soap."

They were a mixed lot of long-tailed mustangs, a couple of ewe-necked old geldings Hewey would bet were spoiled outlaws and one black stud that bared its teeth at any animal that dared come near. "What's Fat tryin' to pull?"

"I just work here. You'll have to talk to him about that."

"I'm fixin' to do that very thing!" Angrily Hewey jumped down from the fence. The impact sent pain lancing through his knees, but he paid little attention to that or the sudden hurting in his belly. Biscuit seemed to sense his agitation, for the brown horse lifted its head high, ears and eyes alert. Hewey swung onto its back, not waiting for Tommy to catch up. He put Biscuit into a long trot.

The Gervins had a home in town, but they freely used the Tarpley house when they were at the ranch. It would be theirs anyway when C.C. passed on to glory.

Fat must have been watching through a parlor window, for he came out onto the veranda and stood there, nonchalantly picking his teeth. Hewey would bet his meal had been a lot better than the one put up by the bunkhouse cook.

Fat's wife, Ellie, a frail-appearing little woman, stood just inside the screen door. Most people in town used to regard her as pretty, but Hewey had always suspected they were influenced more by her father's money than by her features. Even granting that she was good-looking, Hewey doubted that she had inherited old C.C.'s smarts, or she would not have wasted herself on Fat Gervin. Two children peeked out from behind her long skirt.

"Fat!" Hewey shouted. "What're you tryin' to get away with?"

"What's the matter? You don't like them horses?"

"They're supposed to be young broncs of Alvin Lawdermilk's raisin'. I'll bet Alvin never laid eyes on a one of them."

"I didn't say they were of his raisin'. I said they came from his ranch, and they did. They was driven right through it." He grinned in appreciation of his own cleverness.

"There's even a stud amongst them. They were all supposed to be geldin's."

"You've got a knife, ain't you? I don't see where it's any skin off of your nose anyway. You said yourself, you're just a hired hand. The deal was between me and Jenkins."

"But I'm here in his interests, and I sure ain't interested in takin' him them snides you've got out yonder."

"Then he'll have to send somebody else, because those horses are his. I've already got the money."

Hewey dismounted and dropped the reins, knotting his fists as he strode toward the veranda steps. "Fat, you've had a good whippin' comin' to you for a long time."

The woman and children quickly disappeared into the darkness of the hall. Gervin stepped back into the doorway, then forward again. He leveled a shotgun at Hewey. "You take one more step, Hewey Calloway, and they'll tote you away from here in a box."

Hewey stopped short, a chill in his belly. The muzzle of that shotgun looked as wide as a milk bucket.

He choked, "I ain't armed." He never carried a gun because he considered them too dangerous, especially those assumed not to be loaded. He had an old pistol in his war bag back at the Jenkins ranch, but he had not cleaned it in so long that it could have a dirt-dauber nest in its barrel for all he knew.

Fat's hands shook. Ordinarily Hewey would not consider the man dangerous, but anybody that nervous was dangerous when he had a shotgun in his hands. "I'm phonin' the sheriff that you came out here and tried to provoke a fight. Now you get back in that saddle, Hewey, and you take them horses and git. If you ain't gone in ten minutes, I'll file on you for trespass."

Hewey feared he might accidentally squeeze the trigger. "I'm goin', but I ain't forgettin'. Just because Mr. Jenkins is old don't mean he's to be trifled with. And I ain't either."

Tommy's face was two shades paler than normal. The boy had never faced a gun before. Hewey had, but repetition did not make the experience easier. He said to Fat, "I don't suppose C.C. knows anything about this."

"It's my deal, not his. Now git!" Fat made a poking motion with the shotgun.

Hewey mounted and turned away, toward the corrals.

Tommy could hardly speak. "He'd've shot you."

"Not on purpose, but Fat's subject to accidents. Anytime a man points a shotgun at you, you better tell him he's right and you're wrong. There'll come another day."

The cowboy with no name opened the corral gate and helped push the horses out into the open. Hewey saw nothing to thank him for, so he did not speak as he and Tommy rode past and lined the horses out on the trail that led toward town. He would put them in a corral at the wagon yard tonight and talk to Sheriff Wes Wheeler. He doubted Wes could do anything, but it wouldn't hurt to talk. He considered talking to C. C. Tarpley also but decided against it. The old man had too many worries already.

He did not have to look up Wheeler. Wheeler came to meet him several miles from town, a big man riding a big horse. Wheeler's back was straight as a ramrod, his manner friendly but somewhat formal. He reined up and let Hewey come the last short distance to him. He frowned as the loose horses trotted past him, Tommy trailing. "Are these what all the fuss was about?"

"Wasn't much of a fuss to it. Fat threw a shotgun on me, and the fuss was over with. Howdy, Wes."

"Howdy yourself, Hewey." Wheeler had a deep, commanding voice that could bring a roomful of drunks to immediate attention, and a handshake that could crush bones. "Fat told me his side of it over the telephone. What's yours?"

Hewey explained about the sale. "Mr. Jenkins was given to understand that they was of Alvin Lawdermilk's raisin', but they wouldn't fool a blind man."

Wheeler gave the horses another study. "I remember these skates. A ragged-britches horse trader brought them into town from way down on the Devil's River. I wondered what Fat was goin' to do with them."

"What he done was run them in as ringers on his deal with Mr. Jenkins. Can you do somethin' about it?"

Wheeler's mouth turned downward. "I wish I could, but this is a case for the lawyers to fight over. I expect Fat was real careful how he described the horses when he wrote his letter. He's gotten awful bold since C.C. took down with his miseries."

"I'd call this theft. Grand larceny, maybe."

"I can't argue the point, but I'm a sheriff, not a judge. Mr. Jenkins'll have to get a lawyer if he wants to fight the case."

"He's got a low opinion of lawyers. If he was younger, he'd just show up with a bullwhip and make Fat come to Jesus."

"And I couldn't blame him none, but this is 1910, and that's not the way folks do things anymore."

"More's the pity. I'd be sorely tempted to do it myself if I caught him without that shotgun."

"I couldn't allow it, Hewey. It's a matter for the court."

"There's more than one kind of court, and sooner or later Fat'll come up for judgment." Hewey grimaced. "Lord, I wish I didn't have to be there when Old Man Jenkins sees these horses."

CHAPTER

7

The horses traveled easier than Hewey expected, probably because they had been trail-broken coming up from the lower country, so he was early in reaching the outskirts of Upton City. He looked at the sun and tried to judge how much daylight he could count upon.

"Wes," he said, "I believe we'll shoot for Walter's and Eve's before me and Tommy quit for the night. We'll circle around town."

That would probably spare the feelings of housewives who had freshly washed clothing hanging on their lines. Even a small band of horses could stir a lot of dust. They would also rouse up the town dogs and perhaps result in a stampede. There was no limit to the damage twenty frightened broncs could do.

Wheeler said, "I'll help you." Some of the complaints would surely be brought to him, so he was saving himself some aggravation.

If anyone should ask, Hewey would say he was simply trying to make all the miles he could, but the principal reason for avoiding town was that he did not want everybody to see this string of third-rate horseflesh and know how badly Fat had snookered him and his boss.

When they cleared the far edge of town Wheeler reined up. "I'll bid you adios, Hewey. Ain't no tellin' what crimes have been committed in my absence."

Hewey nodded toward the horses. "This one was bad enough."

"I wish there was more I could do. Nothin' would tickle me better than to have Fat be a guest in my jailhouse. But don't you do somethin' that'll put *you* in there. Or that boy yonder." He jerked a thumb toward Tommy.

Hewey said, "I've been a guest in a few jailhouses, but Eve would never let me hear the end of it if Tommy was to be locked up with me. Right now all I intend to do is deliver these horses . . . such as they are."

He got to watching the stud in particular, for the black displayed signs of antisocial behavior that bordered on the criminal, biting, kicking at every other horse it could reach. It even took a notion to charge at Biscuit, and Hewey had to beat it off with the doubled end of his rope. He strongly considered leaving the stud behind and telling Jenkins it had gotten away, like the bull he and Skip Harkness had released. But that would be a dirty trick to play on anybody whose good mares took up with this sorry excuse for crow bait.

Just at dusk Hewey saw the familiar homestead and loped ahead to open a corral gate. Walter spotted him coming and reached the gate first. "Thought you might not come back by," he said.

"I hope Eve has got over bein' provoked at me. I been tastin' her biscuits ever since we left C.C.'s place."

"She gets mad easy, but she don't hold it long."

Tommy brought the horses in. Hewey observed his brother's expression as the horses passed by him and through the open gate. Walter did not have to say anything. His frown told it all.

Hewey said quickly, "Fat has run a sandy on us."

Walter latched the gate. "If those are of Alvin's raisin', I'll eat your hat."

"My hat is safe, but I don't know about my job. I been thinkin' about lookin' for work over in the Guadalupes anyway."

Eve was more cordial than Hewey had thought she might be. She hugged her son and gave Hewey a greeting that was civil enough, though not what he would call enthusiastic. She said, "You-all have got plenty of time to wash before supper." She pointed that remark especially at Hewey.

Tommy was eager to tell her about the day. "We had some excitement over at Mr. Tarpley's. Fat . . . Mr. Gervin . . . he aimed a shotgun at Uncle Hewey."

Eve's mouth fell open. Hewey tried to explain what Fat had done, but all she heard was that a shotgun had been pointed in her son's general direction. "Hewey Calloway, it's bad enough that you've lured him away to wander around like a gypsy. Now you've come close to gettin' him killed."

"You know Fat Gervin. He ain't goin' to kill anybody. He's full of wind, and I'll bet that shotgun wasn't even loaded."

He knew better, for he had been shaken all the way to his toes looking into that wide, dark muzzle. But surely the Lord made allowances when a man lied to a woman for her own good.

She burned the biscuits, always a sign that she had lapsed into a bad humor.

After breakfast Tommy stood in the kitchen doorway, a leftover biscuit wedged in his teeth, and fidgeted to be on his way while Eve handed him a sack of food and repeated the previous day's instructions and admonitions. Giving Hewey a distrusting look, she warned, "Don't you do everything your uncle Hewey does. Use your head and don't let him get you hurt."

Hewey said, "Tommy's levelheaded. Like as not he'll be lookin' after me more than I'll be lookin' after him."

"That is exactly what I'm afraid of."

Tommy finished the biscuit and peered into the sack to see what his mother had fixed for him. "Mama, I'm grown, almost."

"I want to see you live to *get* grown. It's a wonder to me that your uncle Hewey has survived this long."

Hewey said, "Caution and clean livin' is what has done it." He swung into the saddle. "We'd better be startin'. It's a long ways to Alpine."

As Hewey had expected, Old Man Jenkins's reaction to the horses was not pleasant to watch. He feared at first his employer would burst a blood vessel, the way the veins rose in his neck.

Hewey said, "I talked to the sheriff. He said there wasn't nothin' he could do. Said you'd ought to get you a lawyer."

"I don't trust lawyers, and from now on I ain't trustin' bankers, either. Since you knew him, why didn't you warn me about Frank Gervin?"

"I did. I said all you could be sure of was that he would do the wrong thing. Anyway, you'd already made the deal."

Jenkins stewed, studying the horses corraled at the J Bar headquarters after a three-day walk and trot from Upton City.

Hewey offered, "At least we got them here in good shape. Didn't lose a one."

"Might've been better if you'd lost them all. Especially that one yonder." He pointed to the black stud. "Acts like he's been on locoweed."

"He needed a good cuttin' and didn't get it."

"We'll do it when the almanac says the signs are right. 'Til then, watch out for him. He'll hurt somebody."

Hewey had never liked castrating studs, but in this case he would consider it a privilege. "You goin' to do anything about Fat Gervin?"

"I paid seventy-five dollars a head. That's fifteen hundred dollars for twenty head. Takin' him to court would cost me that much or more, and it'd all go into the lawyers' pockets." Jenkins's eyes took on a wicked gleam. "But there's a Mexican *curandera* woman over in town that claims she can put a curse on anybody she wants to. She put one on me once, and I never had so much bad luck at one time in my life. I'll see what she can do about Frank Gervin."

Hewey would have favored something more direct, but it was Jenkins's money. "If she can put a curse on people, reckon she could turn it the other way around and do somebody some good?"

"I'll ask her. You got anybody in mind?"

"Old C. C. Tarpley. Considerin' the sort of man he is, he ain't a bad feller. He needs all the help he can get."

"I'll talk to her, but you'd do better with a preacher." Jenkins watched Tommy unsaddle his dun and begin brushing him down. "I wasn't sure you'd bring the boy back with you."

"I hinted every way I knew how for him to stay home, but he's bound and determined to learn the trade. Says he wants a ranch of his own someday."

"He's got a good spirit, and there's a lot he can learn from you."

"I didn't set out to be no teacher."

"For forty dollars a month you can add that to your job." Jenkins turned his attention back to the horses. "They ain't much, but I'd like you and the boy to take them down to the Circle W. Maybe the hands can teach these skates a little somethin'. Then I can resell them and recover some of my investment."

"What you want us to do after we've made delivery?"

"Stay there. The crew's brandin' calves, and you'll be a right smart of help." Jenkins squinted one eye again. Hewey had learned that was a sign he had something on his mind, sometimes good but more often not. "Since you couldn't see your way clear to take the foreman's job I offered you down there, I've hired another man. Name's Ralph Underhill. You'll report to him."

Hewey nodded. For forty dollars he didn't much mind who he reported to.

Jenkins added, "I've made it clear to him that I don't want you ridin' any broncs."

Hewey protested, "You know I can do anything them boys can, and make a better job of it."

"Dammit, Hewey, I know how old you are even if you've forgot. These broncs are for Aparicio and the younger hands."

Hewey felt a spasm of insubordination coming on. "Next thing, you'll be tellin' me to swamp for Blas around the wagon."

"There's plenty of cow work you can do better than most. Ain't no call for you do it ridin' a bronc." Jenkins turned away, then came back. "Underhill's a top hand with horses and cattle, but he don't get along with men too good. You'll find him a little on the touchy side."

Old Man Jenkins was touchy. *Anybody* he *regards as touchy must be a bearcat sure enough,* Hewey thought.

He wished Bige Saunders could be foreman at the Circle W, but Jenkins needed him here on the home place.

Jenkins's auto driver, Peeler, had stood off to one side, eyeing the newly arrived horses with silent disapproval. He wore jodhpurs and tall lace-up boots, which Hewey thought looked plumb disgraceful on a cowboy. After Jenkins walked away, Peeler sidled over. "Looks like you and Mr. Jenkins took a skinnin'."

"It was his money."

"But it'd be your skin if you had to ride any of them outlaws. The whole outfit would be ahead if you'd drive these snides up onto the rimrock and jump them off."

Hewey had had the same thought. "I'm tempted, but I never killed a horse in my life, no matter how much they deserved it."

"Had you rather have these horses on your conscience, or some poor cowpuncher?"

"Neither one. But I *would* like to tie Fat Gervin to that black stud and turn him loose on the side of a mountain. I could sell tickets to every man, woman and child in Upton City."

"It's horses like these that convinced me I'd rather be drivin' an automobile." Peeler rolled a cigarette and offered the sack to Hewey. Hewey accepted with a nod. Peeler said, "You want one more piece of advice?"

Hewey knew he was going to get it whether he asked for it or not. "Can't hurt none."

"Don't forget what Mr. Jenkins said about Ralph Underhill. He's got sore toes on both feet. Even his mama probably didn't like him much."

"I get along fine with most people."

"Ralph Underhill ain't most people. Me and him almost came to a knuckle-bustin' before he went down to the ranch. We would've if it hadn't been for Mr. Jenkins."

"I'll tiptoe when I'm around him. Got to set a good example for Tommy."

The only good news he had heard since arriving with the horses was that Blas Villegas was at the lower ranch, cooking for the hands while they branded the J Bar on Jenkins's newly acquired calf crop. Branding could not be done at the time the cows were being counted because ownership had not been legally transferred. The deal could have collapsed, as it almost did over the value of a crowbar. Because he had bought the rights to the Circle W brand along with the cattle, Jenkins would not have to change brands on the older animals. Attrition would gradually phase out the Circle W.

Trailing had become almost routine for the horses, so all but the black stud gave Hewey and Tommy little trouble. It often tried to pick a fight and kept the other horses in fear except for one wiry little paint, short of leg and shorter of patience. After feeling the sting of sharp teeth, the squealing paint landed a solid kick to the stud's belly where it would inflict the most pain. Afterward the black was selective in its bullying and kept a wary eye on the paint.

Ordinarily Hewey had a low opinion of paint horses, but he decided this one had special virtues. He said, "I'd like to set Fat Gervin behind that kickin' paint and see how fast he could dodge."

Tommy grinned, savoring the image. "Mama would say revenge is a mean and hollow thing."

"But thinkin' about it is like music to the mind."

It was good not to have to open any more pasture gates once they were inside the Circle W's perimeter fence. The horses acted as if they sensed that the journey was almost over, and even the stud settled down to purposeful traveling. Hewey let Tommy lope ahead to open the corral gate. He contented himself to stay behind the horses at a slower pace, for jolting across rough ground had stirred a pain in his side. That seemed to be happening a lot lately.

As the horses began filing through the opening, Hewey gave his attention to a horseman who had stationed himself on the opposite side from Tommy to make sure none doubled back. The rider sat rigidly, one hand on his hip, his attitude that of a man who controlled all creation. Even before the introductions, Hewey decided this was the new foreman, Ralph Underhill.

His surmise was confirmed by a challenging tone of voice as the man ordered Tommy to shut the gate, then rode up to Hewey. "I thought you were supposed to be bringin' me a string of *horses*."

The attitude rankled Hewey. "They ain't burros."

"I've seen burros that looked better. You pick these yourself?"

"I'm not any happier about them than you are. Mr. Jenkins made a deal with a four-flusher, and this is what he got."

The man frowned. "I'm guessin' you'd be Hewey Calloway."

"That'd be a right fair guess."

"Mr. Jenkins told me you'd be comin' along with some broncs, though he didn't expect you quite so soon. Said you was takin' a little vacation."

"It don't take me long to vacate."

"You won't get any vacation here. This is a workin' outfit."

Hewey sensed that Underhill had a mad on about something. He supposed it was the poor quality of the horseflesh, which was understandable, but there wasn't any point in taking his frustrations out on Hewey.

Underhill didn't take them out on Hewey alone. He hollered harshly at Tommy, who remained at the gate afoot, awaiting instruction. "Hey, button, don't just stand there with your thumb in your butt. See them boys brandin' calves in that corral yonder? Fall in there and see if you can be some help."

Chastened, Tommy swung quickly into the saddle and rode away in a long trot.

Hewey felt a prickling along his backside. "You got no call to talk to the boy thataway. He's my nephew."

"I don't care if he's the Prince of Wales. If he works here, he *works* here."

Hewey felt a streak of rebellion coming on. He saw Blas Villegas's chuck wagon standing idle beneath the trees. Blas would be cooking in the bunkhouse kitchen as long as they were at headquarters. "It's been a long ride. I'm goin' for some of Blas's coffee."

"You can drink coffee when everybody else gets to drink coffee." Underhill pointed at the horses. "Go in there and show me what you brought."

Underhill gave orders the way Hewey remembered army sergeants doing it. A thoughtful ranch foreman would usually be more subtle in exerting his authority, framing his orders in the form of a request rather than a command. Hewey said a crisp and exaggerated "Yes, *sir*," the way he had addressed officers in the Spanish war. It was a way of telling Underhill he was two sizes too big for his britches. Underhill got the message, for his face turned red.

Hewey liked the Circle W, but his stay was likely to be short if this was the way he and Tommy were going to be treated.

Underhill pointed his chin at Biscuit. "Is that your own horse or the company's?"

"He belongs to me."

"Most places I've been, they don't allow private horses eatin' company feed."

"Mr. Jenkins has never had any objections." *I wonder if he's like this with everybody or if I'm a special case,* Hewey thought.

Underhill accepted the situation but not in good grace. "If he sees fit to allow it, it's his ranch and his feed. But if it was up to me . . ." He did not finish. He proceeded through the gate and left it for Hewey to close. He walked toward the horses, most of which faced around to watch him suspiciously. A man afoot in a corral had never been good news to them. The stud bared its teeth.

Hewey said, "I'd keep an eye on that one."

Underhill must have heard, but he made no response. He walked directly toward the black. It backed its ears and made a bluffing start in his direction, paused, then came forward again with serious intent. Underhill stood his ground, waiting until the stud was almost upon him, then shouted loudly and slapped his hat across its nose. Startled, the black pawed at him, missed, then turned and ran back into the bunch, eyes rolling. It looked as confused as when the paint kicked it in the belly.

At least the son of a bitch is not afraid of horses, Hewey thought. It took nerve to stand and call a bluff like that. *I'll give him a little time before I haul off and punch him in the nose.*

Underhill walked among the horses, which drew to one side or the other at his approach, all giving him their full attention. He studied them one by one. Hewey suspected when he was done he could probably turn away and give a pretty good description of each animal without looking back. He had the marks of a horseman, even if he *was* a son of a bitch.

Underhill said, "You can tell by the saddle marks that most of them have been ridden before, or ridden at. They're mostly outlaws and knotheads. But we'll stake some of them after supper like they were all young broncs. Might be somethin' we can salvage."

"It'll be like tryin' to find a ripe peach in a barrel of rotten apples," Hewey said. "But we can try."

"We?" The wrinkles went deeper in Underhill's face. "Mr. Jenkins gave me strict orders that you're not supposed to ride any broncs. Seems like you're some kind of privileged character."

So that *was it,* Hewey thought. Underhill resented his being considered a special case.

"Mr. Jenkins has a notion I'm gettin' a little too much age on me to ride the rough string anymore. But what he don't see he don't need to know, and what he don't know won't hurt him. I'll do my share of the ridin' along with everybody else."

Underhill shook his head. "When I work for a man, I do what he tells me. These broncs are for the *young* hands."

Hewey wanted to argue the point, but he had already lost that argument with Jenkins, and it was clear that once Underhill took a stand, wild horses could not drag him from it. Hewey had never understood such stubborn people. He said, "I'll ride broncs if I'm a mind to."

"Do and I'll fire you."

"Try to fire me and I'll quit."

Underhill turned to face him. "Looks like me and you ain't goin' to get along very good."

"Sure looks like."

"Mr. Jenkins says you're a top hand, so I'll try and put up with you for a little while. Maybe we can come to an accommodation."

"Ask anybody. They'll tell you I've always had a smilin' disposition."

Underhill peered closely at him, and Hewey tried to force a smile. Underhill stalked through the gate and left it open. Hewey hurried to close it so the horses would not get out.

He sensed that even in silence, Underhill had had the last word. Almost, anyway. Hewey walked up to the bunkhouse to get that cup of coffee.

While he sat at the long table, the cup in his hand, he questioned Blas about the new foreman. Blas shrugged, evasive. "He is a boss. I have had many bosses. He is not the worst."

"How do you get along with him?"

"I do as I am told." He left unstated the fact that as a Mexican working for gringo bosses, he had always done as he was told. That was the key to survival.

Hewey said, "He seems to have a burr under his blanket. Maybe a bunch of them."

"It is said that his wife left him and took their child. That is a hard thing for a man to bear."

"She probably had reason enough."

It occurred to Hewey that he did not know if Blas had ever even had a wife. He had accepted Blas for what he had become, a wagon cook, and had never asked questions about his past. Feeling guilty, he asked now, for he realized that the old man's friendship was important to him.

Blas said, "Once, in Chihuahua. She was the daughter of a farmer, a *campesino*. The fever came, and she died."

"I'm sorry."

"It was a very long time ago. It is hard even to remember her face.

I try to see her in my mind, and I cannot. It would be an old face now, so perhaps it is as well."

Hewey stared into the cup. He found it easy to conjure up Spring Renfro's face in all its detail. It was hard to imagine that someday he might not be able to. "You ever still miss her?"

Blas stared across the room at nothing in particular. "Sometimes at night, when I am dreaming, she comes and lies beside me. I can feel her body, but in the darkness I cannot see her face." He turned back to Hewey. "At least I have something to remember. What have you to remember, Hooey?"

Hewey had never spoken of Spring to anyone here. "A lot of country, a lot of horses, a lot of good times."

"But there should be more. For every man there should at least be one woman."

The remnant of coffee had become cold in the cup. Hewey walked to the door and flung it out onto the ground. He put the cup in Blas's tub. "I reckon the boys may need some help with the brandin'."

Blas said, "At night, when you dream, is that all you can dream of, the branding?"

"No, sometimes it's horses."

Aparicio was roping calves by the heels and dragging them toward the branding-iron fire. Tommy was partnering with one of the young Mexican hands to throw the calves down as Aparicio brought them by, then hold them still for branding.

Aparicio motioned as Hewey climbed over the fence rather than walk all the way down to the gate. He would sooner ride a mile than walk a hundred yards. "My arm is tired, Hooey. Would you like to heel for a while?"

Anybody could flank calves or wield the hot irons, but not everyone was good at roping heels in a branding pen. As Aparicio handed the reins to him, Hewey glanced toward Underhill. The foreman was watching. Hewey promised himself he would make every loop a good one, and he roped at least twenty calves before he missed one. By then Underhill was no longer paying attention, or appeared not to be.

At last Hewey searched through the calves, his loop ready, but found none still unbranded. Underhill counted the bloody-edged pieces of ear notched from every calf. That tally jibed with the one he had taken before the calves were branded. "All done," he announced.

Hewey could have told him so. He felt as if Underhill was checking up on him. They turned the calves into a larger pen with their mothers to allow them time to pair before being released back into the open. The bawling was loud but more pleasant to Hewey's ears than a lot of human conversation he had heard lately.

Tommy dusted himself off. "I'm sure ready to put away some of Blas's cookin'."

Underhill said, "Before anybody stops for supper, we'll stake out some of these broncs."

The job consisted of roping the new arrivals, earing them down and in a few cases even throwing them to the ground to get a hackamore over their heads. Horsebackers then led them to a stretch of open ground, where a scattering of heavy logs and a couple of big wagon wheels awaited. Most resisted the lead rope, so the riders had to wrap the long hackamore reins around their saddle horns and half lead, half drag the broncs.

Hewey saw that Tommy was eyeing the black stud with misgivings. He said, "You're still a little short in the britches to be handlin' one like that. He's for somebody like Aparicio."

The black seemed to go out of its head when the rope tightened around its neck. It fought wildly, threshing like a fish on a line, even falling on its side, hooves flailing. After it scrambled to its feet,

Hewey worked his way up the rope and grabbed the ears, dodging as the bronc tried to paw him.

"Put the hackamore on him, Tommy." All the time Tommy and Hewey struggled, the stud squealed and kicked. It landed a glancing blow against Tommy's leg, and Tommy fell. Hewey feared the black would stomp the boy, so he bit down on the left ear to give the animal something else to think about. He knew he would be spitting horsehair from now until supper.

Tommy got to his feet and finished knotting the hackamore. Hewey stepped away quickly so a hoof would not strike him. He took a firm grip on the long rein. "Go bring Biscuit."

Tommy limped as he hurried to fetch Hewey's brown horse.

Underhill had been watching while he hackamored the paint that had given the black a dose of humility. "I'll give you this, Calloway: you know what you're doin'."

"I didn't just start yesterday."

"Or twenty years ago, either. You better let one of these young hands wrestle with that black."

"I've got him under control."

The stud tried to shake Hewey loose. Hewey bit down on its ear again, venting on the horse the resentment Underhill had roused in him. Turning loose, he mounted Biscuit and wrapped the long hackamore rein around his saddle horn. "Come on, damn you!"

In response to the tugging of the rope, the stud bared its teeth and charged. Biscuit dodged, almost unseating Hewey but causing the black to stumble and fall.

"You're makin' things rough on yourself," Hewey growled. "But sometimes the worst things that happen to us are the things we do to ourselves." As the black regained its feet, Hewey put Biscuit into a trot that did not allow slack enough for a fight. Instead the stud pulled back on the rein in a contest of wills. Biscuit plodded ahead, the black hopping unwillingly on braced legs.

Hewey chose a heavy log that lay a safe distance from where the other broncs were being staked. Tommy rode along behind, ready to help.

Hewey said, "When I get down, you take Biscuit and lead him out of the way. I'll tie this outlaw."

He expected the black to run at him once he was afoot, so the sudden lunge did not surprise him. He jumped to one side and jerked on the long rein, bracing it around his hip. While the black floundered, Hewey wrapped the end of the rope around the log and took a quick half hitch. He stepped back out of the way as the black ran at him again. The log's weight brought the bronc up short at the end of the rein, almost throwing it off its feet.

Hewey watched in satisfaction as the black transferred its frustrations and began trying to drag the log to death. Each run moved it only a few inches.

"Time you've jerked that thing around for an hour or two," Hewey said, "you're liable to be about half civilized."

The stud fought its head, trying in vain to free itself from the tyranny of the hackamore.

Tommy watched with doubt. "Reckon he'll tame down?"

"There's only one thing he'll ever be fit for, and that's a bar of soap. It'd probably blister the hide off of anybody who used it."

Underhill finished tying the paint to a log. He came over to look at the black.

Hewey said, "Luckiest thing that could happen would be if he fell over that log and broke a leg."

Underhill shook his head. "Mr. Jenkins spent good money for that skate, so it's up to us to try to make somethin' of him." He turned to Tommy. "You think you can ride him?"

Tommy swallowed. "I don't know."

Hewey quickly put in, "He's just a boy. He's got no business on a loco outlaw like this."

"He's bein' paid a man's wages. He'll do a man's work." Under-hill rode away.

Hewey felt a rising dread as he studied Tommy. "I sure wish you'd stayed home."

CHAPTER

8

Tired though he was, Hewey did not sleep much. He lay on his cot, staring at the moonlight through the narrow bunkhouse window, listening to others snore. He had heard Tommy turn several times and guessed that his nephew was awake too, thinking about that outlaw black. Tommy had broken broncs for Alvin Lawdermilk, but Alvin didn't raise any like the loco devil hitched to a log out on the flat.

Underhill had not exactly said he would order Tommy to ride the stud, but the implication had been plain enough.

It's on account of me, Hewey thought. *Underhill doesn't like me, so he's taking it out on Tommy. And he's liable to get the boy hurt bad.*

Hewey would send his nephew packing home tomorrow if he could, but he knew Tommy would refuse to go, fearing it would look as if he were running away. Hewey would not leave under those circumstances either, and Tommy was trying to model himself after his uncle.

Why can't he model after somebody else, like his daddy? Or even Old C. C. Tarpley? After some consideration he eliminated Tarpley.

He could slip out yonder right now, shoot that stud in the belly and tell God it died of colic. But Hewey had not fired his pistol in a long time. The barrel might be rusted enough to blow up in his hand. He was not even sure he had any cartridges in his war bag. He felt about guns much the same way he felt about posthole diggers; they were simply a working tool that he took no pleasure in.

Besides, as he had told Peeler, he had never killed a horse in his life. The thought repulsed him.

In any case, Underhill was likely to want to see the stud remain staked for several days before it was saddled. A lot of things could happen in that length of time.

Hewey tried to think what they might be and how he might help them along, but no good ideas reared up and showed themselves.

The branding continued, and each evening the hands staked broncs to spend the night contemplating the authority of the long rope rein that tethered them. The animals were freed each morning to water and to graze under the loose supervision of a young Mexican horse jingler. Spoiled though they were from previous misuse, most seemed to show an educated respect after a couple of days. Their noses were sore from the hackamore's stern discipline, imposed each time they resisted being prisoner to log or wagon wheel.

The stud, however, remained unbent. Though the hackamore had burned a raw sore across its nose, the black fought like a caged cat each time it was caught and led to the log.

Underhill watched each day's struggle without comment. The fourth evening, the branding was finished earlier than usual. Peeler had driven Old Man Jenkins out in his touring car to see how the work was progressing. Underhill announced, "Them broncs've had time enough to learn that the rope is boss. We'll start ridin' them this evenin'."

Hewey thought he was applying the word *we* a little loosely. It was not a foreman's job to ride raw broncs; it was his place to see that the others did. Underhill assigned them, starting by giving Aparicio Rodriguez the paint. It might never be a good cow horse, but Hewey was willing to forgive its shortcomings out of respect for the way it stood up for its rights against the black stud.

The stud was the last to be assigned. Underhill turned toward Tommy, but his gaze settled upon Hewey as he spoke. "They tell me your uncle was a real bronc stomper in his day. Reckon it runs in the blood?"

Hewey listened for a trace of malice.

Tommy was hesitant in answering. "I don't know."

"Then we'll have to find out. If you can handle that stud, you ought to be able to handle anything that comes along."

Hewey was not in the habit of arguing with foremen, but this was a time to make an exception. "You know this boy ain't ready to ride a horse like that. He'd be a handful even for me or Aparicio."

"You're out, and I've already given Aparicio his mount. It's time to see if this boy can pull his weight."

Tommy's words were strong, but Hewey heard doubt in his voice. "I can do it, Uncle Hewey."

Underhill grunted with satisfaction. "You heard him yourself." He walked away, putting an end to argument. Hewey stared after him in frustration, trying to decide which to do first, fight him or quit.

Tommy said, "Would you help me saddle him, Uncle Hewey?"

Dread stirred like acid in Hewey's stomach. "It'd be smarter to roll our beddin' and leave here right now."

"But we're not goin' to." Tommy's voice had picked up determination. "We're not goin' to let some old bronc scare us."

"He scares me."

"Daddy always said it's best to spit in the eye of whatever scares you and go ahead with what you have to do."

That had usually been Hewey's philosophy, though circumstances from time to time had caused him to back away and rethink his principles. "Your daddy may not've taken a good look at that black stud."

Aparicio was the first to saddle and ride. The paint gave him a creditable fight but was no match for the vaquero's skill. After a few jumps, the paint began to race around the corral. Clearly it had been ridden before but perhaps had been given up as a bad job by someone who lacked Aparicio's touch. The cowboy let the horse run until it was lathered with sweat, then force-reined it to left and right until the paint surrendered. A couple more cowboys rode their broncs, one being thrown but immediately getting back on and staying until the horse quit bucking.

Underhill jerked a thumb in Tommy's direction. "Let's see what you can do."

The black fought so hard that Hewey had to rope it by its forefeet and trip it, then tie up one foot while the horse was down. Even on three feet the squealing stud was formidable, lunging against the rope, eyes rolling and nostrils flaring as Tommy kept trying to place the saddle blanket on its back. It attempted to paw first Tommy, then Hewey, falling each time but showing no sign that it had learned anything.

Hewey grumbled, "This horse is crazy as a bedbug."

They managed finally to get Tommy's saddle on. While Hewey gripped the black's ears, Tommy attempted to fit his left foot into the stirrup.

Hewey did not know how the stud managed it on three feet, but it kicked Tommy on the hip and sent him spinning back, falling in the dirt.

"That settles it," he declared. "Tommy ain't ridin' this loco son of a bitch. Aparicio, grab ahold of him."

Tommy had ridden a bronc once for Skip Harkness, who was no kin. Hewey would ride this one for his nephew.

The vaquero took Hewey's place, holding the ears, biting down on one as the black kicked at Hewey and grazed his leg. Hewey gritted his teeth against a flash of pain and grabbed for the bouncing stirrup. He shoved his foot into it and grasped the horn, swinging up, leaning forward to offset the pull if the bronc should suddenly surge ahead before he was firmly set. He considered keeping his hold on the horn, but he let pride prevail over prudence. A real bronc stomper did not grab leather. The black lunged forward, nearly falling.

Old Man Jenkins's stern voice boomed from outside the fence. "Hewey Calloway, what the hell do you think you're doin'?"

Hewey saw no reason to answer. Jenkins had eyes to see.

"All right, Aparicio, untie his foot."

The vaquero loosened the rope and scrambled out of the way. Loosing a furious sound that reminded Hewey of the bull he and Skip had brought down, the stud seemed to twist halfway around in midair and come down at a ninety-degree angle from where it had started. The impact of hooves against the ground jammed Hewey's teeth together so hard he feared some might shatter. The bronc bawled in fury.

Before Hewey could regain his balance the black was in the air again, repeating the twisting motion. Hewey tried to anticipate and counter the move, but he seemed always a second behind. He felt his head twisting and thought he could imagine how a chicken felt as its neck was wrung. He knew he showed daylight between his seat and the saddle. He tightened the grip of his knees and tried to contemplate the virtues of a nice soft job in town.

He saw the fence coming at him and realized the bronc was going to strike it a glancing blow. He could do nothing to protect himself from the impact. His right knee seemed to explode as it smacked against a post. The shock set Hewey's head to reeling. He forgot about pride and grabbed the saddle horn, trying to steady himself. He was sure the pounding had broken something loose inside—his lungs, his liver . . . he had no idea what. He hurt like he had never hurt in his life.

The black made another high jump but somehow failed to land solidly. The legs buckled, and it slammed down hard on its right side, pinning the already-injured knee. The horse rolled half over, threshing to find its feet. The saddle horn punched against Hewey's ribs. He felt as if he were sinking into a deep pit of agony.

A thousand bright suns circled around him. The black scrambled to get up. Instinctively Hewey's hand found the horn again. He heard the shouts of the cowboys, but the only voice that came through clearly was Aparicio's. "Jump, Hooey! Jump!"

He felt the stud surge ahead, then slam hard against the fence. The force of the sudden stop hurled Hewey forward. He smashed against the fence and fell away. The back of his head slammed against the ground. For a panicked moment he wondered where the bronc was, but he could not see. He feared the strike of the hooves, or perhaps having his foot caught in the stirrup so that he would be dragged around the corral.

Strong hands tugged at him, pulling him away from the fence, but he could not find the faces through the brilliance of all those whirling suns. He fought for breath and tasted the sticky salt of blood on his lips. He wanted to cry out but could not muster the voice. He heard a weak groan and knew it came from somewhere deep inside.

He heard Underhill's voice. "I believe that crazy bronc broke his neck."

Whose neck? Hewey wondered. *Mine or his?*

Old Man Jenkins's voice said, "We ought to've shot that outlaw. Now we won't have to."

The black's neck, then. But Hewey felt as if it might be his own as well. He hurt from his feet to the top of his head. He tried to move his hands, but his left did not respond. The sharp pain told him the arm was broken. So was every other bone in his body, for all he could tell.

Jenkins said, "Damn it, I've kept tellin' him one of these broncs would kill him someday. Salinas, ride to the bunkhouse and tell Peeler to fetch that automobile down here. Spur like hell."

Hewey lapsed into semiconsciousness, though he was aware when they lifted him from the ground. He heard Jenkins's voice. "Gentle with him, boys. If he's got any broken ribs, they might punch a hole in his lungs."

A sharp pain pierced his left side, and his arm felt as if it were wrenching itself loose from his shoulder. He was vaguely aware of being carried and of the misery that compounded with every stride.

Tommy's anxious voice demanded, "You don't reckon he's goin' to die?"

Hewey had wondered now and again how death must feel. At this point he thought it might come as a relief. But amid all those whirling flashes of light he glimpsed Tommy's face, beseeching him to live.

He drifted off somewhere far away and remained there awhile in some vague sort of limbo. He was only dimly conscious of the automobile's roar.

Jenkins said, "Ease him into the backseat, boys. Careful. Ain't no tellin' what all may be broke."

Tommy said, "He's my uncle. I want to go with him."

Jenkins replied, "All right. You may have to hold him down if the pain really hits him. I think he's got a busted arm and leg, and maybe some ribs. His innards may be a mess, too."

Aparicio said, "*Mala suerte.* He is a good one, that Hooey."

"*Was,*" Jenkins said. "If he lives, he won't ever be the same again." His voice darkened with regret. "He was a great cowboy in his day. I wish he'd quit while he was still in one piece."

Peeler said, "You sure that stud is dead? If he ain't, I'll cut his damned throat."

Somebody replied, "A hundred years from now he won't be any deader."

Tommy sat on the edge of the backseat, beside Hewey. He

pleaded, "Don't you die, Uncle Hewey. Don't you die on me like Skip did."

The starting of the trip was a nightmare of agony, the automobile jolting unmercifully on the rough trail that passed for a road. Hewey awakened sufficiently to know that he lay stretched out on the backseat, his legs bent because the car was not wide enough to accommodate the length of his body. Tommy perched precariously beside him, insurance against Hewey's rolling off the seat. Jenkins sat in front beside Peeler.

He heard Jenkins complain, "A good forty-dollar cowboy busted to hell by a bronc that wasn't worth twenty. Why does this bad luck always happen to me?"

Peeler said, "Maybe Doc Evans can fix him up."

"You can patch an old shirt, but it'll just be an old shirt with patches on it. Maybe someday I'll learn to fire every cowboy as soon as he turns thirty."

Hewey wanted to protest that he wasn't as old as Jenkins made out, but he could not muster voice except for an occasional groan. He was not even sure that what he was hearing was real. All kinds of images ran through his mind like a magic lantern show gone berserk. Some were memories, but some were hallucinations, flitting dreams and nightmares prompted by the pain. He heard Tommy tell him, "You oughtn't to've done it. I could've handled him."

Hewey wanted to say he doubted it, but he could not form the words. Gradually consciousness fell away, and with it much of the hurting. Through a haze he saw Tommy leaning protectively over him. Strangely, his nephew seemed to change, to grow younger and smaller. He was as Hewey remembered him from four years ago, when Tommy had bid him a tearful good-bye and said, "You'll be back, won't you, Uncle Hewey? You ain't goin' to let some old bronc kill you?"

Maybe he had. Maybe he *had* let that black stud kill him.

Hewey realized that the pain was draining away from him. Everything that had hurt so terribly was going numb. Gradually he began feeling warm and safe and comfortable, as if he were floating free on a soft cushion of air or a gentle south wind. A sense of euphoria came over him, a sense of peace so total that he could compare it with nothing in his experience. He knew in some deep corner of his subconscious that it was a dream, but it seemed much more than a dream. It was as real as life.

I'm dying, he told himself, and wondered that the thought brought him no fear. He found himself welcoming it.

Faces came to him, dear faces out of his past—his mother, whom he barely remembered because she had died so young, and his father, who had never quite found his way. He wanted to call to them but had no voice. They seemed to want to speak to him but made no move to come closer. They faded as in a twilight mist, and in their place came his old sidekick Grady Welch, flashing a wide, happy grin that had been his trademark. He and Snort Yarnell had been a pair to draw to, so much alike they could have been brothers. Grady waved and turned to mount a black horse that appeared out of nowhere.

A horse like the one that got me, Hewey thought. He saw that the horse had four stocking feet, like the one that had stomped Grady to death. Hewey tried to shout a warning, to tell Grady not to get on him, but he still had no voice. Grady and the horse drifted away into the same twilight mist that had taken Hewey's mother and father. Hewey was alone.

He wanted to follow, for the mist seemed friendly like an easy April rain, but he could not move. The warm glow enveloped him once more, and he would have been content to remain in its embrace forever.

He felt as if someone were tugging on his arm, trying to pull him back toward the darkness. He resisted, for he did not want to go back. He did not want to leave this cradle of peace, but the tugging was insistent.

He saw Spring Renfro. She held his hand, bidding him to follow her, but the direction was wrong. It led back to the pain. She smiled with reassurance, and it was the smile she had shown him the day he first met her, long ago. He tried to pull away from her grip, for death seemed preferable to the agony. Sadness came into her blue eyes, the sadness he had seen the day she had released him from his promise so he might ride away once again, a free spirit seeking a place that did not exist and perhaps had never existed, where time would stand still and he would always be twenty years old.

In her eyes he saw what those four years of freedom had cost him, for now she belonged to another. She gave him a faint smile that seemed to say good-bye, and a terrible loneliness settled upon him. He reached for her, but she was gone back into the mist from which the vision had come. He tried to call to her, but he could summon no voice.

The regret lasted only a moment, for he settled again into the peace of this strange place into which he had drifted. He did not want to leave.

He felt himself being pulled away once more and fought to remain where he was. He had never realized how easy it would be to accept death when it came with the faces of his mother and father and good old Grady Welch. But the hand he could not see kept pulling him away against his will.

"Let me go!" he shouted in his mind. "It's better where I am."

He saw a face forming in the mist, and it was his nephew's. Tears welled in Tommy's eyes. He held firmly to Hewey's right hand. "Hang on, Uncle Hewey. Don't you die and leave me."

Hewey wanted to tell him, *I did die, and you pulled me back. I wanted to stay there, but you wouldn't let me.*

The misery returned, strong as before, and told him he was still alive. Tears stung his eyes and warmed his face as they trickled down. *Alive. But alive for what?*

The sun was down, and darkness came. At times the weak headlights caused Peeler to let the automobile stray from the poorly defined road. He sped along, almost high-centering the car a couple of times lurching through cement-hard ruts left after the drying-up of a mud puddle. A particularly severe jolt sent a shock coursing through Hewey and caused him to lapse into unconsciousness again.

Spring Renfro came back to him, telling him he was going to be all right. He reached toward her, but he could not find her. She had disappeared into a gray haze, gone with a man named Farley Neal.

Hewey had but little concept of the time spent on the road to Alpine. He was aware of Tommy jumping out to open gates, but he had no idea how many there were. He realized the car had come to a stop, and he heard Peeler pounding on a door, calling for Dr. Evans. Hewey cried out as they picked him up and carried him inside. The next thing he knew he was lying on a bed, his boots and clothes off, and the doctor was feeling his arms and legs, trying to locate broken bones. He caught the unpleasant odor of medicines and disinfectant.

Hewey cried out again as hands searched down his right leg.

Evans asked, "Is that where it hurts?"

Miraculously, it seemed, Hewey could speak. "It hurts every place there is."

"That knee looks bad."

"I can't raise my left arm."

"It's broken. Didn't anybody ever tell you that riding broncs is a job for the young?"

They had, often, and Hewey's stock reply had been that whenever a man had a sitting-down job he should hang on to it. But that did not seem funny now. Nothing seemed funny now.

Jenkins said, "He done some talkin' out of his head. From what he was sayin', I'm afraid he's probably tore up inside, too."

The doctor's face was grave. "I can wrap his ribs and his knee. I can put a cast on his arm. But as to internal injuries, they will either heal themselves or they won't. I am afraid they are beyond any abilities of mine."

Jenkins said, "Do what you can. He's been a good hand, even if sometimes he hasn't got the judgment God gave a jackrabbit."

Hewey was not too far out of it to grasp what Jenkins was implying. *He's been a good hand. Been!* Like it was all over with. Like he really had died.

He tried to raise up but fell back. Somewhere inside, something was badly wrong.

Tommy bent over him. "You'd better lay still, Uncle Hewey."

Hewey squeezed his eyes shut, as if that would block off the pain. He felt tears burning. Crying like a baby . . . hell of a thing for a grown man.

When the worst of it was past, he managed a weak voice. "Did they say that black stud is dead?"

"Broke his neck when he hit the fence."

"I almost wish he'd broken mine, too. Seems like he broke everything else." Hewey remembered the brief period of peace, when death had come to him like a friend and had taken away the pain. It still seemed as if he should be able to reach out and grasp it and leave this suffering behind.

The doctor told Tommy, "Son, you'd better wait out in the front room. I'm going to set his arm, and it won't be something a boy would want to watch." To Peeler he said, "Would you mind helping me?"

Tommy said, "I'll be close by, Uncle Hewey. If you need anything, just holler."

Hewey would holler, all right. He would holler like hell when they set that arm.

The work done, Dr. Evans brought something in a glass. "Drink this. It should dull your senses and help you sleep."

"Is it whiskey?" Cold sweat running down his face and burning his eyes, Hewey would give a week's pay for a double shot of bourbon or rye. He would even settle for tequila.

"Not quite, but it should have some of the same effect."

It certainly was not whiskey, Hewey found as soon as he gulped it down. The worst rotgut he had ever tasted was ambrosia in comparison. But in a while he felt more at ease and dropped off to sleep. When he opened his eyes, daylight through the window made him close them again quickly.

He heard Tommy's voice. "You awake, Uncle Hewey?"

"I ain't even sure I'm alive." He knew he must be, however. A dead man wouldn't hurt so much. His ribs were wrapped tightly. He moved his right arm, then tried to move his left but found it in a cast, tightly bound. His right leg was immobilized. It felt as if it weighed a hundred pounds. Trying to lift it sent pain lancing through his body.

"I've roped and tied cattle that wasn't as helpless as this."

"I wish you'd had more faith in me. You wouldn't be here if you hadn't taken it on yourself to try and ride my bronc."

Hewey thought he detected a touch of resentment. "I was afraid he'd hurt you."

"I'm younger than you are, and not near as brittle. Now we'll never know if I could've ridden him."

"You'd've wound up where I'm at."

"Maybe, maybe not." Tommy turned to stare out the window. "I can't be mad at you, seein' you layin' here all busted up. You thought you were doin' what was right for me."

"I promised your folks I'd look out for you."

"You sure did that, all right. Now I'm feelin' guilty because you got yourself tore up takin' my place."

"There's no cause for you to feel guilty about anything. I didn't give you time to have a say about it." Hewey tried again to raise up but could not. "Besides, I'll be back amongst them before you know it."

"That's not the way the doctor talks. For a while he wasn't even sure you'd live."

"Ain't the first time some horse busted my arm. I was always a quick healer."

"You weren't always this old."

Dr. Evans heard their voices. He walked into the room carrying a steaming cup. Though Hewey had always enjoyed coffee, he found the aroma strangely nauseating. "I don't believe I can handle any coffee."

"It's mine, not yours. A man in your condition shouldn't be drinking coffee." The doctor swallowed what remained in the cup. "At least you seem to have gotten some sleep. That's more than your nephew did. He sat up in this room all night."

It was Hewey's turn for guilt. "Wasn't no need in that. Boy his age needs his rest."

"I dozed some," Tommy said. "That big chair is pretty comfortable."

Evans felt Hewey's forehead, then stuck a thermometer in his mouth. "Feeling any better?"

Hewey could not answer without biting down on the glass and risking a mouthful of mercury. He was not certain what he would say anyway. He knew only that it would be hard to pick out one place that hurt worse than another.

Tommy said, "I wish I could let Mama and Daddy know."

The doctor said, "You could telephone them."

"They don't have a telephone. It costs too much to run a line. But there's one in the sheriff's office. I could tell Wes Wheeler."

When the doctor removed the thermometer, Hewey protested, "Ain't no need gettin' your folks all upset. I'll be back at the ranch in a few days."

Frowning in disagreement, the doctor turned to Tommy. "Have you ever talked on a telephone?"

"No, sir, never was any reason to before."

"Then I'd better ring Central for you. It's a complicated business, talking long distance."

"I'd sure be obliged, sir."

Walter and Eve had brought the boy up to have good manners, Hewey thought. He wished they had taught him not to get people unnecessarily excited over something that time would heal.

Though the telephone was two rooms away, Hewey could hear the doctor's and Tommy's voices clearly, for they had to shout to be heard. Tommy sounded nervous, not just because of the message but because he had never talked on a telephone before. Hewey had done it a couple of times, though he never had quite trusted the contraption. There was something unnatural about carrying on a conversation with somebody miles away, somebody you couldn't see.

Tommy came back. "Mr. Wheeler said tell you to hurry up and get well. Said he'd ride out this mornin' to tell Mama and Daddy."

"It's a waste of a public servant's time and a burden on the taxpayers."

"How much tax have you ever paid, Uncle Hewey?"

"A right smart of whiskey tax, I expect."

Later in the day—he judged it to be around noon—a booming voice awakened him from a light doze. Blinking the sleep from his eyes, he saw a tall, lanky, slightly stooped figure standing in the doorway, hat crushed in his big hands. A false smile revealed a gold tooth.

The voice declared, "Hewey Calloway, you've got awful lazy in your old age, layin' in bed plumb to noontime."

"Snort Yarnell! I thought I was in the midst of a nightmare, but it's turned out real. What're you doin' in town this time of the day? Get fired again?"

"I ain't been fired in my life. I always quit before they got the chance." Though he forced himself to grin broadly, Snort could not control the anxiety in his eyes. "I hear you finally found a bronc too tough for you to handle. I'll go out and ride him for you."

"That won't be hard to do. He's dead."

"Probably died of fright, knowin' I'd be comin' to turn him wrong side out. You ain't goin' to be in here long, are you? I've got plans for the two of us."

"Plans?" Snort always had plans. Most of them led to calamity of one sort or another.

"Figured we'd go down into Mexico this fall and buy us a bunch of raw broncs real cheap. We could spend the winter ridin' them, then bring them north in the spring to sell. Our pockets would jingle like a wagonload of trace chains."

"Last time we went to Mexico we were lucky to get out of there with a horse apiece and the saddles to put on them."

"That was on account of bad tequila. This time we won't drink nothin' but the best." Snort laughed, but Hewey sensed that the laughter was as fake as the gold tooth. That notion about Mexico had probably just popped into his head as a way of making conversation. There was not a career politician in the Austin statehouse who could outlie Snort Yarnell.

But Hewey was not exactly an amateur at the game. "I'd sort of figured we might go down into South Texas and rope outlaw steers out of the brush this winter. Them ranchers down there pay pretty good for clearin' the mossyhorns out of their pastures."

"That sounds like fun, too. We'll take Tommy with us and show him what *real* cowpunchin' is like. Think you'll be able to ride in a few days?"

"Why not? May need somebody to help me onto my horse at first, 'til this bum knee heals a little, but once I'm in the saddle I'll be as good as I ever was."

"All right, old pardner, I'll be lookin' in on you again." Snort turned to go but stopped in the doorway, his head down. He twisted the hat in his hands before turning and coming back. His eyes brimmed with tears.

"Damn it all, Hewey, who are we lyin' to? That doctor says you'll be lucky if you ever get back on a horse again. Your cowboyin' days are over with."

Tommy was dismayed. "Snort, you shouldn't . . ."

Hewey tried to say the doctor was wrong, that he would be out of this bed and riding again in no time. But his throat tightened up so that he could not speak.

Snort placed a strong hand on Hewey's good shoulder and squeezed. "Best friends I ever had in this world was you and Old Grady Welch. Grady's gone, and now you . . . Damn it all, life just ain't fair." He cleared his throat. "I promise you ain't goin' to ever need for nothin', old pardner. Anything you want, just let me know. Old Snort'll be here before you can draw a second breath."

A tear on his cheek, Snort turned quickly and strode out of the room. Tommy spoke to him as he started out the front door, but Snort gave him no answer.

Damn that doctor, getting Snort all upset for nothing. Of course

I'm going to ride again. I'll keep cowboying 'til I'm a hundred years old and get myself killed by a jealous husband.

Hewey turned his head away from the door. His throat felt as if he were about to choke, and his eyes burned like fire. He supposed it was the fumes from all that medicine in the doctor's cabinet.

CHAPTER
9

Old Man Jenkins came that afternoon. Peeler trailed behind him in his jodhpurs and lace-up boots, offering no more than a quiet "Howdy" so long as his employer was there.

Jenkins sat beside Hewey's bed. "By rights I ought not to pay none of your expenses. You got yourself hurt doin' exactly what I told you not to. But I've always had a generous heart. I'll go halves with you."

"I hate to put you to all that expense."

"I've arranged for you to be moved to a boardin'house soon as you're able. It'll be some cheaper. This old quack charges like his place was the Menger Hotel in San Antone."

"I figure to be back at the ranch pretty quick."

Jenkins's eyes showed strong doubt, but he made no direct comment. "By rights it's Frank Gervin who ought to pay the bills, foistin' off that bunch of snides on us. But I sicced the *curandera* woman on him. She claims she can give him a case of the itch, at least. Maybe even the piles." Jenkins arose to leave. "The next place you work, I hope you follow orders better than you did for me."

By that, Hewey assumed he was out of a job. Well, he had been out of a job many times but had never had much trouble finding someplace to work. There was always call for a good cowpuncher. Soon as he knitted a little he might take Biscuit up into the Guadalupes, as pretty a country as he had ever seen. Tommy too, if the boy wanted to go. They would have their pick of places to work.

Peeler had been so quiet, Hewey had almost forgotten he was still there. The chauffeur moved nearer the bed and gazed down on Hewey with sympathy. "I wish there was somethin' I could do for you."

"There is. Next time you go to the ranch, tell Aparicio and the boys I'd be obliged if they'd look after Biscuit for a couple of weeks 'til I'm in shape to come and get him."

Peeler looked at him askance. "A couple of weeks? Don't you know how bad you're hurt?"

"I've been hurt worse than this fallin' off a wood-haulin' wagon."

Peeler carefully gathered his words. "You're not goin' to want to hear this, but I wouldn't be honest if I didn't say it. While you're layin' here you'd best be thinkin' about what you'll do from now on. Your wild-ridin' days are over. Even a gentle horse like Biscuit may be too much for you. But you've got to keep on livin'. You'd better start figurin' on how you're goin' to do it."

He did not wait to hear Hewey's protests that this was just a temporary setback, that he would soon be making a hand again.

Hewey stared in frustration at the open door through which Peeler had gone. He made a fist with his right hand, for he could barely move the fingers on his left. He would have thought everybody knew him better than that, already giving up on him when it hadn't even been twenty-four hours since his little accident. It would take more than a crazy black stud to set him permanently on the ground.

Tommy came into the room. "Need anything?"

"I need for everybody to quit tellin' me what a hopeless wreck I am. I've had toothaches hurt me worse than this." His left arm and his right leg both pulsed with pain, and each time he moved he felt as if someone were running a sword through his lungs. He moved no more than he had to.

Tommy did not answer. Hewey changed the subject. "You'd better be findin' a way to get back to the ranch. You ain't been fired too, have you?"

"I'm stayin' here to look after you."

"The doctor's supposed to be doin' that, and at considerable expense, the way Old Man Jenkins tells it. If you're goin' to be a cowboy, you'd better be out there cowboyin'."

Tommy's face was sad. "I had no idea it was goin' to be like this. First Skip, then you."

"The cowboy life ain't all roses. It sticks a thorn in you from time to time."

"Home looks a lot better to me than it used to. But right now the main job I've got is takin' care of you."

"I always took care of myself."

"Let's see you walk to the toilet."

"You know I can't do that."

"Then there's no use in us talkin' any more about it." Tommy looked into a water pitcher on a small table beside Hewey's bed. "I'll go pump some fresh water for you."

"A stiff drink of whiskey is what I need."

He knew he would not get it, not until he was out of this place and away from the doctor's close scrutiny. He had been looking at a pair of crutches leaning in a corner, propped between a medicine cabinet and the wall. He had never used any before, but it stood to reason that a man who could ride broncs should be able to master a pair of crutches. He imagined the surprise he would see on bystanders' faces when he entered the saloon and bellied up to the bar with an arm and a leg wrapped like Christmas packages. They would know then that Hewey Calloway was made of sterner stuff than they had given him credit for.

He appraised the distance. He would be unable to put weight on his right leg, but he could hop on his left, holding on to the bed partway, then the table and finally the medicine cabinet.

The first step was to get out of the bed. That, he reasoned, might be the hardest part, for he had lain here since last night, hardly changing position. His body would be stiff, resisting movement. He tried sitting up, but he immediately fell back on his pillow, stricken by an internal wrenching so intense that it left him in a cold sweat and breathing hard. He rested a bit until the pain subsided, then decided to try a different way. Carefully he slid his left leg to the edge of the bed and dragged the bound leg after it. He swung both legs off, twisting his body around to a ninety-degree angle without his back losing contact with the mattress. The left leg bent normally at the knee, but the bound right leg extended straight out, stiff as if splinted between boards. He gritted his teeth.

The really hard part would come now, raising his upper body off the mattress. He had little control over his left hand, but with his right he gripped the edge of the mattress and pulled himself to a sitting position so quickly that he was up before the pain had time to register. It came with such a blinding force that he bit his tongue to keep from crying out, and he almost fainted. The room seemed to swing back and forth like a pendulum. Nausea brought his breakfast up into his throat, burning hard, and he thought he would lose it.

Gradually the dizziness diminished, and with it much of the hurting. He felt sweat, cold and clammy, running down his face, tickling his chest. But he was still sitting up. He wished Old Man Jenkins could see him, and Peeler and Snort.

When he thought he was steady enough, he eased forward until his left foot touched the floor. He tested his weight on it and decided it would hold him. The right leg remained stiff and useless, but he could hold the edge of the bed with his right hand. He pushed himself the final inches to clear the mattress and was standing on his left foot. Holding to the edge of the bed for balance, he made the first hop.

The internal pain came roaring back. This time he could not help crying out. Nausea came upon him again in a rush, and with it the dizziness. He could not hold on to the bed. He fell forward, unable to help himself. He struck the floor on his stomach, then his face. Most of the breath gusted from his lungs, and his nose smarted as if a fist had struck him. He felt he was still falling, far into some bottomless black hole.

Tommy hurried into the room. "Uncle Hewey!"

The doctor was only a few steps behind. "Come, son, help me lift him back onto the bed. Careful. He may have undone everything we did for him."

Hewey had never felt agony more intense. All the bright suns he had seen yesterday came back, spinning as wildly as before. He had but a fingernail hold on consciousness.

The doctor's voice was angry. "He thinks he's a bronc rider, and he can't even stay on a bed. We may have to tie him like a horse."

Hewey tried to explain that he was trying to reach the crutches, but he was just mumbling. He could not even understand himself. The doctor felt over his leg and his arm, then his ribs and his chest. Hewey groaned at his touch.

Evans told Tommy, "These old cowboys get to thinking they're made of rawhide. They're more like eggshells, and nobody ever put Humpty Dumpty back together again."

Hewey spent a miserable night, all of yesterday's pain reawakened and intensified. Trying to get out of bed too early had been a mistake, a lesson learned the hard way like so many others in his life. But if he had not tried, he would not know.

The doctor took the precaution of removing the crutches to another room. "I should have done this in the first place. You don't leave candy in front of a child and expect him not to eat any."

If Hewey had felt better he might have taken offense, but a few disparaging words carried no sting compared to the injuries imposed upon him by that black stud. He lay half awake, half dreaming much of the night, trying to conjure up appropriate measures of vengeance against Fat Gervin but finding none that seemed devilish enough to fit the crime. The one or two that came closest would probably result in his taking a trip to the Huntsville penitentiary, much too far from cow country.

At least Tommy did not spend a second night sitting up in a chair. The doctor admired the boy's loyalty but had arranged for him to sleep and eat in a nearby boardinghouse. Nevertheless, Tommy was at his uncle's side soon after sunup, asking how he felt.

"A whole lot better," Hewey lied. "That medicine is doin' me a world of good." In fact, when the doctor was not looking he had poured much of it into a bottle provided for him to empty his bladder. If a medicine had to taste bad to do a man any good, this one ought to cure everything from warts to double pneumonia.

He still judged distances by the length of time it would take to travel them on horseback. Though he had ridden in automobiles several times, he never had gotten used to the notion that they could carry people as far in an hour as a good horse might go in the better part of a day. He was not surprised that Walter and Eve showed up, but he was amazed that they arrived so soon. He would have thought they would come in a wagon, the way they usually traveled.

Walter said, "Alvin Lawdermilk brought us in his automobile."

"Alvin's got him an automobile?" Alvin had always been a horseman and had preached mightily against the motorcar. First Blue Hannigan and now Alvin Lawdermilk. "The world's changin' too fast."

Walter said, "We came all this way and didn't have to fix but four flats. That's some travelin'."

Eve hesitantly took Hewey's right hand after seeing that it was not injured. "Tommy says you're in this shape on account of him."

"I'm in this shape on account of Fat Gervin."

"When we asked you to look out for Tommy, we didn't mean for it to come to this."

"He was a little put out with me for not lettin' him ride that bronc, but I was afraid he didn't have a chance."

Eve blinked away tears. "Damn you, Hewey Calloway, you're the most aggravatin' man I ever knew."

She took Hewey by surprise. "How do you figure that?"

"You do the most thoughtless things sometimes without givin' any consideration to the consequences, and you make me mad enough to want to shoot you. Then you do somethin' like this and make me want to hug your neck. I would, but I don't know where all you're busted."

"I'd appreciate the hug. What I'd appreciate a lot more would be for you-all to take me away from here. I'm damned tired of this bed."

Walter shook his head. "The doctor says you'll be on your back for some time yet."

"If I had Biscuit here, I'd saddle up and ride off right now." He knew better, but he did not want them thinking of him as an invalid. They would want to start doing things for him, and he had always been most comfortable doing for himself.

Walter said, "Alvin's waitin' in the next room. He's anxious to see you."

Hewey warmed with pleasure at the thought of seeing his old friend and sometime employer. He had intended to stop by Alvin's place for a visit when he and Tommy went to Upton City to receive the broncs from Fat, but his unexpected encounter with Spring

Renfro had gotten in the way. "Good old Alvin. I wonder if he's ever got any better lookin'."

"Judge for yourself," Walter said, and went to fetch him.

Alvin grinned like a new cat in a barnful of mice, his false teeth a little too large, his pudgy face a little too red. He looked older than Hewey remembered him, though he lacked a lot being as old as Jenkins or C. C. Tarpley. People had said Alvin had to slow down, which was the reason he had employed a ranch foreman to help ease the burden of labor and responsibility. His longtime love for good whiskey probably bore much of the fault.

Hewey grasped Alvin's hand. "Did you bring me a drink?"

Alvin winked at Eve. "Eve drank it all up on the way here."

She made a fist as if to punch him.

Alvin said, "But soon's you get out of that bed we'll make up for lost time. About four years' worth."

"Four years is a lot of whiskey."

"We won't drink it all at once. We'll spread it out over a couple of days."

Eve said, "You know you've stopped drinkin', Alvin. You've been quit for two years."

Alvin looked about as if to see who might be listening. "What did you have to go and say that for? You'll ruin my reputation."

Hewey made a halfhearted grin, trying to play along with their joking, though he did not find it funny. He remembered when Alvin used to hide bottles from his wife, Cora, all over the ranch so he would never be without. If he really had quit after having loved whiskey so much, that was another indication he was slipping.

Damn it, why do my friends have to get old while I've got my back turned?

Alvin said, "Everybody back home is anxious about you . . . Cora, even her mother."

Hewey believed what he said about Cora, but not his comment

167

about Cora's mother. Old Lady Faversham never had liked Hewey, but then, she didn't like her son-in-law either. Hewey waited for Alvin to mention someone else. When he did not, Hewey asked, "How's Miss Renfro?"

Alvin said, "You can ask her yourself." He turned and beckoned.

A shadow moved through the doorway, almost hidden behind Walter and Eve and Alvin. Spring Renfro stepped around them. She gave him only a thin and fleeting smile, but it was like someone had lit up all the lights in the house.

"I'm sorry to see you like this, Hewey."

He pulled up the sheet to cover his shoulders. "I feel fine. Just a bruise here and there." He reached for her hand, but she was not close enough. Even so, the sight of the teacher was like a tonic to him. Some might regard her as a spinster and even say she was plain, but each man's standard of "pretty" was a personal matter. She could probably still have her pick of Upton County bachelors, age forty and over, and there were a good many of them. Hadn't somebody told him she and Alvin's foreman—what was his name?—had been seeing one another?

"I sure didn't expect you to come, Spring . . . Miss Renfro. But I'm glad you did. I can already feel the hurt fadin' away."

Spring's lips tightened as she stared at him. "I . . . everybody's been very concerned about you."

"You don't have to be. I'll be up from here in a few days." He looked at Alvin. "I'm out of a job. Reckon you've got one for me? I wouldn't ask for full pay. I know it'll be a month or two before I can do anything heavy."

The fun went out of Alvin's eyes. His gaze drifted to where the sheet covered the bound arm and leg. "Sure, Hewey. You'll be as good as new in no time, and there's always more work than we can get around to."

His words were confident, but their tone said they were empty.

Alvin could not see the future as Hewey chose to see it. He saw only a crippled-up cowboy. He had seen a lot of them in his time.

But Hewey had no intention of remaining this way. He would be as good as he had ever been . . . better, even, because every year he lived made him a little smarter.

Hewey's visitors stayed a couple of hours, the talk rambling around like a blind sheep over subjects of little or no interest to Hewey. He only half listened to most of it, putting in a word here and there. He concentrated his attention on Spring. He remembered with pleasure the summer they had come to know one another, and with regret the promises spoken, promises broken.

Four years. It seemed not half so long since they had talked of buying the Barcroft homestead and settling down together to a life of farming. But Hewey had been too restless to walk long behind a plow. Spring had released him, and he had ridden away to seek new country, hoping to find a place where life would remain as it had been in his youth, never changing, never making him feel like a stranger lost and passed up by time, trapped in a world he no longer understood.

Surely somewhere there must be such a place. Maybe he would find it in the Guadalupes, when he was well.

There was no question of the visitors returning home that evening, for the drive from Upton City had killed most of the day. They took rooms in the hotel. That was enough to tell Hewey his brother and sister-in-law were coming up in the world. In earlier times when they had to be in town overnight they carried their bedrolls and put up in a wagon yard.

They came again after breakfast. Hewey talked with everyone, but his gaze remained mostly on Spring.

Alvin took a watch from his pocket. "I hate to bust up a good party, but we'd better start if we're to get home before dark. No tellin' how many flats we may have to stop and fix."

Eve tried to talk Tommy into going home with them, but Tommy declined. "I need to stay and watch out for Uncle Hewey. Anyway, my horse is still at the Circle W."

Hewey said, "I can take care of myself. I'll be up and out of here in a week or two, and I'll get our horses."

Tommy had a stubbornness in his eyes that Hewey had often seen in his mother's. When Eve got that look, not even an earthquake could shake her. "I'm stayin'."

Alvin, Walter and Eve said their good-byes and walked out with Tommy, leaving Spring alone for a private moment with Hewey. She gripped Hewey's hand, as if on impulse, then quickly released it. "Please do whatever the doctor tells you."

"Can't do much else as long as I'm layin' here. But I won't be here long." He wished she had held on to his hand, but she had moved back a step. He got an inkling of the hurt he had caused her, the hurt she must still be feeling. "How about you, Spring? Are you happy?"

"I'm making a living."

"But are you happy?"

"It depends on what you consider happy. I guess I am. Are you?"

"I was. Thought I was, anyway, 'til this happened to me." He struggled for the words. "Everybody tells me Farley Neal is a good man."

She was a moment in answering. "He is."

"You-all plannin' on gettin' married?"

The question took her by surprise. "Would it bother you?"

"I've got no right to be bothered. I went off and left you a long time ago."

"It was a decision we made together. If you'd stayed you'd have had to change too much, and you weren't ready for that."

"I still ain't changed. Not much, anyway."

"If you did, you wouldn't be Hewey Calloway." She reached as if to take his hand again but changed her mind. Before he could say anything more, she was gone.

He stared at the empty doorway, remembering the way she looked, the way she talked, her gentle fragrance, and he pondered the imponderable price of freedom.

He hated the crutch. Though it gave him limited mobility, it was unwieldy and kept threatening to throw him to the floor. Because of his broken arm, he could use only one. That kept him off balance. Each step aroused sharp protest somewhere inside, so he ventured out of the room only to take advantage of the doctor's indoor plumbing at the end of the hall. Tommy was usually there to support him, but Hewey made him stop at the bathroom door. Some activities were meant to be private.

Peeler visited every day that he was not driving Old Man Jenkins somewhere. Blas Villegas and Aparicio Rodriguez dropped in once. Aparicio said little, but Hewey could read the thought in his eyes: *This could have happened to me. It still might.* Blas said, "Maybeso now you will learn to cook, like me."

"One day of my cookin' and the whole outfit would up and quit. No, I'll stick to punchin' cows."

Jenkins did not appear. Hewey asked the doctor about him.

The doctor said, "He inquires after you almost every day, but he won't come by. I think you trouble his conscience."

"But not enough for him to pay all my doctor bills."

"The age of miracles is past."

It bothered Hewey that Snort Yarnell had not visited him again. He assumed at first that Snort was in a distant camp on the Slash R and could not come to town. Then Tommy told him he had bumped into Snort on the street. Snort had asked about Hewey, then hurried away.

That he had not come by to visit hurt almost as much as the broken arm and the bum knee.

About a week after the accident Dr. Evans said Hewey was doing well enough to be moved to the boardinghouse where Tommy was staying. He brought a wheelchair. "It's too far to walk on that crutch. Tommy can push you over there in five minutes."

Hewey took an instant disliking to the chair. Among other things, it reminded him of Old Lady Faversham. She could walk when she wanted to, but she favored a wheelchair because it was a way of seeing to it that others waited upon her. "Can't we hold off 'til dark so everybody won't be lookin' at me? I don't want them all thinkin' I'm a cripple."

"They might as well get used to seeing you as you are."

"I don't intend to stay this way. The healin' is just takin' a little more time than I expected."

"You'd better get used to the idea, Hewey. I don't know to what extent you will eventually recover, but I can tell you this: you'll never be the same as you were."

"Bet you."

Getting out of bed and into the wheelchair involved considerable internal pain, but the embarrassment of being watched by strangers was almost as bad. Hewey kept his head down and his hat low as Tommy pushed him along. They had almost reached the boardinghouse when Hewey's eye caught a familiar figure on the opposite side of the street. Tommy said, "There's Snort Yarnell."

Snort stopped to look, and for a moment he seemed about to hurry away. Instead, he reluctantly crossed the street, pausing to let a wagon go by.

"Howdy, Hewey." His subdued voice sounded guilty as if he had been caught sipping whiskey in church.

"What you been doin' that you couldn't come to see me?"

"I wanted to, God knows I did. But I couldn't bring myself to look at you in this shape."

"I won't be like this for long. Tommy says he saw you a couple of days ago. You must have an easy boss if he lets you hang around town."

"Ain't with the Slash R anymore. I quit."

Hewey was not overly surprised. It had not been in Snort's nature to stay with one job long enough to wear out a pair of pants, but Hewey had thought he might have found a home at the Slash R. Even someone restless as Snort needed to light in one place eventually.

"What're you goin' to do now?"

"Got me a job here in town. Night watchman."

Hewey could hardly believe. "Walkin' around in the dark, jinglin' keys and checkin' doors? That don't sound like a job for Snort Yarnell."

"I hate to admit it, Hewey, but seein' you the other day scared the hell out of me."

"Why? That was nothin' compared to the time you saw a horse stomp Old Grady Welch to death."

"But that was years ago, and we're older now. After seein' you I went back out to the ranch, took a look at them owl-headed broncs and got the shakes so bad I couldn't hold a cup of coffee. I asked for my time."

"You'll get over it. Me and you'll be ridin' the rough string together before the snow flies."

Snort's voice cracked. "Ain't you figured it out yet? You ain't ever ridin' the rough string again. Neither am I. It's a fool's game, and we sat at the table too long."

Hewey stared at Snort's back as the cowboy's long legs carried him quickly away.

Tommy seemed shaken. "I never thought I'd see Snort Yarnell boogered over anything. You reckon he's right?"

"You can't pay attention to what Snort says. He changes his mind a lot oftener than he changes his socks." But Hewey had a cold feeling in the pit of his stomach. He tried to dismiss it as foolishness, but it would not go away. His broken arm hurt, and his knee, and something inside. He tried to roll a cigarette, but his hands shook and he spilled his tobacco.

Damn that Snort! Whatever he's got is contagious, and he's given it to me.

The boardinghouse room he shared with Tommy was on the ground floor so he did not have to contend with the stairs, though getting up the two steps to the front porch was a challenge. Because of that, he did not try to venture beyond the porch the first three days. He gradually learned to manipulate the crutch with some dexterity.

He could see an improvement in his right knee when the doctor unwrapped it. Most of the angry red was gone, the blue was fading, and the external damage was healing over. The knee remained stiff, however. He could not straighten the leg.

He said, "This *will* keep gettin' better, won't it?"

The doctor said, "That knee took a lot of punishment. It's like a twisted hinge. You hammer it out the best you can, but it may bind and never work again quite the way it did when it was new."

"You're tellin' me I could have a gimpy leg from now on?"

"It's a mark of your trade. How many *old* cowboys do you know that don't limp or walk with a cane? The body can take only so much."

"What about my arm?"

"It may never be strong again, but at least the elbow is intact."

Hewey resisted the doctor's appraisal. "Maybe you just ain't run onto a patient as determined as I am."

"Keep that attitude. Determination may be better than any medicine I can give you."

But determination and faith both began to flag. Each morning when he arose, Hewey sat on the edge of the bed and tried straightening the right leg. He attempted to convince himself that it was getting better every day, but after five or six days he realized that any improvement was marginal or perhaps even imaginary. At least the knee was giving him less pain day by day. He could put a little weight on it. The doctor said perhaps soon he could discard the crutch and get along on a cane.

The day came when he told Tommy, "I want to go to the wagon yard and take a look at Biscuit." Aparicio had brought the brown and Tommy's dun to town.

Tommy eyed the crutch with misgivings. "It's a good ways down there."

"Fine. I need to get as far away from this place as I can."

He shrugged off Tommy's attempt to help him down the porch steps. "Let's see how good I can do on my own."

The knee hurt less than he expected, though he felt a sharp pain inside. Whatever had shaken loose was still floating around. It was only a couple of blocks from the boardinghouse to the wagon yard, but it felt like a mile. Sweat ran down his face by the time he got there, and the breeze was cool blowing through the wet spots in his shirt.

Tommy said, "You better sit down awhile."

"Been sittin' too long already. The only place I want to sit down is in a saddle."

He whistled, and Biscuit ambled up to the fence. Hewey rubbed the horse's nose, then moved through the wooden gate. Biscuit watched suspiciously, for Hewey's movements were strange to him, and he took the crutch as a potential threat. Hewey talked softly, whistling under his breath until the horse ventured up to nuzzle him, hoping for some kind of handout. Hewey patted him and rubbed his good right hand up and down the brown neck. His eyes burned a little. Cooped up indoors so long, he was not used to this bright sunlight.

He told Tommy, "Saddle him for me."

Tommy protested, "Uncle Hewey, you can't."

"Saddle him."

Tommy fetched a bridle, then led Biscuit to where the saddle had been placed on a wooden rack. "You oughtn't to do this."

Hewey knew he could not mount from the ground. "There's a hay bale on the ground yonder. Lead him over there."

Hewey had some difficulty in stepping up onto the bale, but the crutch gave him leverage. Tommy led the horse up close. Hewey handed him the crutch. Gripping the horn with his right hand, he made a little hop, fitting his left foot into the stirrup and swinging the stiff right leg up and over the saddle. It extended awkwardly out to one side. He could not bring it in close enough to touch the stirrup. The effort set the knee to throbbing. But Hewey was in the saddle; that was the important thing.

"Come on, Biscuit, let's mosey a little."

He set Biscuit into a walk, then a trot out into the large corral. Almost immediately Hewey had to slow him back to a walk, for his knee felt as if it were afire, and the internal pain was like a sword thrust between his ribs. Nauseous, he leaned out to one side, expecting to vomit.

Tommy saw his distress. "I tried to tell you." He came running, bringing the crutch. "Let me help you down."

"I can make it by myself." But Hewey quickly found that he could not. He had to lean heavily on Tommy for support to dismount.

He fitted the crutch under his right arm and felt cold sweat breaking on his face. The nausea was slow to pass.

Biscuit seemed confused. Hewey patted him on the neck. "It ain't your fault, old friend."

Tommy's voice was quiet and sympathetic. "I'll unsaddle him for you while you rest awhile. Then we'll go back to the boardin'-house."

Hewey dropped down on the bale of hay, his shoulders slumped. He watched while Tommy removed the saddle, blanket and bridle and fed Biscuit some oats out of a barrel.

All the discouraging words he had heard from Snort and Peeler and the doctor seemed to be shouting in his ears.

What if they were right? What if he never could ride again?

He bowed his head so Tommy could not see him drag a sleeve across his eyes.

CHAPTER
10

Hewey sat in a wicker chair on the front porch of the boardinghouse, absently tapping the end of a cane against the wooden floor as he gazed morosely out into the street. He observed people going about their end-of-the-day business as if the world were not skewed off its proper axis and they had never heard of such a thing as an outlawed black stud.

Tommy sat sideways on the top step, leaning against a post and positioned so he could watch his uncle, his guileless eyes full of concern. He had remained close after the incident at the wagon yard. "Uncle Hewey, you ain't taken a decent meal in three days. Ain't slept much either."

"It's hard to sleep good when you've had the slats kicked out from under you."

Hewey had not summoned the nerve to go back to the wagon yard, much as he wanted to. Seeing Biscuit, knowing he could not ride him, would only renew the bitter disappointment.

Tommy said, "It ain't healthy, sittin' around here mopin' and spendin' money you ain't got. You'd be better off at home with the folks. How about me telephonin' Alvin or Wes Wheeler?"

"They got more important things to do than drive all this way for a cripple who ain't in shape to do anything for anybody."

"You've done a lot of good things for a lot of people."

"That was before. I ain't worth much to anybody now."

"You're worth a lot to me, and Mama and Daddy. And to Miss Renfro too, I'll bet."

"Miss Renfro and Alvin's foreman have got an understandin', or so I heard."

"She came all the way here to see you."

Hewey did not feel like putting up with Tommy's pestering. "I wish you'd go down to the wagon yard and make sure they fed Biscuit this evenin'."

"I fed him myself, remember? He's gettin' fat, standin' in that pen. He's liable to try and throw you off the next time you get on him."

The next time. Hewey wondered when the next time would come, or if it would ever be.

"Well, go see if he's got enough water. The worst thing that can happen to an animal is to run out of water."

He knew Tommy was not fooled; Hewey was trying to get rid of him for a while. Tommy pushed to his feet. "I'll go see if they need help puttin' out hay for the night." He had been doing some work around the wagon yard to pay for the two horses' keep.

As Tommy started up the street a chugging noise made him stop and look back. He returned to the edge of the porch. "I think that truck yonder is Blue Hannigan's."

Hewey had not reconciled himself to the thought of Blue Hannigan retiring some of his freight wagons for a truck. It was like surrendering and taking up the enemy's flag.

The truck pulled to a shuddering stop in front of the boarding-house, its engine clattering before it shut down. Hewey expected to see one of Hannigan's drivers, but Blue Hannigan himself stepped to the ground. He extracted a wad of tobacco from his mouth and dropped it in the dirt before starting toward the porch.

"Damn if this ain't a sight to behold, Hewey Calloway in a rockin' chair. Ain't you ashamed of yourself, lollin' around in idleness while there's still daylight left?"

He walked up onto the porch and extended his hand.

Hewey said, "No more ashamed than you ought to be, turnin' good mules out to pasture and scarin' horses off the road with that stinkin' contraption."

"At least it hasn't throwed me off and stomped on me." Hannigan's forced smile faded as he stepped back to give Hewey a deep-frowning once-over. "You look better than I expected, goin' by what I heard. Can you navigate with that cane?"

"Fair, but I couldn't even footrace Fat Gervin." He enjoyed a moment's fantasy of outrunning Fat and administering a few good cane licks to that broad backside. He tried to flex his left arm, but the cast would not give. "I don't know how much it'll bend when the doctor finally cuts this thing off."

"Time and patience, Hewey."

"Worst thing is somethin' busted loose inside. The doctor says he can patch up an arm and a leg, but he can't do much for my vitals."

Blue blurted, "How would you like to go home?"

Home had always been whatever ranch he was working for, and at the moment he was unemployed. "I don't have a home except for Walter's and Eve's place, and that's theirs, not mine."

"I brought a load of freight, and it's too late to start home tonight. I've got room for a passenger if you'd like to go back with me in the mornin'."

Tommy had come up to join them on the porch. "Why don't you, Uncle Hewey? I can take the horses home."

"By yourself? I'd never stop catchin' hell from your mama."

"I can handle it, like I could've handled that black stud."

"But what use would I be to anybody? What could I do besides maybe swat flies?"

"What're you doin' *here?* At least we wouldn't be runnin' up a board bill."

Hannigan put in, "He makes sense, even if he *is* kin to you. Maybe you'll heal faster, bein' amongst family and the people that know you best."

The thought set Hewey's skin to prickling. This was an eye-filling country to be in, surrounded by the rock-crowned peaks of the Davis Mountains, but even a mountain got old when watched too long from a rocking chair.

"I won't be able to get out and open gates for you."

"Any gates get in our way, we'll just bust through them."

Hewey found Tommy nodding hopefully. The boy had grown up a lot in a short time, and he was ready to go home. "All right, Tommy, but don't you tarry along the road, and be sure you go way around Pecos City. It's too rough for a farm boy."

Hewey tried to look stoic while the doctor carefully unwrapped his knee, though it remained sore enough to make him grit his teeth. The surface appeared to have healed over fairly well. "Bend it a little and let's see what happens. Slow and careful now."

Hewey tried, cautiously. The knee felt as if he had jammed a hot coal into the joint.

Evans said, "I don't know how much more it will improve. I'll rewrap it, and you'd best abuse it as little as possible until the healing is complete."

"What about my arm?"

"That cast had better stay on it another month."

"It itches under there like a nest of lice have found a home."

"That is altogether possible."

Hewey could not tell when the doctor was joking with him, for his face never changed. The only hint of a smile was a slight twitching at one end of his gray moustache.

"Doc, I'm obliged to you for takin' such good care of me. I'll start payin' you soon as I'm able to work again."

"Don't you worry about that. Jenkins is paying me."

"Only half. He said half the expense is mine."

"That's what he thinks. But I quoted his share at double my normal rates."

"Is that honest?"

"Of course not. Do you think cowboys are the only liars in the world? One of the first things a young doctor learns is how to look regretful when he asks a well-heeled patient for twice what the treatment is worth." He motioned that he was finished. "Let me know how you get along." He put the bandage roll back in a cabinet. "And do me a favor, will you?"

"What's that?"

"Leave the broncs to the young men. Their bones knit better."

Hannigan and Snort Yarnell waited for him on the porch rather than go inside. Snort swore that the smell of medicine made him sick, and the only cure he had found was whiskey. When he had money or his companions did, he took a lot of curing. He walked with Hannigan and Hewey to the truck, which he eyed with silent disapproval.

Hewey said, "You won't last another week on that night-watchman's job. You'll be bustin' broncs again before I get this cast off my arm."

"I wouldn't want to take your money, not that you've got any. I know how Old Man Jenkins pays." Snort's eyes watered a little. "I do hate to see you leave here in this shape. I've got half a mind to go along and see that you're took care of."

"Don't worry, I can't afford to die. I'm too broke to bury."

Snort gave him a grip that threatened to put Hewey's right hand in a cast along with his left arm, then helped him up into the truck.

"Don't you let Blue run you off in a ditch. Them trucks is dangerous."

Hannigan picked his way along a crooked old wagon trail to which rubber tires were still something new, out beyond the Glass Mountains, then across the dry greasewood flats toward Fort Stockton. The truck was rough even on an average stretch, and the jolting was severe in places where wind had blown out the ruts or where they crossed over deeply worn cattle trails. Hewey ached inside, but he would not complain. Now and again when a relatively smooth surface presented itself, Hannigan would step on the accelerator and push the truck to twenty or twenty-five miles an hour. The speed almost took Hewey's breath away.

Hannigan said, "I've owned many a good mule in my time, but I never had one that could go like this."

Hewey remembered Hannigan's frustration with this truck on the street in Upton City. "When a mule acted up, though, you could kick it in the belly. Kick this thing and all you'll get is a broken foot."

The freighter said, "What would you think about drivin' one of these things?"

"I think I'd rather have *both* legs broke." Hewey frowned. "Are you serious, or just makin' talk?"

"Just makin' talk right now, but someday when you've healed up as much as you're goin' to, I might get serious. Like them or not, these trucks are a comin' thing. I took a look at the wall a couple of years ago and saw the handwritin' all over it. The day'll come when you'll stand at the road and see a car or a truck pass by every ten or fifteen minutes. Horses and mules are fixin' to go the way of the buffalo."

It was a sobering thought, one Hewey did not tolerate for long. "Nope, these gasoline buggies are a big thing right now, but they'll fade out like chin whiskers when everybody's had a bellyful of tryin' to keep them runnin'. There'll always be horses and mules."

Hannigan shook his head. "Even Alvin Lawdermilk sees what's comin'. He's sellin' off a lot of his mares and increasin' his cow herd to take up the slack. Ain't you read about the big oil booms over in East Texas? It's on account of everybody needin' gasoline."

"I heard those oil fields stink worse than a den of polecats."

"Not if they belong to you. They smell like money."

"But I don't own one. I've always been happy just bein' a cow-puncher."

"If that leg don't straighten up, and that arm, you may not be a cowpuncher anymore. What you goin' to do then?"

Hewey swallowed hard. He did not want to admit how many nights he had lain awake wondering the same thing. He certainly did not care to start driving a truck. He fell back on one of Eve's favorite sayings when doubt intruded. "The Lord will provide."

"The Lord generally provides best to those that help theirselves."

Late in the afternoon, Hannigan pulled into Upton City. He had repaired three flat tires along the way, which he said was not bad for the distance. Hewey figured it would have taken three days to make the same mileage on horseback if one did not want to pun-ish the mount. But time had seldom been of premium value to him. He had rather have made the trip on Biscuit.

Hannigan said, "I need to stop by the office and see if the roof has fallen in. Then I'll take you on out to Walter's."

A sinking sun had turned the clouds to gold low on the western horizon. If Hannigan drove out to the place now, he would finish the trip in the dark. Hewey said, "It's late, and I've already put you to too much trouble as it is. I'll tote my bedroll down to the wagon yard."

"I ain't keen on drivin' after dark, so I won't argue with you. There's a cot in my office that don't get used much. It's better than any at the wagon yard, and free."

Free sounded good to Hewey in his present financially stressed condition. "I ain't quite flat busted. I'll set you up to supper down at the chili joint. It's little enough to pay for the ride home."

Hannigan's schedule was so erratic that his wife never put anything in the oven until she saw him coming. "It's a deal."

Hewey fumbled his tarp-covered roll down from the bed of the truck with his right arm, making a grab with the fingertips that stuck out from the cast on his broken left arm. He dropped it. Hannigan said, "Let me." He picked up the roll by the rope that bound it.

Hewey said, "Damn if I ain't come down in the world. Can't even handle my own bedroll."

Leaning on the cane, he followed Hannigan up onto the narrow porch. Out back was a complex of corrals that used to be home to a considerable aggregation of horses and mules when all the freighting was done by wagon. Now only a few remained, milling around wooden racks piled high with hay. Hewey saw a new sheet-iron garage, and in front of it a couple of barrels with pumps attached to dispense gasoline and oil. At the distance he could not actually smell them, but he imagined he did.

Hannigan had surrendered to the new times. It seemed to Hewey that most people had. Regret gripped him, then turned into something akin to grief at an old friend's funeral. The world he had known—the world in which he had been at home—was slipping away from him piece by piece.

What he called a chili joint was actually more than that, though it had not always been. It had begun as a hole-in-the-wall café started by a one-time wagon cook who decided he wanted to spend the rest of his nights sleeping under a roof instead of a tarp. Now it was operated by a couple of widows who had little experience with the open range but knew their way around a wood range. Though their fare was lacking in fancy appearance, it compensated in flavor and generous quantity. *Fancy* was all right for city folks, but *filling* was what a cowboy wanted. And Hewey was hungry. He and Hannigan had made their noon meal, such as it was, on cold biscuits, bacon and coffee boiled in a black pot Hannigan carried in the bed of the truck.

The two middle-aged women bustled about in the kitchen. One had a daughter who might be eighteen or twenty—Hewey had difficulty in guessing the ages of people that young. She waited the tables, taking orders from the customers and from the two older women. In Hewey's view she was pretty as a speckled pup, slender where she ought to be and plump in the right places, but he suspected she might be a little lacking in smarts. She seemed to have to be told everything twice.

Hewey remembered one of the older women and her husband, who had been only moderately successful as a farmer. In Hewey's view he had worked himself to death trying to make crops on land better suited for grass.

The widow came out of the kitchen to sympathize with Hewey. "I hope you'll soon be back to your old self."

Hannigan said, "I don't know if we want him that way or not. There was things about his old self that needed improvement."

"One thing I ain't done," Hewey responded, "I ain't surrendered to trucks and automobiles."

The girl brought out two platters with steak, gravy and fried potatoes. "Maybe you won't mind surrenderin' to this."

Hewey took up his knife and fork and quickly capitulated. Even Blas Villegas did not cook this well.

Hannigan watched Hewey cut into the steak, swabbing each piece in the gravy. He told the women, "If Hewey ever decides to give up his bachelor ways, he's liable to come lookin' for one of you."

The farmer's widow said, "As I recall, there was talk a few years ago that he might be about to jump over the broomstick with that schoolteacher, Miss Renfro."

Hewey swallowed and laid down his fork. "I figured everybody had forgotten."

Hannigan said, "In a small town, everybody knows everything and nobody forgets nothin'."

"It was best for her that it didn't happen. I wouldn't've been no catch."

The conversation dampened his appetite; then Fat Gervin came into the restaurant and finished it. Gervin stopped just inside the door to grin at the girl. "Howdy, sweetness." Embarrassed, she looked away.

Her mother called from the kitchen door, "Annabelle, you come in here and start a new pot of coffee. I'll wait on Mr. Gervin."

Relieved, the girl hurried into the kitchen.

For the first time, Gervin saw Hewey. He seemed about to turn and leave, then changed his mind and walked with heavy steps to the table where Hewey and Hannigan sat.

"Hadn't heard you was back in town."

Hewey was about to say he had just arrived, but a stubborn streak cut off the words. He didn't have to explain a damned thing to the likes of Fat Gervin.

Gervin stared at the cast on Hewey's left arm and the bulge in his trousers leg caused by the heavy bandage on his knee. "Somebody told me you ain't the bronc stomper you used to be. Looks like they was right."

In spite of himself, Hewey said grittily, "It was that loco black stud you palmed off on Old Man Jenkins."

Hewey thought he could see gloating in Gervin's eyes, though perhaps it was imagination. Gervin asked, "How did the old man like them horses?"

Hewey decided there was no reason he should be the only one here with worries on his mind. Fat Gervin deserved a few. "He throwed a ring-tailed fit. Last time I saw him, his Fort Worth lawyers were gettin' ready to file a lawsuit against you." Fort Worth lawyers had a reputation for being among the toughest in Texas, unless it might be the ones in Galveston. But those were too far away to carry much weight here.

Gervin's smile died a sudden death. "A lawsuit?"

There was no use in settling for a small lie when a big one would do so much more good. "His lawyers said you pulled a fraud on him and he ought to be able to collect at least fifty thousand dollars. Maybe a hundred."

Gervin gripped the back of a chair, his heavy jaw sagging. "A hundred thousand dollars?"

"Plus lawyers' fees."

Doubt came into Gervin's eyes. "They can't do that."

"Mr. Jenkins has got the same lawyers that almost throwed the T&P Railroad into bankruptcy."

Arms folded, the woman said with exaggerated politeness, "We've got a nice table for you in the corner, Mr. Gervin."

Gervin turned and walked out, dragging his feet. The woman went to the window and stared after him, puzzled but not disappointed over his abrupt departure. She said, "I never saw such a shameless flirt. It's a good thing all the young ladies around here know him for what he is. And him a married man with two young'uns."

To Hewey, how Fat Gervin had wooed and won C. C. Tarpley's daughter was a mystery as profound as the afterlife.

Hannigan held back a laugh until Gervin was well out of sight. "I'll swear, Hewey, you're still the best straight-faced liar in West Texas. Fat won't get a bit of sleep tonight."

Hewey should have felt a surge of triumph, but anger came instead, and a sharp pain in his side. "I ain't had a good night's sleep since that black stud did this to me. That stud and Fat Gervin."

He did not seem likely to sleep well tonight either. He lighted a lamp, then spread his blankets and sat on the steel cot in the back of Hannigan's office to roll a cigarette. He shifted his weight as the frame's sharp edge bit into his legs. He had found no way to be completely comfortable, whether sitting or lying down. He was tired from the trip, but the anger Gervin aroused had swept away any sleepiness he might have felt. He was wide awake and itching to move.

The cigarette was bitter, its smoke burning his eyes. He took a couple of unsatisfactory drags on it, then tossed it into a metal can filled with ashes to catch cigarette butts and tobacco juice. Tobacco had not tasted right to him since the accident.

He limped out the door and looked down the street. He saw lamplight in Dutch Schneider's saloon. A drink couldn't hurt, and it might even help a little.

The little German was dismayed to see Hewey's condition. He expressed his regrets. Hewey saw a couple of cowboys at the bar, men he did not know. At a table toward the rear, C. C. Tarpley was hunched alone, as he had been the last time Hewey had seen him. He saw Hewey and beckoned.

Hewey asked Schneider, "Is C.C. doin' any better?"

Schneider shook his head. "About the same. Always he was a fighter. Now the fight is gone, and he only sits, sipping a little whiskey."

"I know how he feels. I'll go back and jaw with him a bit."

Tarpley gave Hewey the same study that the Dutchman had. Hewey knew the sympathy in his voice was genuine. "I heard tell you got busted up. I'm sorry."

"It's what I always got paid such high wages for."

"Sit down and have a drink. We can share miseries."

Hewey pulled out a chair and stretched his good leg. The other would not bend. "You ever gone and seen a doctor, C.C.?"

"I don't need a doctor to tell me I ain't long for this world. He'd charge me for information I already know."

Hewey pondered the logic in that. If C.C. died, the money he saved would do him no good . . . unless he figured on taking it with him. If anybody could do that, it would be C.C. "Maybe whatever's wrong with you can be fixed."

"Can what's wrong with *you* be fixed?"

"I wish I knew." Hewey did not like admitting to his doubts, but there were times when they bore down on him like the chill of a cold winter norther. They came now as he stared into the melancholy of the old man's eyes.

Tarpley said, "I was like you once, wilder than a March hare. Rode anything with hair on it and roped anything that'd run. Came a time, though, when I had to start doin' my ridin' in a buggy. Hated it at first, 'til I figured out I could hire men to do the things I couldn't do for myself, and I could concentrate on puttin' my ranch and my bank together."

"I ain't a rancher or a banker."

"I wasn't either, then, but I learned there's bigger and better things to do than ride broncs and rope wild stock. Gettin' stove-up was the best thing that ever happened to me." Tarpley's voice dropped, and his eyes were bleak. "Now that I got all that stuff put together, what's fixin' to happen to it?"

"You've got a daughter, and she's got a couple of young'uns. It'll go to them."

"Time them kids get grown, there won't be nothin' left of it. That son-in-law of mine is just waitin' for me to cross over Jordan, then he'll run through it like a drunken mule skinner. Some gold-diggin' woman'll flare a skirt and show him an ankle, and he'll be gone. Fat Gervin ain't got the judgment God gave a goose."

Hewey doubted that Tarpley knew of the swindle Gervin had run on Old Man Jenkins. He saw no reason to burden his already troubled mind by telling him.

Tarpley said, "If I knew just when I was goin' to die, I might go shoot Fat on my last day. We could make the trip to hell together."

With a little luck, Hewey thought, some affronted father or husband might beat Tarpley to that pleasure. Most women shied away from Fat like quail from a bird hound and giggled behind his back, but a few would probably be impressed by the wealth he was in line to inherit. "You could put it in your will that Fat ain't to have anything to do with anything."

"But I've already made the mistake of lettin' him pretty well take over the bank and the everyday runnin' of the ranch. And whether I like it or not, he's my daughter's husband and the daddy of my grandkids."

Hewey shrugged. "Looks to me like the only choice you've got is to be stubborn and outlive him. You used to be a fighter, C.C. I can't see you just givin' up."

"Are you any better? You used to be full of piss and vinegar. Now you've got a look about you like a whipped dog, with your tail between your legs."

They sat in silence, together but each alone, agonizing over his individual troubles. Schneider came over to see if their glasses needed refilling, but they did not, so he retreated quietly, careful not to disturb their solitary deliberations.

The whiskey made Hewey's stomach uneasy. He decided he had had enough. Staring into the old rancher's sallow face only depressed him. He stood up to go.

"I do wish you'd see a doctor, C.C."

The old man did not answer, and Hewey did not push him. He said, "Good night." Tarpley did not reply.

Hewey slept fitfully and was up before good daylight, boiling coffee in a can on top of a wood heater in Hannigan's office. Hannigan came along about sunup and invited Hewey down to his house for breakfast, but Hewey begged off. His stomach was none too stable. He had not drunk much last night at Schneider's, so he blamed his problem on his brief encounter with Fat Gervin, author of his difficulties.

Hannigan was gone awhile, then came back. He cranked the truck motor, but it would not start. He used mule-skinner language on it to no effect.

"Told you," Hewey said. "You oughtn't to've sold the mules."

"It probably needs a rest after goin' to Alpine and back. My other truck's out on a trip. Looks like I won't be gettin' you out to Walter's and Eve's today."

"No hurry. I'd be nothin' but a burden to them anyway." Perhaps someone would come to town from over in the direction of Walter's, and Hewey could get a ride home in a wagon or buggy. If not today, maybe tomorrow. Time didn't mean much when a man couldn't do anything useful with it.

Hannigan still had a couple of wagons and a load of freight to haul in them, but they were going in the wrong direction. Hannigan said, "Make yourself to home. You're welcome to stay here as long as you want to."

Hewey had no wish to impose upon hospitality. As soon as Hannigan and a driver left with the wagons, he began looking around for something practical to do. The office had not been cleaned in a while. Hannigan's wife probably figured she had chores enough in keeping their house clean. Hewey found an old rag and wiped dust from shelves and cabinets. Then he took a broom from the corner and began sweeping the floor. His impairments made him awkward, and he knew the effects of his labor would be short-lived. As soon as the wind arose, dust from the street and corrals would blow in through the open windows and door. At least when Hannigan came back he would find new dust instead of old.

"Ah, Hewey," said a voice in the doorway. Turning, Hewey saw Schneider, the saloonkeeper. "It is a good thing you are doing. If a job you are looking for, there is more of the same at my place of business."

Hewey felt a little embarrassed, being caught with a broom in his hand. "I've drunk a saloon dry a time or two, but I've never swamped one out. And I've never herded sheep." He did not know which job would be the most humiliating.

Schneider said one of Hannigan's trucks was supposed to have brought him a supply of whiskey from the railroad at Midland. They looked around but did not find it.

"Blue said he had a truck out. It must be bringin' your whiskey." Hewey explained that he needed a ride to Walter's. "If anybody comes in from that direction, I wish you'd tell them. I don't want to impose on Blue any longer than I have to."

"He does not mind. He is your friend, and I am your friend, too. Come visit my place as long as you wish."

Hewey warmed with gratitude. He had never had much money in his pockets, but he had never lacked for friends. Fat Gervin had access to C. C. Tarpley's bottomless bank account, but he had no real friends. Hewey would not trade places with him for all the money he could load upon both of Blue Hannigan's trucks.

"I'm obliged to you, Dutch. Maybe it's time I learned how to swamp out a saloon. Then about the only thing I can say I've never done is to herd sheep."

After Schneider left, Hewey walked down to Pierson Phelps's

store and told Phelps about his need for a ride if anybody came to town from that direction. Phelps expressed concern about Hewey's injuries. Hewey said, "I'll be as good as new pretty soon, and maybe a little smarter." His voice sounded hollow, for he felt he was lying to himself as well as to Phelps.

Phelps said, "I hope you'll be smart enough to quit ridin' those bad broncs."

Schneider kept a pot of coffee in the saloon and urged it upon his customers when he felt they had had enough of his other merchandise. Hewey had rarely seen him drink anything other than coffee. Schneider contended that whiskey was made to sell, not to drink.

Hewey accepted his invitation to a cup of coffee, then asked where Schneider kept the broom. After a mild protest, the Dutchman handed him one from his storeroom. It probably pained the man more to watch Hewey work than to do it himself, but Hewey persevered until he swept the dust out the front door. Then he went back to the storeroom and began cleaning it, too.

He heard a familiar voice from inside the saloon. At the storeroom door, he saw Fat Gervin buying two bottles of bourbon to take to the ranch with him. Gervin spotted Hewey, standing with the broom in his good hand. Surprise faded to a look of satisfaction. "You've finally found a job that fits you, Hewey Calloway."

Hewey's skin prickled. He wanted to say, *You're the son of a bitch that put me here,* but he bit back the words.

He had always been generous with whatever little money he had. Often he had lent it to down-on-their-luck friends and strangers without worrying about getting it back. But Fat Gervin owed him, and sometime, the good Lord willing, that self-important gentleman would pay up.

"If I was you, Fat, I'd be off to Fort Worth or someplace, findin' me some lawyers like Old Man Jenkins has got."

Gervin said, "I don't believe that lawsuit business. You're just hoorawin' me." But his eyes revealed doubt.

I've got him on his left foot, Hewey thought. *And I'm going to keep him there.*

CHAPTER

11

For lack of something constructive to do, Hewey was lying on the cot with his right arm over his eyes in Hannigan's office when a tall man walked in. "Didn't mean to wake you up," the intruder apologized.

"Wasn't asleep," Hewey said, though he had been napping, compensating for another restless night spent mostly awake.

"You may not remember me. I'm Farley Neal. Mr. Phelps told me you're needin' a ride."

Hewey blinked sleep from his eyes. He recognized the man who it was said was keeping company with Spring Renfro. He arose and shook Neal's hand. "I do remember you." He could not have forgotten. He gave Neal a long study, wondering how serious he really was about Spring.

"I've got a wagon, and I'm goin' to Alvin Lawdermilk's this afternoon. Somebody can carry you on over to your brother's place in the mornin'."

Hewey had reservations about riding with Neal, but he did not want to remain in town, either. "You sure it won't put you out none?"

"I've been stranded myself, and somebody always came along."

He seemed genuine enough, though Hewey kept a few reservations just in case. "I'll leave Blue a note." At Hannigan's paper-strewn rolltop desk he found a pencil advertising the Fort Worth stockyards and scrawled a few lines on a ruled tablet. "I don't like for people to worry about me. Blue's got troubles enough of his own."

Neal helped Hewey roll his bed, though Hewey would rather have done it for himself. He was not keen on getting in Neal's debt. He was indebted to too many people already for favors he might never be able to repay. Neal tied the roll and carried it outside. Hewey dragged his saddle, blanket and bridle until Neal came back to take them from him.

Two young horses hitched to the wagon appeared to be in training. Alvin Lawdermilk had long made a business of raising and training horses and mules for the saddle or for harness.

Neal said, "You don't need to worry about them runnin' away and spillin' you. They're pretty well broke."

"I'm pleased to hear that." A wreck could undo all the healing he had accomplished and add to the damage.

Neal gave him a boost up, not loosing his hold until Hewey was safely set on the wagon seat. Hewey thanked him and tapped his cane gently against the sideboard. "Never thought I'd ever need three legs to get around."

"Things happen no matter how careful we try to be. It's nobody's fault."

Hewey saw Fat Gervin climbing into a red automobile in front of the bank and figured he had bought it with his father-in-law's money. Resentment warmed him, but he said, "No, it's nobody's fault."

He studied Neal, trying to find something about him to dislike. As Neal took hold of the leather lines, Hewey saw that he had big workingman's hands similar to his own, rough and calloused. One knuckle was knocked down like Hewey's, probably the result of an accident suffered in the line of duty. His face was lined with the marks of living, of working in the sun. His gray eyes were crow-tracked at the corners and had a way of looking straight at Hewey, unflinching, yet making no judgment.

Hewey took him to be just what he appeared, a cowboy through and through. He could find no reason not to like him, apart from the fact that he was keeping company with Spring Renfro.

The road to the Lawdermilks' was long. Neal seemed to sense that Hewey did not feel like talking much, and he did not push him for conversation. Hewey felt more at ease riding on the wagon seat than in Hannigan's truck. Even when one of the horses broke wind, the smell suited him better than the odor of gasoline.

He wanted to ask about Spring, but he was a long time in gathering the nerve. Instead he asked, "How's everybody out at Alvin's? Is Julio Valdez still there?"

"Julio's the top horse and mule man, after Alvin himself."

"He always was. How do you get along with Old Lady Faversham?" Hewey regarded Alvin's vindictive mother-in-law as being a few bricks shy of a full load, a woman who could find fault in Jesus Christ.

"I get along with her just fine. For some reason she seems to like me."

"I'm glad she likes somebody. She used to pray for lightnin' to strike me and Alvin both." Hewey fretted awhile before he asked, "And Miss Renfro?"

"A fine lady. But you know that."

"I do for a fact."

Neal stopped the team at a fence line. Hewey apologized for being unable to climb down and open the gate.

Neal said, "I'd have to open it anyway if I was by myself, and I'm pleased to have the company." He handed the lines to Hewey. "Reckon you can drive them through after I open the gate?"

Hewey took the reins in his right hand and flexed the stiff fingers of his left, which protruded beyond the cast at the first joint. He did not want to admit to any doubt about his ability to handle the green team, though that doubt was substantial. "Nothin' to it."

He eased the team through the open gate. Though one of the young horses began acting up, Hewey kept a firm grip on the reins and brought the pair to a stop. His right hand was slick with sweat, but he felt a sense of minor victory. So far as he could remember offhand, it was the first substantial challenge he had met and mastered since his big bronc wreck.

He handed the lines back to Neal and rubbed his sweaty hand against his trousers. "Like I said, nothin' to it."

The horses surged against the harness. Silent a while, Neal finally said, "Spring tells me you and her once came close to marryin'."

"She told you about that?"

"We don't have any secrets. I've told her all about my first wife. Ada was a good woman, patient and kind, a lot like Spring. Saw most things the same way. She was . . ." Neal's voice thinned, and he looked away. However long it had been, it was obvious that he still grieved a little.

Hewey said, "People say you and Spring may marry up."

"Everybody's talked about it but us. How would you feel if we did?"

Hewey had to be honest. "I don't know."

"Do you feel like you still have some claim on her?"

"No claim. I don't reckon I ever did have. But to be honest, I still think about her a lot. Sometimes I wish . . ." He felt his hand sweating on the cane. "I wouldn't blame you none if you put me off right here and let me walk back to town."

"I wouldn't deserve her if I did a thing like that. I can understand you still thinkin' about her. After my wife died, I roamed around a long time tryin' to find someplace I belonged. Then I met Spring.

She'd come close to marryin' once even before she knew you, but the poor feller died in Cuba durin' the war. Did you know about that?"

"She told me."

"She made me feel like I'd finally found a home. I expect it was that way for you, too."

"For a while, 'til the old ways got the best of me and I thought I just had to leave."

"I had the travelin' fever once. Finally got over it. Have you?"

Hewey rubbed his hand against the bandaged knee, which ached from the jolting of the wagon. "I don't know. Maybe. That crazy black stud may have put the fire plumb out."

Hewey had worked for Alvin Lawdermilk for short periods, so the ranch headquarters was like a second home to him. It was comforting to see it ahead as they passed through the final pasture gate. Several goats, unafraid, clustered at the roadside and watched like kids at a parade. A burro stubbornly stood its ground in the middle of the road and would not move until Neal got down from the wagon and threatened it with a stick.

The place appeared but little changed from the last time Hewey had seen it except that a modest new house had been constructed to one side of the sprawling single-story one that was home to Alvin, Cora and Cora's mother. Hewey surmised that the smaller house had been put up for Neal, who could not be expected to sleep in the combination bunkhouse and toolshed indefinitely, though Julio Valdez had done it for years.

The small schoolhouse had a fresh coat of white paint that gleamed in the sunlight like vanilla frosting on a cake. There Spring taught children from several miles around because town was too far away. To their regret, Alvin and Cora Lawdermilk had never had children of their own, so they had built the country schoolhouse on their place that they might enjoy the sight and sound of others' sons and daughters. Spring lived in a corner room of the L-shaped Law-dermilk house and took her meals with the family.

Hewey was not sure if school was out for the summer, but cer-tainly it must be out for the day because the sun was almost down. He watched the white building nevertheless, hoping he might see her step outside at any moment.

A screeching peacock heralded the wagon's approach, and a couple of blue-gray guinea hens trotted out of its way in a flutter-ing panic. The Lawdermilk headquarters had always been some-thing of a menagerie. Whatever the species—beast, fowl or fish—if it was not carnivorous and would survive here, Alvin had it. It was Noah's ark without the water.

Julio Valdez heard the trace chains and came out of the barn as the wagon passed on its way to the big house. He shouted a greet-ing and trotted alongside, extending his hand. "Hey, Hooey, you come to stay?"

"Just the night, Hooley. Ain't caught you a *señorita* yet?"

"They run too fast for me."

Alvin Lawdermilk strode onto the broad porch of the big house, a jolly smile breaking across his ruddy face. "Well, looky what just dragged in. Couldn't stay away from Cora's cookin', could you, Hewey?"

"Been tastin' it in my dreams."

Alvin helped him down and hollered for his wife. "Cora, put an-other plate on the table. Better make it a platter. Look who's come for supper."

Hewey had noticed a telephone line strung above the barbed-wire fence that paralleled the wagon road. Alvin had a telephone now, but Hewey doubted that he needed a phone to talk to anyone within less than two miles. His voice would carry that far.

Cora came out onto the porch, wiping her hands on a white apron edged with lace. There had always been something of gentle elegance about Cora Lawdermilk, even when she and Alvin had started their married life thirty-something years ago in an unpainted one-room shack. She had spent those years guiding and cajoling her husband past his various weaknesses, the worst being whiskey and cussing, so that they might not be parted in the hereafter. If Alvin had truly quit drinking, as was claimed, the hereafter seemed secure. He was in other ways an upright citizen, a substantial rancher who his neighbors repeatedly re-elected to be a county commissioner. Everybody in the community would turn out for his funeral someday. Hewey hoped that was still years in the future.

Cora already knew of Hewey's injuries, but even so she seemed dismayed. She was the caring kind of woman who would bandage a sparrow's broken wing and raise dogie calves on a bottle. "Alvin, you help him up the steps and into the house so we can feed him. There's nothin' like good solid food to hurry the healin' process."

The screen door was bumped open, and a heavyset woman pushed onto the porch in a wheelchair, her gray hair atangle, her voice belligerent. "I can't hear myself think for all the commotion." Her accusing eyes lighted upon Hewey and did not soften as they took in the cast and the bandaged knee. "Some people are like a bad penny. They keep comin' back."

"Mother!" Cora admonished her.

Hewey could not remember anybody ever shutting Old Lady Faversham up before she had her say. "First cowboy I ever saw that was bound up tight enough to suit me. He ain't in no condition to be a danger to poor weak womenfolk."

No matter how well Alvin had provided for her daughter in later years, Mrs. Faversham had never forgiven him for having been a poor man at the start. She had always felt that Cora had settled for too little in marrying him. She had become equally protective toward Spring Renfro, fearful that some lusty rakehell might despoil her innocence.

Hewey had always felt a little guilty in the old woman's presence whether or not he had done anything to feel guilty about. "I'll just be spendin' the night and movin' on, Mrs. Faversham."

She raked him up and down with what the vaqueros out at the J Bar would call an evil eye. "Been many a young maiden's life ruined in just one night. But I reckon you're not in a shape to do much damage."

Her eyes softened as Farley Neal came up onto the porch, carrying groceries in his arms.

Anybody that old woman likes has got to have something wrong with him, Hewey thought. But for the life of him he had not seen it, and he had been looking.

Hewey used the cane to hold the screen door open for Neal, who had both hands full. Cora said, "Go on in, Hewey. You know where the washpan is, on the back porch."

Washing one-handed, he dried his face on a towel and cast the pan of water out into the yard, scattering several chickens and a guinea hen that had been pecking around in the dirt. He walked back through the hall into the dining room.

There stood Spring Renfro, blue eyes wide. He had taken her by surprise. She brought both hands up to her face. "Hewey! I thought you were still in Alpine."

"I left," he said, realizing how silly that sounded. Of course he had left, if he was here.

She stared at him for a long, quiet moment. Once the surprise was gone, her eyes guarded whatever thoughts lay behind them. She said, "You're looking better than when I saw you last."

He wanted to say, *You've always looked good.* But all he managed was "Pleased to see you again."

She came closer, looking at his arm. "I hope it's knitting all right." Her voice was neutral, with the kind of general solicitude she might have given to anyone, even a stranger.

He wished for more. "If itchin' means knittin', it is."

"It's good to see you at home, Hewey."

"I ain't home yet."

"You're among friends anywhere you go. You're always at home." She gave him the smallest of smiles, finally, and Hewey melted.

Old Lady Faversham wheeled her chair down the hall and stopped in the doorway to the dining room, shocked at seeing the two together. "Farley Neal, you better get yourself in here. A wolf is after your lamb!"

It had been Lawdermilk family custom to gather around the piano in the parlor at night and sing while Cora or Spring played. Hewey's singing was more appropriate for night guard at the edge of a cattle herd than for a parlor, so he kept his voice low. Spring's clear soprano carried the melody in perfect pitch, and Hewey thought Neal's smooth baritone would serve well in a church choir. The two made pleasant harmony together. Much too pleasant, Hewey felt.

Old Lady Faversham had a strong voice better served in yelling than in singing. She could not carry a tune in a milk bucket.

Cora said, "I haven't had a chance to buy any new sheet music in a while, Hewey. Surely you have learned a few new songs."

He had, but they would not do for a family parlor. "I'm afraid I don't have much ear for music."

"But you've got big eyes for a nice-lookin' woman," said Mrs. Faversham, her gaze switching to Spring, then back to Hewey.

Hewey felt his face flush. If Spring had any reaction, he could not see it.

Eventually the piano went silent and the conversation began to lag. Old Lady Faversham slumped in her wheelchair, mercifully quiet, her eyes closed. Alvin yawned, and Cora laid down the knitting that had occupied her hands. Hewey reluctantly pushed himself to his feet, leaning heavily upon his cane.

"It's high time I let you-all get your rest." He turned to Spring. "You've got school to teach tomorrow."

"School's out for the summer," she said. "But it *is* late."

"I'll be takin' my bedroll out to the toolshed."

Neal said, "There's an extra bed in my house. No need to wake up Julio."

A house would be more comfortable than the shed, though Hewey wondered that Neal was being so kind to him. Perhaps he was trying to make a good showing for Spring. Hewey saw nothing wrong with that so long as it got him a good bed. "I'm obliged."

Spring said, "Be careful on the steps, Hewey. Help him, Farley."

Hewey appreciated her concern, though it rankled that she had to see him this way, unable to take care of himself without help the way he used to do.

Damn you again, Fat Gervin.

He and Neal said their good nights and walked to the smaller house, which Hewey assumed would be Neal's and Spring's together if they married. Just inside the door Neal struck a match and lighted a lamp. The house still had a new-lumber smell and the faint odor of recent painting. Hewey recognized a couple of pieces of furniture as having come from the Lawdermilk parlor. The rest appeared new but plain and utilitarian.

He said, "High livin' for a cowpuncher."

"I'd've settled for much less, but Cora insisted. She wanted it to be nice for Spring . . . if things go that way."

"They will, won't they?"

A tone of doubt crept into the slow answer. "I was figurin' they would." He looked at Hewey, then turned away. "I'm not sure now."

Hewey wondered what he meant by that.

Neal showed him a spare bed in a small room off the kitchen. Hewey tried to keep his eyes closed, hoping to bring on sleep, but he kept opening them, looking at moonlight reflected from the window. He was as wide awake as if it were the middle of the day. He thought a long time about how he must look to everybody, especially Spring, hobbling around on one leg and a cane, one arm useless except for limited movement of the fingers.

The doctor had told him to keep the knee tightly bound at least a couple more weeks, but now of a sudden the binding seemed oppressively heavy and hot and restrictive. He flung the thin covers aside and sat up on the edge of the bed. He had cut off the right leg of his long underwear above the knee to accommodate the binding. Even then it had been difficult to pull the shortened underwear and his pants on over the bulge of cloth.

With no light except what came through the window, he found the knot the doctor had tied in the gauze covering. He could not untie it with his fingers, so he cut it with his knife and began to unwrap the binding, slowly and carefully at first, then quickly, wanting to be done with it.

When the cloth lay like spaghetti on the floor he cautiously tried flexing the knee. It moved, though stiffly, like a tight hinge badly in need of oiling. With the movement came pain like a knifepoint punching into the joint. He worked for several minutes, improving the flexibility, though he could not straighten the leg completely. When he had worked up enough confidence he reached for his cane and stood, putting his weight first upon his left foot, then increasing it slowly on the right.

He found himself shivering and realized he was sweating profusely. A night breeze through the window was chilly upon his skin. He wanted to close it but feared he would wake Neal. He raised the tip of the cane from the floor and tested his full weight on the leg. He found he could stand, even if shakily. When he tried to walk, however, the leg gave way with a stabbing pain. He caught himself on the cane, stopping a fall, but the impact made a loud thump. It had almost been another disaster like his first attempt to walk on a crutch. He felt dizzy and sat back on the edge of the bed.

A match flared, lighting Neal in his underwear. "Are you hurt?"

Hewey's face warmed with embarrassment. "My feelin's are shot to hell. I think I'm all right otherwise." He felt like ten kinds of a fool.

The flame curled the match down near the end, burning Neal's fingers. He quickly dropped it and struck another, lighting a lamp on a small bureau. He touched his tongue to the burned fingertips. "You weren't supposed to take the wrappin' off so soon, were you?"

"That doctor doesn't know how helpless I feel when people have to take care of me like a baby. I'm a grown man."

"Let me look at that knee." Neal knelt, gently probing it with his fingers. The joint remained sore, but the surface looked almost normal except for a reddish scar.

He said, "Let's see how far you can bend it."

Hewey showed him. "It won't straighten all the way."

"It's been bound hard and fast. You have to expect it to be stiff at first."

Hewey felt a rush of disappointment that left him empty and a little angry. "If I was a horse they'd shoot me."

"A horse and a man ain't the same."

"They are in some ways. When a horse gets too old or too stove-up to use, you shoot him or turn him out to pasture. I ain't ready for the pasture."

Neal smiled. "Surely you don't want me to shoot you."

"No, but if the chance comes my way, I may shoot Fat Gervin."

"Want me to help you rewrap the knee?"

"No, I'll leave it like it is. That doctor's way off in Alpine. I won't tell him if you won't."

Hewey managed a little sleep, once he forced down his disappointment. He awoke to the crowing of a rooster and the neighing of a horse in a corral, letting everybody know it was time to feed.

The knee felt lighter with the binding off. Hewey tried bending it again. At first it was tighter than when he went back to bed, but after a few attempts he got it to flex as far as it had last night. He tried standing on it without the cane, though he held to the bedstead as a precaution. After a few tentative steps he decided he could not throw away the cane as he had thrown away the binding, not for a while.

Peeking into the room where Neal had slept, he found the bed made and the man gone. Through the open window floated the distant sound of conversation from the corrals. In the early morning light, he could see Neal and Alvin forking hay to horses and mules. Julio was probably milking the Jersey cows.

I ought to be out there helping, he thought, feeling guilty for having slept almost to sunup, but he knew he would be more a liability than an asset. Some of last night's anger revived.

He limped to the barn, leaning on the cane, his eyes squinted against the first bright sliver of sunrise on the horizon. Alvin hollered, "Sleepin' late, ain't you, Hewey? The Bible speaks hard against sloth."

Hewey tried to think of an appropriate rejoinder, but none came. He was not in a joking mood. He guessed that Alvin and Neal had close to thirty young horses and mules in the big corral. These would be in training for riding or working to wagons or plows. Alvin no longer broke them himself. He farmed them out to various young bronc riders such as Tommy Calloway to be ridden several times, wearing the rough edges off so they were ready to start their real lessons administered by Alvin, Julio and, Hewey supposed, Neal. Hewey had rough-broken a good many himself in times past, turning them over to Alvin to be honed into useful shape.

As always, Alvin picked out favorites for special treatment. He moved close to a young red roan and caught a handful of mane high up on the neck. He led it out to the fence where Hewey stood. It walked along obedient as a pup. "I wisht you'd look at this colt. Smarter'n my mother-in-law and ten times easier to get along with. If you ever get tired of Biscuit, this one would make you a good hand. He already watches a cow like a cat watches a mouse."

"Me and Biscuit are figurin' on gettin' old together . . . someday." The rate he was going, Hewey thought darkly, he might have little use anymore even for Biscuit, much less a young colt.

Alvin patted the colt on the neck and let it go. He unlatched the gate and came outside, waiting for Neal. Julio walked up from the milking pen, carrying a pail in each hand.

Alvin said, "We'll eat breakfast, then I'll take you over to Walter's and Eve's in my automobile."

"I hate to pull you away from your work."

"Farley and Julio do most of the work anyhow. I'm gettin' too stove-up. Comes a time when we all have to settle for less than we used to."

Hewey sensed that Alvin was not just speaking about himself.

Through breakfast Hewey sat across the table from Spring. He stole glances, trying not to be obvious, and often found her staring at him. She would avert her eyes, hiding her judgment, whatever that might be. Neither said much. Old Lady Faversham held the floor through most of the meal anyway, talking about the hardships women had to endure living in an uncivilized environment, not the least of them the ingratitude of their men. That train of thought led her to a lecture about the faithlessness of cowboys.

After breakfast Alvin asked, "Cora, how would you and Spring like to go with us? You-all ain't had much chance to visit with Eve lately."

Cora begged off, saying she had too much work stacked up. She said, "Spring, why don't you go? You could return those dress patterns I borrowed from her and take her some of the preserves we put up last week."

Spring seemed caught in a bind. She glanced at Hewey, then at Neal. His nod told her it was all right to go, but his eyes wished she would not. She shook her head, not looking at Hewey. "There *is* a lot of work to be done. Perhaps another day."

Hewey stared at the ground in regret. He had much to apologize to her for if he ever got the chance, and if he could work up the nerve. Likely as not it was too late anyway. The time for apology had been four years ago.

Alvin went to start the automobile and back it out of the hay shed where it was kept safe from the weather. Shortly the roar of the engine told Hewey that Alvin had pulled the car up to the front of the house. He gave Spring one more quick glance. "I'll go fetch my roll," he said, and left as hurriedly as the cane would allow.

He heard Old Lady Faversham behind him, telling Spring she had made the right decision. "I don't blame you, not wantin' to go with Alvin and that fiddle-footed cowpuncher. His kind are a dime a dozen and badly overpriced."

Neal came into the little house as Hewey finished tying his bedroll. "I'll carry that for you," he offered.

Hewey said, "It wasn't my idea to invite her in the first place. She belongs to you."

"She doesn't *belong* to anybody. She's a free woman."

Hewey wondered if the man wasn't too good to be real. "Lots of old boys I've known wouldn't have so much trust."

Regret pinched Neal's eyes. "I didn't always have. I was young and green and a little jealous when I married. Kept a tight rein on Ada when there wasn't any reason for it. I realized that after I lost her, and I didn't like myself much." He hoisted Hewey's bedroll over his shoulder. "I wouldn't want Spring to look back years from now and have regrets on my account."

You're the right man for her, Hewey thought. But the thought was too painful to speak aloud.

Cora gave him several messages to take to Eve. Hewey assured her he would deliver them, though he knew he would forget most of them before he got there. For the hell of it he waved good-bye to Old Lady Faversham, who sat in her wheelchair on the porch. She did not respond. She was not there to wish him farewell but simply to be certain that he left.

Spring and Neal stood side by side. Neal nodded at Hewey, and Spring made a weak smile that carried a hint of sadness. Hewey forced himself to look away, facing forward. The automobile backfired, and Alvin came within inches of running over a flustered peacock that contested him for the right-of-way and yielded just in time. Alvin laughed. "Them peacocks belong to my mother-in-law. When she ain't screechin', they are."

Though getting in and out of the car was a struggle, Hewey insisted upon opening and closing the gates. The wooden ones were little challenge, but the tight wire gates were almost more than he could handle. Alvin was sensitive enough to Hewey's pride that he let him wrestle them alone, though it must have taken all the patience he could muster not to get out and take over. Alvin would never be a good poker player; whatever he was thinking showed in his face, and his pity was apparent.

It only made Hewey feel worse. "Sometimes I almost wish that stud had killed me instead of leavin' me in this shape, havin' to depend on everybody."

Alvin frowned. "Have you talked to the Lord about it?"

"Pray? I've prayed for other people, but it always seemed selfish to do it for myself."

"Not when you've got a real need. The Lord generally answers, though not always like you hope for. You remember how fond I always was of whiskey? It got to a point that I was sick a lot of the time, so me and the Lord had a long talk about it. Well, I done the talkin', but I could tell He was listenin', because pretty soon it got to where it tasted so bad to me that I didn't want it anymore.

"When He takes things away from us, He usually gives us somethin' in trade. We lose the energy we had when we were young, but He gives us more wisdom. And as He takes away our ability to do one thing or another, He also takes away most of the want-to so we can be content with what we've got left."

"I ain't content with the way I am, and I don't intend to settle for it."

"Fine. The Lord loves a man who won't give up tryin'."

"It wasn't the Lord that put me in this shape; it was Fat Gervin. Be damned if I'll let him win."

Alvin nodded approval. "You're gettin' mad, and that's good. As long as you're mad, you'll keep fightin'. But when you go as far as the Lord intends for you to, you'll have to make your peace and be glad for what you've still got."

"What *have* I got? The shape I'm in, I'll do well to swamp out Dutch Schneider's saloon."

"You told me Morgan Jenkins offered you a job as foreman. You wouldn't have to ride no rough horses to do that."

"I couldn't take care of a ranch afoot."

"The wheel has been around for thousands of years. Every buggy and buckboard has got four of them."

Hewey noticed dust rising to the south. Alvin pinched his eyes almost shut, trying to see through the haze. "Looks like horses run-nin'. You don't reckon somebody's rustlin' a bunch of my stock? I ain't got a gun with me."

Hewey doubted that Alvin had ever pulled a gun on anybody in his life. It was not his style. He was a peacemaker, like Walter.

Rustling had become rare in this big country because the horse had not been born that could outrun a sheriff's telephone calls. In these vast distances a thief would have to travel far and hard to re-move himself from harm's way.

Alvin left the road and set the car bouncing across the open pas-ture. Hewey held tightly with his good hand to keep from being tossed around in the seat. He could only imagine what this jarring might do to his innards.

When they were close enough that Alvin could see the horses clearly, he braked to a slow stop, relieved.

"They ain't mine. I wouldn't allow any on my place as sorry as them."

Two riders were driving a remuda of thirty or so runty-looking Mexican ponies. A horseman with his shirttail hanging out reined toward the car. Hewey recognized the no-name cowboy he had met on the C. C. Tarpley ranch.

Alvin shouted, "Where you goin' with them broomtails?"

The cowboy's clothes were dirty, and he had several days' growth of whiskers, showing he had been on the trail. "We're takin' them to Mr. Gervin for delivery to a buyer. They come from down on the Pecos."

Alvin said, "It'd be a lot easier to take them along the road than to cut across my ranch."

"It was Mr. Gervin's orders to bring them this way. We'll be off your place before they have a chance to eat much of your grass. Adios." The cowboy spurred off after the horses.

Alvin said, "Now, why would Fat give an order like that?"

"So he could tell a buyer that they came from your ranch and not exactly be lyin' about it." Hewey explained about the bunch Gervin had sold to Old Man Jenkins under false pretenses.

Alvin swore. "The duplicitous son of a bitch!"

Hewey was surprised to hear such language come from Alvin. He didn't used to say words like *duplicitous*.

CHAPTER

12

The sound of an automobile was still so uncommon in the countryside that it brought out everyone within hearing distance to see who was coming or going. Walter appeared in the door of the toolshed, and Eve stood on the step in front of her kitchen, shading her eyes with her hand. The black dog trotted to meet the car, barking all the way.

Out in the field, someone halted a team and turned to look. Hewey could not be sure at the distance, but he supposed this was Lester the nester boy, hired on a day basis to help Walter with his crops. Lester never lacked for excuses to halt work. Hewey would bet a dollar that he would leave the mules standing and come all the way to the house to find out who had arrived, though it was none of his business.

Eve waited for the dust to settle after Alvin braked to a stop; then she walked to the car. "Hewey! We didn't expect to see you home so soon. Is anything the matter? Are you all right? Where's Tommy?"

That was a lot of questions, and Hewey lumped the answers together. "I'm doin' fair to middlin', and Tommy ought to be along in a day or two. He's bringin' our horses."

"That boy? All by himself?"

"By the time I was his age I'd seen all of Texas and half of hell." Lately he had seen the other half.

Alvin asked, "How long 'til dinner?"

Eve said, "If I'd known you-all were comin' I'd've killed the old red rooster. I'm afraid you'll have to settle for mutton stew."

"Mutton?" Hewey demanded.

"Didn't Tommy tell you that Walter bought us a flock of sheep? They pay better than cattle when we can keep the coyotes off of them."

A bad taste came into Hewey's mouth, as if he had been chewing tobacco. He had boasted to Dutch Schneider that there were two things he had never done: swamp out a saloon and herd sheep. He had then proceeded to sweep Schneider's floor. Now he might find himself herding sheep.

Stove-up and not worth his beans, he could sink no lower, it seemed.

As Hewey stepped out of the car, bracing himself on the cane, the old dog moved up close and barked at him. It never had accepted him as a member of the family.

Hewey had to limp all the way around the car before he could satisfy Walter that he was not a total invalid. Alvin declared, "He's gettin' pretty good with that cane. Before long you'll have to run to keep up with him."

Alvin was trying to make him feel better, but his solicitude only sharpened Hewey's sense of being less than whole.

Lester stopped twenty feet short of the car and stared without speaking. It was just as well; Hewey could not remember ever hearing him say anything worth listening to. Lester welcomed any chance to get away from the plow a while. Sooner or later, Hewey figured, he would wangle himself a job at the courthouse. Things there moved at about his chosen speed.

Hewey said, "Lester, would you mind takin' my bedroll to the barn? I'll be sleepin' down there."

Eve said, "You'll do no such of a thing, Hewey. You'll sleep in the boys' room like kinfolks, not in the barn like a hired hand . . ."—

she turned severe eyes toward Lester—"one that's fixin' to get fired if he doesn't go back to the field and do a little work."

Walter said, "Now, Eve . . ." Walter's peacemaker trait was often called upon when things did not go Eve's way.

Lester turned and started toward the field in a trot, though he soon slowed to a walk, and he climbed over the fence rather than take the trouble to open a heavy gate.

"That boy's poor mother," Eve lamented, "I can imagine the tribulations he's put her through."

Though he was a brother-in-law rather than a wayward son, Hewey had given Eve more than her share of tribulation over the years. He said, "Soon as I get this cast off my arm and my knee is a little more limber, you can send Lester home."

Eve said, "You wouldn't be in that shape if you hadn't tried to spare Tommy from gettin' hurt. You're here to rest, Hewey Calloway, and you'll do it if I have to tie you to a rockin' chair."

Alvin asked again, "How long 'til dinner?"

After three days Hewey feared he would wear a hole through the seat of the rocking chair. He was restless to be up and doing something, even if it was wrong. The dog's barking gave him reason to arise and hobble to the door.

"Looks like Tommy's comin'," he told Eve, then went outside. He was halfway to the barn when he heard the screen door slam as Eve came out to look for her son.

Tommy was not alone. Long before he could see the face, Hewey knew the rider. He could usually recognize his friends at a distance by the way they sat on their horses, and no one rode with quite the same easy slouch as Snort Yarnell. Hewey was not sure whether to whoop for joy or give in to dread. With Snort, there was never any knowing.

Tommy was riding his own dun horse, leading Biscuit on a long rope knotted so it would not choke. As soon as Tommy released him, Biscuit headed straight for the feed trough; he knew exactly where it was.

Hewey said to Tommy, "You're kind of careless who you let ride with you."

Snort grinned at Hewey, showing his gold tooth in full glory. "You still gimpin' around, tryin' for sympathy?"

"What happened to that night watchman's job? They catch you openin' the bar after hours?"

"Me and a runny-nosed constable had a little set-to. It was his fault, not mine, but you know how narrow-minded them small-town John Laws can be. After a few nights of walkin' the streets, I decided I'd rather take my chances on bein' killed by a horse than die of boredom."

Snort's grin died, and he looked Hewey up and down with a sober eye. "We've come to help you get well, me and Tommy. We're goin' to work you and make you exercise 'til that arm and leg move better than the day you was born."

"It's more likely you'll kill me, if I don't kill you first." Hewey turned back to Tommy. "You took your sweet time gettin' home."

A hint of guilt came into Tommy's face. Hewey noticed a bruise on his cheekbone. "Snort had to go by Pecos City to see a man about a horse."

"I warned you to take roundance on Pecos. It's too lively a town for a boy your age."

"It sure was lively after Snort got there. We had to leave in kind of a hurry."

Snort was all innocence. "It was their fault. They ain't as friendly anymore as them old-timey Pecos folks used to be."

Eve was walking out from the house. Hewey cautioned Tommy, "I wouldn't say anything to your mother about Pecos. She might run us all off."

Eve hugged her son, then stepped back to examine the bruise. Quickly Tommy said, "Dunny spooked at a rabbit and caught me off guard. I took a fall."

Somebody's been teaching that boy to lie, Hewey thought. He gave Snort an accusing look.

He doubted that Eve was taken in. She had seen through windies told by far better liars than Tommy. Her voice had a crisp edge of suspicion as she asked Snort, "You *are* stayin' for supper, I suppose?" It was less an invitation than an expression of resignation.

Snort was notoriously unreliable. He might stay a month, or he might ride away in ten minutes without saying a word. Hewey hoped he didn't stay a month. Eve would be chewing up nails and spitting them out long before then.

Snort said, "Eve, the angels in heaven could take lessons from you. I'll be here for supper tonight and many more after that. Poor old Hewey needs my help."

Eve frowned. "God had better help us all."

After she returned to the house, Snort poured oats in a trough for his horse and dropped the bucket back into the barrel from which it had come. "First thing we got to do, Hewey, is cut that cast off of your arm. How do you expect to move your elbow with it all trussed up thataway?"

Hewey had been toying with the same notion. His leg had not collapsed when he unwrapped his knee. It was becoming a little more flexible every day, though he could not straighten it fully. He could even take a few rabbit-hopping steps without the cane. "Since when have you been practicin' medicine?"

Snort said, "I've doctored many a horse. In your case there can't be much difference."

Gratitude made tears come into Hewey's eyes. "You don't know how much it means to me, Snort, you comin' all the way back here to try and help."

Snort's face went dead serious. "You're my friend, Hewey. I've moved around a lot and rode with a lot of good fellers, but I ain't ever had many real close friends. Mainly there was just you and Old Grady Welch. I lost Grady. Time we got to him, there wasn't a thing I could do to help him. In Alpine, I was sore afraid I was fixin' to lose you, too."

"I'm figurin' on bein' around for a long time yet."

"And I'm here to help you."

At the supper table, Lester the nester boy listened with mouth hanging open as Snort told stories. Some contained a grain or two of truth, though not enough to hurt them much.

When Snort paused to poke half a biscuit into his mouth, Tommy told Hewey, "Mr. Jenkins asked about you. Said he was sorry you left without sayin' good-bye. He wanted to proposition you again about that foreman's job at the Circle W."

"He hired him a foreman."

"Seems like him and Mr. Underhill got in an argument over the way to handle those broncs he got from Fat Gervin."

Eve corrected him. "*Mr.* Gervin."

"Mr. Fat Gervin. Anyway, Mr. Underhill left, and Mr. Jenkins needs a foreman."

Hewey felt a stirring of interest. The Circle W was as pleasurable as any place he had ever worked, situated in a valley with sheltering mountains on either side, a clear creek meandering unhurriedly down the length of it, and not too many fences or gates. It was far enough from town that a man wouldn't be bothered by a lot of uninvited company.

"I can't think of a place I'd rather go if I was inclined to take on the responsibility and if I wasn't busted up like an eggshell. I can't even ride a horse."

Snort argued, "What responsibility? You just tell the boys what you want done and they do it. A foreman don't even have to ride a horse. I've worked for several that rode around in a buggy like they owned the bank. Even had somebody hitch up their team. It's like havin' a gravy bowl that don't ever run dry."

With Snort around, it would need to be an awfully deep bowl, Hewey thought, watching him take another helping of mutton stew. Snort probably didn't recognize what it was, for he had a cowboy's unreasoning prejudice against sheep and everything associated with them.

Hewey said, "I don't know that I could give orders and stand back, and the shape I'm in, I couldn't do much else."

After supper Snort jerked his head toward the door. "Come on out to the barn with me, Hewey. We'll do somethin' about the cast on your arm."

Eve protested, "That time Walter broke his leg, we had to leave the cast on for three months."

Snort assured her, "An arm heals faster than a leg."

Hewey wondered where that piece of wisdom came from. Probably out of Snort's imagination. But he was ready to shed the cast anyway. It itched as if a nest of wood ants had hatched under it, and it gave off a smell that reminded him of a dead mule.

Snort rummaged among Walter's tools. Cotton had been methodical, making sure every piece of equipment had its proper place and was returned to it immediately after use. When Cotton left home to seek his own way working on automobiles, that sense of good order went with him. Snort said, "Walter's bound to have a set of hoof trimmers around here someplace."

He found them and began to nip at the edges of the cast, breaking it away one small piece at a time. Hewey winced, for Snort's twisting and straining made the arm hurt. Hewey was almost ready at one point to call a halt, but by then half the cast was in shreds, and he saw no choice except to go ahead. Both men had worked up a healthy sweat, Snort through exertion and Hewey through fighting pain. Snort stopped to roll a cigarette. He offered it to Hewey.

Hewey said, "I've quit. Since the accident they've got to where they taste like cow chips." Not only could he no longer work as he used to, but one of the simplest of his pleasures had abandoned him as well.

"Never tasted a cow chip," Snort said, "so I wouldn't know."

Tommy and Lester had come to the barn and watched in silence as Snort methodically demolished the cast, passing the elbow and working along the upper arm. Finally he pulled the last of it away. The rough barn floor was littered with bits of plaster and cloth.

Hewey carefully felt the arm. It still hurt to the touch where the bone had been broken just above the elbow. "Looks sort of crooked, don't it?"

Snort shrugged. "Nobody'll see it. Your sleeve'll cover it up." Snort had one leg twisted and scarred from an argument with a horse. He maintained that it still worked all right, even if it looked like a bear had chewed on it. A cowboy hadn't graduated to the top ranks until he was marked up some.

Hewey tried working the elbow. Like the knee, it resisted. The arm bent only a little.

Snort said, "You need to squirt some axle grease in there."

Lester was awed. "You reckon that'd work?"

Tommy elbowed him. "Don't you know when Snort's kiddin'?"

"It makes sense to me."

Snort gripped Hewey's arm above and below the elbow and tried to force it to bend. Hewey hollered out and jerked free. He rubbed the arm in an attempt to smother the fire Snort's abuse had aroused. "If that's the way you've doctored horses, you probably had to shoot them afterwards."

"Some of them got well. Your arm is goin' to take a lot of work."

That night Hewey lay in bed awake, the arm throbbing so hard from the strain that tears forced their way through his clenched eyelids. He was bitterly disappointed that it had not healed straight, that it seemed so weak. He kept trying to work it, but the elbow moved only a little, and every attempt was like dipping the arm in hot coals.

He had been resisting what Alvin had suggested. Now, through the pain, he whispered a prayer.

Hewey paused from hoeing weeds in Eve's garden to wipe sweat from his face. Snort leaned on a fence post and rolled a cigarette. He hollered, "Don't stop now. You need to keep workin' if you're goin' to free up them joints."

Hewey considered breaking the hoe handle across Snort's head, but that would probably violate some stupid law passed by city folks who had no idea of the emergencies that might arise in the countryside. He looked out into the field, where Walter and Tommy were working. Lester the nester boy had gone home.

Hewey said, "There's weeds enough here for both of us."

"You're the one that needs the exercise. Just keep doin' what you're doin'. I think I'll go see if there's any coffee left from breakfast."

Snort entered the frame house. Shortly Eve came out, walking to the garden, her arms folded. She looked back over her shoulder, a frown set deeply. "You reckon Snort has got a tapeworm?"

"Nothin' about Snort would surprise me."

"I asked him if he was hungry. He said no, he just wanted a cup of coffee. Then he mixed half a pound of butter into a plateful of molasses and started swabbin' it up with cold biscuits. I never saw a skinny man who could eat so much. How much longer does he figure on stayin' here?"

"He ain't said, but I'm wishin' he'd take a notion to leave. Every day for two weeks it's been 'bend that arm, work that leg,' over and over. And when he gets tired he sics Tommy on me. He's about wore me down to a nub."

"They say absence makes the heart grow fonder. I would sure like to get a lot fonder of Snort Yarnell. I guess he's done you some good here, but in the long run he's a bad influence. He'll try and lead you back to the wanderin' ways you and him shared for all those years."

"Snort's a good old boy at heart. He don't mean any harm."

"Take a real hard look at him. He's got nothin', he's got nobody. He drifts from one place to another. God knows what he's lookin' for. I doubt Snort knows himself."

"He seems happy enough."

"It's all a show. He's lonely and miserable, and he tries to cover it up with bluster and hooraw. You've been enough like him that it scares me half to death. He'll never change, Hewey, but you can. You just have to make up your mind. It wouldn't hurt you to call on the Lord for help."

"I already have," he admitted. "And maybe He heard me. See my cane hangin' on the fence yonder?"

She suddenly realized. "You're walkin' without it."

"Can't hold a cane and a hoe both at the same time."

Eve was so pleased she kissed him on the cheek. "Mind what I said about Snort. The world's not big enough to hold two like him."

When she returned to the house, he noticed that Biscuit had walked up to the garden fence and stood there, watching. Hewey laid down the hoe and limped over to the horse, which stood still while Hewey rubbed and patted its neck. "You're gettin' fat, old boy. All them oats and no work. But I don't know what I can do about it." Tommy had been riding the horse a little, though not enough to wear off much weight.

Biscuit turned his head, pointing his ears toward the road. An automobile was coming. Hewey said, "It's a disgrace for company to catch a cowboy with a hoe in his hand. But it'd be worse if I was herdin' Walter's sheep." He patted the horse once more and turned away, propping the hoe against the fence and picking up his cane.

The car was Alvin's. Snort came out of the house, eating a biscuit. He walked to the garden to join Hewey. "Just because we've got a little company don't mean you need to quit work. Ain't nobody except Alvin and his womenfolks."

Spring was in the backseat, behind Alvin and Cora. Hewey glanced down at his clothes, dirty from the garden work. He tried to brush some of the dust away, but he did little more than move it around. He felt awkward about going out to greet Spring, but it would be even more awkward if he avoided her. Every time he saw her, old emotions began to stir, regret for old decisions still painful though they had seemed right.

Snort sensed his indecision. "Careful, *compadre*. You got away once by the skin of your teeth. You may not be that lucky again."

Hewey limped to the car, tipping his dusty hat to the women and shaking Alvin's hand. Alvin said, "Farley Neal and Julio are behind us a ways. They're bringin' a set of green-broke ponies for Tommy to work to the harness."

Walter and Tommy had seen the car and were on their way in from the field. Eve hugged Cora and Spring. "Everybody come on into the house. I'll make us a fresh pot of coffee." She gave Hewey a quick, furtive nod that told him to join Spring. "You too, Hewey."

Hewey said, "I still got a lot of work to do." Reluctantly he pulled away from Spring and the others, earning a reproachful frown from Eve. Spring's face was without expression; he could not tell what she was thinking. He returned to the garden, Snort walking with him.

Snort said, "You done right, not goin' in the house. Womenfolks are always workin' and schemin' to get somebody hitched up. They can't stand to see a man stay free."

"They never got *you* hitched up."

"And they won't. There ain't no bigger threat to a man's freedom than a good woman. Once they set a hook in him, he's a fish on a line. The kind of women I like don't ask for much, a few dollars and a little of your time. They smile when they see you comin' and they smile when you go. No tears and no regrets."

Hewey nodded. It sounded good if he didn't examine it closely. "But someday you'll be old and all by yourself, and even your money won't make them smile at you."

"I don't figure on ever gettin' old. I'll just turn into a gray mule and go around kickin' the people I don't like."

Hewey retrieved his hoe and chopped a few more weeds. Snort sidled up to him and elbowed him in the ribs. "Look out. She's comin'."

Hewey turned. Spring was at the garden gate. The sight of her stirred a warm feeling.

Her voice was pleasant enough, though her smile was tentative. "Are you going to work all day?"

"The weeds are tryin' to take Eve's garden. And I need the exercise to get my joints limbered."

Snort said, "I been workin' real hard on him. Want to get him back to where he was before that bronc messed him up."

Hewey sensed that Spring wished to talk but did not feel free while Snort stood there. He said, "Snort, you look like a man that needs a cup of coffee, or somethin'."

"I had my coffee already." He caught on. "Oh! Sure, reckon I do." He made his misgivings plain as he moved toward the garden gate, looking back. "Don't you forget what I told you about them good women."

Spring gave Hewey a quizzical look. Hewey shrugged. "Don't pay no attention. Half the time Snort don't know what he's sayin'."

When Snort was out of hearing, Spring nodded toward Hewey's

cane hanging from the top wire of the fence. "It appears you're making good progress if you don't need that cane all the time. I'm pleased for you, Hewey."

"It's Snort's doin', mostly. He keeps workin' me 'til I'm about ready to bust him with an ax handle."

Biscuit remained near the garden fence, grazing. Spring said, "Are you riding your horse yet?"

"Ain't tried. It hurt too much the last time."

"Perhaps it's just as well. As soon as you could ride you would probably be wanting to leave again."

He thought he detected a faint edge of resentment but hoped it was his imagination. It had been four years, and anyway, she had told him it was all right for him to go. He hoed a few more weeds, waiting for her to say something else to give him some gauge of her feelings.

She said, "This may all have happened for a reason. It may be a way of turning your life around and setting you off on a new road."

"I liked the road I was on, and my life the way it was."

"How well I remember."

"Look at me, all busted up, can't do an honest day's work. What am I worth to anybody?"

"You're worth a lot to Walter and Eve and Tommy."

He hoped she might add *And to me,* but she did not. He was not sure how he would react if she had. Four years ago he had shut a gate and locked it behind him.

She asked, "So, what next, Hewey? What do you do now?"

"Ain't much I *can* do. Cowpunchin' was the only life I ever knew or cared to know. I may not be able to do it anymore."

"You have to accept that some things may never be the same. There've been changes in what you can do, but there doesn't have to be any change in what you *are*."

"And what is that?"

"You're a good and decent man at heart. Alvin once said you're an eagle on the wing. That's why I let you ride away, because I couldn't bear to tie up an eagle or put it in a cage. You're still the eagle you always were."

"I'm afraid I got my wings clipped."

"But I think your eyes are still on the sky, Hewey. And my feet are still on the ground."

She walked back to the house. Hewey kept hoeing the same weed over and over.

Neal and Julio brought the young horses. Hewey saw the eagerness in Tommy's face at the challenge of training them, and he felt a glow of envy. At least Eve wouldn't have to worry about her son leaving again for a while. He had something to stay for.

Hewey stood outside the corral, looking in. Neal came around and stood beside him, saying nothing at first. Hewey decided one of them had to speak. "Good-lookin' set of horses. Ain't nobody raises better ones than Alvin."

Neal blurted, "I'm goin' to ask her to marry me."

Hewey flinched as if Neal had hit him in the stomach. He forced a smile, but it was thin as water. "I think she'll say yes."

"Maybe she will. Again, maybe she won't."

"Why wouldn't she?"

"Afraid, maybe. She's been hurt in the past."

Hewey gripped the fence so hard that his knuckles ached. "I reckon I know about that." As badly as it pained him, he had to say, "I think you're the right man for her. I wish you luck."

Neal walked to the house alone. Hewey leaned against a post, trying to think of what he should have said to Spring, though it had already been too late . . . four years late.

The two horsebackers left soon after dinner so they could get back to the Lawdermilk place in time for the chores. Alvin, Cora and Spring stayed until mid-afternoon. Hewey remained in the garden for the most part.

Spring made no attempt to be alone with him again, but he was acutely conscious that her gaze followed him when he was in sight. As the visitors prepared to go, she turned to Hewey. "Keep trying. You can do it." She got into the car and did not look at him again.

Eve was keenly watching them both. Once she had pushed hard to make a match between the two, hoping to crowd Hewey into giving up his wandering ways and setting a more stable example for her sons. Watching the automobile pull away, she moved close to Hewey. "You know Spring's concerned about you."

"She's concerned about everybody. She's got a good heart."

"And it could've been yours." She went back into the house.

Snort jerked his head. "Let's go, Hewey. There's still a-plenty of weeds in that garden, and you need to be workin' them muscles."

Instead, Hewey looked for his nephew. "Tommy, I wisht you'd go catch up Biscuit for me."

Tommy's eyes lighted like the Fourth of July. "You goin' to ride him?"

"I'm goin' to try damned hard."

Snort said, "It took you long enough to make up your mind. Or was it that schoolteacher done it?"

Tommy saddled Biscuit and led him out of the corral. He said, "You ain't been on him in a while, so he's fat and frisky. I'd better ride him around a little first."

"The day somebody has to top out my own horse for me is the day I go lookin' for a night watchman's job." He gave Snort a challenging look.

Snort winced. "You goin' to hold that over my head the rest of my life? Just stepped off of the trail one time . . . just once . . ."

Hewey started slowly, patting the horse on the neck, rubbing its ears.

Snort declared, "If you're goin' to do it, do it!"

Hewey hung his cane on the fence. Carefully he lifted his left foot to the stirrup, which forced him to put all his weight on the injured right leg. He gritted his teeth against expected pain, but it was milder than he thought. Tommy's eyes were wide with anticipation. Walter had caught on to what was happening and had come from the milking pen to watch.

Hewey said, "Tommy, you're young and innocent, and the Lord'll listen to you. Talk to Him for me."

"I already have."

Hewey gripped the saddle horn and pulled himself up. The right leg was still stiff, and he dragged it across Biscuit's rump. A less gentle horse might have jumped. Hewey sought the stirrup with his right foot, found it and slid it in past the toes. The leg felt as if it were still bound. He could not bring it tightly against the horse's ribs as he did with his left, and a small ache began in the knee. But these negatives were minor considerations against a much more important fact: he was in the saddle.

Tommy whooped for joy. Walter stood beside his son, an arm around Tommy's shoulder. Snort Yarnell grinned in satisfaction, as if it were all his doing.

Hewey rode Biscuit in a wide circle, walking him at first, then putting him into an easy trot. He hurt in several places; there was no getting around that. But he was riding.

Eve came out onto the kitchen step to watch. Hewey saw her lift the hem of her apron and dab it against her eyes.

After a while his side began to ache, and he knew he had done all he should for the day. But he would ride again tomorrow, and the day after. It would get better. It had to.

He felt like shouting as he slid down from the saddle, avoiding too much weight on the right leg. He patted Biscuit again and handed the reins to Tommy. "Unsaddle him for me, will you? And give him a double bait of oats."

Tommy had a smile a yard wide. "Sure thing, Uncle Hewey."

Walter pumped Hewey's hand, and Snort slapped him on the back so hard that Hewey thought he would lose his breath. Walter said, "Let's go to the house. I think we could all use some coffee."

Hewey retrieved the cane from the fence. He took a couple of steps on it, then detoured over to the woodpile. He pitched the cane onto the top of the chopped stove wood and limped back to join Walter and Snort.

"I don't believe I'll need that thing anymore."

CHAPTER
13

Hewey was half a mile from the house, riding Biscuit alongside Snort Yarnell, when he recognized the open-topped automobile making its way along the wagon road from town. "That's Old Man Jenkins's car. Wonder what he could want?"

"More money. Them old ranchers are always after more money, like they ain't already got most of it corraled."

Hewey put Biscuit into a stiff trot. The jarring touched off an internal ache so slight that Hewey was able to ignore it. The pain had diminished gradually, day by day. He was confident it would soon be gone entirely if he did not do something foolish and undo the progress he had made.

He waved his hat to be certain he was seen. Peeler eased the car to a stop in front of the house and took off his goggles as Hewey and Snort approached. Beaming, Jenkins hollered, "I wisht you'd look at Hewey Calloway on horseback. I expected to see you rockin' your life away on the front porch."

"I wore out that rockin' chair in about a week," Hewey replied, dismounting slowly to shake hands with both men. He still had to be careful how he moved, for his right knee remained tricky. He had limited mobility in his left arm.

Jenkins said, "Then I reckon you're ready to go back to work."

Hewey sobered quickly. "It's better, but it ain't that good. I'm afraid I've rode my last bronc."

Snort eyed Peeler with misgivings. "I remember you. You're the gink that spurred our outlaw bronc to a standstill and cleaned out us Slash R boys."

Peeler grinned. "And you're the man that drank the rest of us under the table. Hard to forget a feller with that kind of talent."

Eve came out of the kitchen, and Hewey introduced her to the two visitors. He said, "You-all go on into the house. I'll unsaddle Biscuit and be along in a minute."

Snort reached for the reins. "I'll unsaddle him. I expect Mr. Jenkins came here to talk to you."

It still made Hewey uncomfortable to let someone else saddle and unsaddle his horse for him, though Tommy had been doing it lately. "I'm obliged," he said, and motioned for Jenkins and Peeler to precede him into the house. Eve set three coffee cups on the table and poured them full in silent invitation.

Jenkins looked Hewey over before he seated himself. "I'm tickled to see you doin' so much better. I've had you on my conscience, seein' as you got hurt workin' for me."

"Wasn't your fault. I got hurt on account of Fat Gervin."

"It was my ranch and my horse. If you've been concerned about your doctor bill, don't be. I paid my half and yours, too."

"I'm obliged." Hewey wanted to smile but didn't. Dr. Evans had been a big winner on this deal. "Did you manage to get rid of them broncs Fat sold you?"

Jenkins scowled. "Only a couple of them. It appears I'm stuck with the rest. Buyers come and take a look, and they leave so fast their shirttails don't touch them 'til they're back on the road. Blas may have to learn how to cook horsemeat and make it taste like steak."

"I wish there was a way you could make Fat Gervin eat them." For whatever satisfaction it might give the old man, he described the lie he had told Gervin about Jenkins planning to sic a battery of Fort Worth lawyers on him. "It's thin comfort, but at least I worried him for a little while."

Not long enough, however, for evidently Gervin had pulled the same swindle on someone else. Hewey told about the day he and Alvin found two Tarpley cowboys driving a remuda across the Lawdermilk ranch so Gervin could trade on the good reputation of Alvin's horses and palm off some scrubs he had bought cheaply down on the Pecos. "I'd bet he's usin' the Tarpley bank's money, but the bank ain't gettin' none of the profit. Poor old C.C. ain't been in any shape to keep an eye on things lately."

He described Tarpley and the old man's troubles. "You'd like C.C., Mr. Jenkins. You and him have got a lot in common."

Both were highly ambitious and tight with a dollar, though this was not unusual among ranchers of their generation. Without those traits they might not have endured and prospered through the harsh challenges of the early years. Hewey was not critical. He understood the men and the drive that compelled them, though he did not share it.

He said, "It'll be a poorer country when C.C. is gone. Fat Gervin ain't fit to polish the old man's boots."

"Gervin!" It sounded like a cussword, the way Jenkins said it. "It's not so much the money. I've lost that much through a hole in my pocket. It's the principle of the thing, lettin' him skin me that way. I shot a man once for stealin' horses, but at least he was honest after his own fashion. He never claimed to be anything but a horse thief."

Eve kept staring at Peeler with poorly hidden curiosity. He must have looked like some foreign being to her, wearing a duster, cap and goggles, jodhpurs and tall lace-up boots. Hewey decided not to tell her he was just a reformed bronc rider. Like as not she would start pointing to him as a potential model for Hewey's own reformation.

Jenkins said, "Looks like all I can do with them broncs is load them on a train and ship them to the Fort Worth stockyards. They ought to fetch a little somethin' for soap, but they won't bring back what I've got in them."

Hewey sympathized. "It's a pity you can't sell them back to the man you bought them from." A glimmering of an idea began forming. "Or maybe you could."

"To Frank Gervin? He wouldn't take them back. I'll bet he's been laughin' up his sleeve ever since he sold them to me."

"There ain't any use appealin' to Fat's good nature. He ain't got one. But maybe we can appeal to his greed."

"How?"

"I've got the first stirrin's of a notion." Hewey arose and looked out the window toward the corral where Snort was helping Tommy and Walter unhitch a raw team Tommy had been working to a wagon. After a minute he turned to stare at Peeler. "Eve, what does Peeler look like to you?"

Eve was caught off balance. "What kind of question is that?"

"If you was to bump into him in town, lookin' like he looks right now, what would you think he was?"

"He looks like a gentleman, of course, dressed for a drive in an automobile."

"Would you figure him for a man of means?"

"How else could he have an automobile? *We* sure don't have one."

Hewey grinned at Peeler. "How are you at catchin' fish?"

"I've hooked a few in my day."

"With a little luck you may hook the fattest fish you ever saw."

The two automobiles moved along slowly, a couple of hundred yards in front of seventeen horses driven by Tommy, Snort Yarnell and two J Bar vaqueros. As they came to a wire gate, Hewey could see the windmill towers of Upton City half a mile ahead. He turned

235

in the seat of Alvin Lawdermilk's car and motioned for Peeler to pull Jenkins's automobile up beside him. Aparicio Rodriguez left his place behind the band of horses and loped ahead to open the gate.

Hewey climbed out of Alvin's car. He had to speak loudly to be heard over the roar of the two engines. "Mr. Jenkins, you'd better get in the car with us. Wouldn't do for Fat to see you and Peeler together."

Jenkins left his own automobile, moving over to the backseat of Alvin's.

Hewey said, "Now, Peeler, we'll let you go on into town ahead of us. You won't have any trouble spottin' the bank. If a red car is parked alongside it, you'll know Fat is there."

Peeler nodded. They had been over this already.

"Now, you're a rich cotton merchant from Dallas. You've just bought a big ranch, and you need a bunch of horses for your hands to ride. You're puttin' all your trust in him to find you some."

Peeler mumbled impatiently, for he already had it memorized. "And my name is Smith."

"Smith, Jones . . . whatever you want it to be. Tell him you're willin' to pay up to a hundred dollars a head. No, better make it a hundred and twenty-five. Mr. Jenkins deserves some profit on this deal."

"And a little commission for you?"

"I don't care about any commission. I just want to see Fat Gervin get his comeuppance. We'll wait at Dutch Schneider's saloon. It's up to you to set the hook, then me and Mr. Jenkins'll try and pull in the fish."

Tommy, Snort and one vaquero pushed the horses through the open gate. Aparicio stood holding it, waiting for the automobiles to pass. Peeler drove through first, Alvin following. Aparicio closed the gate and set his mount into a lope to catch up.

Jenkins said, "If we put this over, I owe them boys a bottle of whiskey apiece. You too, Mr. Lawdermilk."

Hewey said, "Alvin has reformed. But I reckon he'd take a bottle and give it to his friends. How long've we been friends, Alvin?"

Alvin muttered some kind of reply. Hewey suspected his reformation had more to do with Cora than with health or religion.

Tommy and Snort took the lead, guiding the vaqueros to the Upton City wagon yard. Hewey told Alvin, "In case Fat might be lookin' out the window, maybe we ought to pull this car in on the back side of the barn."

Alvin remained far enough behind the remuda to avoid the dust. He stopped and let the motor run while the four riders penned the horses in a large lot. Hewey could not see the bank from here, which meant that Fat should not be able to see them, either. Alvin parked the car at the side of the large red barn.

Snort was explaining to the liveryman that the horses belonged to Mr. Jenkins of the J Bar at Alpine. Jenkins took over the negotiations. He said, "Just throw them a little hay. Not too much. They ain't worth much."

The liveryman grumbled, "Ain't no horses goin' to be worth much if everybody keeps buyin' them damned automobiles. Looks like I may have to turn this place into a garage."

Hewey heard a commotion in a corral back of the barn. Two men were trying to saddle a sorrel bronc, and it was giving them a fight. This was the kind of show Hewey had always enjoyed watching, but somehow it put a cold feeling in the pit of his stomach. He watched as one of the punchers eared the pony down and the other mounted. Turned loose, the bronc pitched hard. Hewey wanted to look away but could not. He seemed unable to move, fascinated like a bird watching a snake.

It became obvious that the rider would not remain in the saddle for long. Hewey held his breath. It seemed the cowboy was suspended in midair for a whole minute before he came down like a sack of bran. The sound of impact was physically painful to Hewey. He could not breathe until he saw the cowboy get up and dust himself off. At least he was not hurt.

Only then could Hewey bring himself to turn away, shaking as if a cold norther had just blown in.

Tommy asked, "You all right?"

"I'm fine. For a minute there it was like watchin' myself and that black stud. I used to love a good bronc ride. Now just watchin' it gave me a chill."

Alvin Lawdermilk said, "It's like I told you. You lose the ability, then you lose the want-to."

They walked out the front of the barn. At the far end of the street stood the bank. Peeler had parked Jenkins's car beside it.

Jenkins said, "Looks like we've got some time to kill. If you gentlemen won't mind, I'll set everybody up to a drink."

Snort said, "Bad as I hate to . . . the saloon's right down thisaway." He led out.

Aparicio had misgivings. "It may be that we are not welcome, Raul and me."

Some saloons did not allow Mexicans or blacks, but Hewey assured him, "Dutch Schneider ain't got an ounce of prejudice in his body." He looked at Tommy. "Except for underage boys. You'd best take you a sody water and stay real quiet."

Schneider came from behind the bar to shake hands with the men as Hewey introduced them. He was as cordial to the Mexicans as to Old Man Jenkins. He seemed surprised to see Alvin Lawdermilk. "It is a long time since you were here to visit me, Alvin."

"I took the pledge."

"That is good. How better it would be if more did the same." Though it went against the business he was in, Schneider could safely make that statement because the pledge was more often honored in the breach than in the keeping among male citizens of Upton City.

Schneider carried glasses and a bottle to a table large enough for all seven. Like Tommy, Alvin settled for a soda water. Cora should be proud of him, Hewey thought, though Old Lady Faversham would no doubt find fault somewhere. She would be terribly disappointed if she were someday to enter the pearly gates and find her son-in-law there ahead of her.

Snort was already on his third drink when a thin figure appeared in the doorway, stopping to squint and accustom his eyes to the darkness of the interior. C. C. Tarpley spotted Hewey and hollered from the door. "Hewey Calloway! I thought I saw you comin' into town a while ago." He strode with a strong step toward the table. His back was straight, his eyes alive and cheerful.

Hewey was taken aback. The last time he had seen C.C., the old man looked ready for the graveyard. Hewey stood up and extended his hand. "You're lookin' real good, C.C."

"I finally decided to take your advice. I went to Fort Worth and let a couple of doctors look me over from my head to my toenails. They said the only thing wrong with me is that I've got a stomach ulcer."

"That's all, an ulcer?"

"That's it. Said I been sittin' around worryin' too much instead of gettin' busy and grabbin' ahold. I need to cut out the whiskey and drink lots of milk. Trouble is, I've got five thousand cows on that ranch and not a one of them I could pen up and milk. You reckon Walter's got a Jersey cow he'd sell?"

"He's got a heifer fixin' to freshen. I'm sure he'd let you have her at a fair price."

"Price is no object, as long as it's not too high."

"I'm sure glad to hear the good news, C.C."

"I owe it all to you, Hewey. The doctors said if I'll take care of myself there's no reason I can't live another ten, maybe twenty years."

"I'll bet Fat was tickled to hear that."

The irony went over C.C.'s head. "Frank didn't seem as cheered up as I thought. I suspect he don't believe them doctors. He'll believe, though, when I grab ahold again out at the ranch, and I'm goin' to take a bigger hand in the bank, too."

"He'll be real tickled," Hewey said.

C.C. paid for a round of drinks for the crowd, though he did not take one for himself. "I'm headed for the ranch," he declared. "Ridin' out in Blue Hannigan's truck with a load of horse feed. There's a couple of Fat's hired hands badly in need of a firin', and I feel just good enough to do it."

He had been gone only a few minutes when Hewey heard an automobile pull up outside. Peeler walked in, pushing his goggles up. Hewey met him halfway. "How'd it go?"

Peeler looked as if he had won a big pot at poker. "If anybody asks you, you're addressin' Mr. Percival Smith, a rich cotton trader from Dallas, who's got more money than he knows what to do with and is willin' to spend a wad of it on horses."

Hewey asked, "You think Fat bit on it?"

"Ever watch a wolf grab a rabbit? I could see the cash register workin' in his eyes. I told him I'd find me a boardin'house and be around town for two or three days."

Hewey said, "We'd best give Fat a little time. If we go over and brace him too quick he's liable to smell a badger game."

Jenkins frowned in Snort Yarnell's direction, his voice a little sarcastic. "I don't suppose your friend Yarnell would object if I bought him another drink?" Snort was two drinks ahead of everybody else and working on another. "I'm gettin' curious. I wonder how much it'd take to fill him up?"

Peeler shook his head. "You don't want to find out."

Hewey's skin prickled with impatience, but he forced himself to wait for what he guessed was half an hour. Peeler still had half of his first and only drink, for he had to drive. Snort had drunk enough for Peeler's share and Alvin's as well. He seemed lost in a far-off solitary world of his own, half humming, half singing a raucous ditty that could get a Baptist thrown out of his church, though that was no hazard for Snort.

The song was happy, but Snort's expression was melancholy. Even with a crowd around him, Snort was somehow alone.

He was always alone, Hewey realized. He had lived his life that way, drifting like a cottonwood leaf on the vagaries of the wind. He reached out for friendship, yet always left for new country before people could come too close. He had many acquaintances but few real friends. It came to Hewey as a sudden revelation that Snort was getting old, too old to continue much longer the kind of life he had led. Hard as he might fight it, trying to live young and loud and reckless, the years were pressing down on him. One day he would look in a mirror and see himself as he truly was.

Perhaps he already had, and that was why he looked sad.

Maybe I ain't far behind you, Hewey thought. A chill ran through him, like the chill he had felt watching the bronc ride.

He asked Jenkins, "You ready to go take Fat's temperature?"

He looked back once at Snort before he left the saloon. Snort had his head down as if he were half asleep. He sat at the edge of the group, but his chair was pulled back a little, not quite in the circle with the others. He was talking to himself, talking about Grady Welch and the way he died. Nobody seemed to be listening to him.

Hewey and Jenkins crossed the street and walked toward the bank that had C. C. Tarpley's name prominently carved across its stone front. Blue Hannigan leaned against a truck parked a little short of the door, a load of feed stacked on its bed. As Hewey and Jenkins neared, Hannigan stepped free and held up his hand, gesturing for them to stop. He looked pleased.

"C.C. is readin' the gospel to Fat. You wouldn't want to disturb a good sermon."

Hewey heard Tarpley's voice inside, loud and commanding. "I'm fixin' to get to the bottom of this, Fat." He never called his son-in-law Fat to his face except when he was provoked. "Now, I want them books brought up-to-date, and I don't mean some time next week. I'll be back from the ranch tomorrow, and they'd better be ready."

Gervin's meek voice answered, "Yes, sir."

Tarpley burst out of the bank with a strong stride that said he was in full charge. He saw Hewey and Jenkins and seemed to feel that an explanation was in order. "Sometimes you've got to hit a mule over the head to get its attention. You-all got business in the bank?"

Hewey said, "We just need to talk to Fat about a horse."

"I don't think he knows which end eats grass, but I'll teach him if it takes me twenty years." He turned to Hannigan. "Ready to go, Blue?"

"Ready and rarin'." Hannigan winked at Hewey.

As the truck pulled away, Hewey said, "Now, that's the C.C. I used to know."

He motioned for Jenkins to precede him into the bank, which he thought was appropriate in view of the fact that Jenkins was much the oldest. It did not matter that he had the most money.

Fat Gervin sat at his desk, his head low. His chubby face was even redder than usual, for he had taken a dressing-down from his father-in-law in front of two harried, underpaid bank employees who probably enjoyed every minute of it. He looked like a man who had just been run over by a team of mules. Glancing up, he saw Hewey first.

"Hewey Calloway, what do you want?"

"I want to introduce you to Mr. Morgan Jenkins of Alpine, Texas.

He's the man who's fixin' to sue you for a hundred thousand dollars."

Jenkins suddenly had Gervin's full attention. "You the man I sold them horses to?"

Jenkins took a cue from Hewey and drew himself up like an officer commanding a firing squad. "I am, and I have come here for satisfaction."

"I sold you them horses in good faith. I don't see where you got anything to sue me for."

Hewey reminded him, "You said they came from Alvin Lawdermilk's ranch. All they did was cross over it."

"A technicality. I didn't claim that Alvin raised them."

Jenkins charged, "But you wrote the letter in such a way as to deliberately mislead me. It's a federal offense to use the mails to defraud. I intend to lodge a complaint with the post office. And sue you besides." He looked at Hewey. "For two hundred thousand dollars."

Hewey took pleasure in the old man's audacity. "You never saw so many lawyers in one bunch as Mr. Jenkins has got."

Cornered, Gervin turned both palms upward as if to say he was helpless. "I got troubles enough right here in the bank. Them horses are way out yonder at Alpine. I don't know what I can do."

Hewey said, "The horses are here, down at the wagon yard. We're givin' you a chance to buy them back before the lawyers get into it. You know what a mess they can make."

It took a moment for the information to soak in on Gervin. His expression made a gradual transition from despair to hope to greed. "They're here? Well, now, that does alter circumstances. It just so happens . . ." He caught himself and did not finish.

Hewey suspected he had been about to say he had a ready and willing buyer but realized that information was best kept to himself.

A calculating look came into Gervin's eyes. "I've always wanted to be fair. If I was to buy them ponies back from you for the same price you paid for them, that ought to set things right. It was fifty dollars a head, wasn't it?"

Jenkins said, "It was seventy-five, and you know it."

Reluctantly Gervin said, "Seventy-five, then."

"But I got a lot of labor and expense in them broncs, and a big doctor bill besides." He motioned toward Hewey. "One of them outlaws ran into a fence and broke its neck. It'll take a hundred a head to square the deal."

"How many head?"

"Seventeen. I sold two."

Gervin tried to look displeased, but his eyes gave him away. Peeler had told him he would pay a hundred and twenty-five dollars. Hewey could see him mentally multiplying twenty-five dollars times seventeen, his potential profit.

Hewey tried to do it himself and came up with four hundred and seventy-five. That didn't seem right, but he had rarely had occasion to tally up large sums.

Jenkins said, "Deal."

Gervin put down a satisfied smile. "I'll write you a check."

"No check. Cash."

Frowning over the imposition, Gervin walked into the open vault and returned with a handful of greenbacks. He counted out seventeen hundred dollars. "I'll want you to sign a receipt."

Jenkins counted the money for himself.

The teller moved up cautiously to Gervin's side. "You'll need to make a note for that cash, Mr. Gervin. Mr. Tarpley will insist on knowing where it went."

"I'll have the cash back in the vault long before he comes in tomorrow."

Jenkins said, "Mr. Gervin, I'll call off my lawyers. I'm glad we got our account settled."

"So am I. Come again."

Jenkins muttered, "When the sun rises up out of the west."

Walking back toward the saloon, Hewey said, "I guess I've settled my account with him too, as much as I ever will."

"I'd love to see his face when he goes lookin' for Peeler and can't find him."

Hewey smiled over an imagined confrontation. "Even more, I'd like to be there when he tries to account to C.C. for that seventeen hundred dollars."

"That would be a show worth stayin' for, but I'd best be gettin' out of town. When he catches on, he's liable to put the sheriff on me and Peeler."

"Wes Wheeler's the law. You don't need to worry about him."

Before they entered the saloon, Jenkins pulled out the roll of bills he had received from Gervin. "I wouldn't have got it done if it hadn't been for you, Hewey. I feel like I owe you a commission." He peeled off a hundred dollars, considered a moment, then said, "Aw, what the hell!" and peeled off a hundred more.

Hewey debated about accepting. "It was worth it to see Fat put up a tree." But he considered his financially embarrassed condition and took the money.

Jenkins said, "I'm still needin' a foreman for the Circle W. Looks to me like you're healed well enough to take on the job."

"I doubt I can do rough work anymore. I'll never wrestle wild cattle again. I won't be able to ride anything but gentle horses, and maybe not all of them, either."

"It's time you learn the difference between a cow*boy* and a cow-*man*. A foreman can point out what's to be done and let the younger hands do it. If he can't ride a horse, he can ride in a buggy. He uses his head and lets the others use their hands and their backs. You've got a head on your shoulders, Hewey. You showed that when you figured out how to snooker Fat Gervin."

Hewey rubbed his neck, wondering. He had never liked having to answer for anything or anybody except himself.

From inside the saloon came Snort's voice, telling again in painful, tearful detail all the facts about Grady Welch's sudden death and how hard it was to lose a good friend when he had so few. The words came slowly and badly slurred. Listening, Hewey felt the chill again.

He said, "I'm afraid Snort's pretty far gone."

Jenkins frowned. "He doesn't know where he's at or where he's goin'. I'd hate to see you wind up like him, Hewey. There's too many lost souls in this world already."

"I'll bet Snort would enjoy workin' at the Circle W."

"He's a good cowboy, but he's not foreman material. You could be."

Hewey reached deep inside for courage. "If I was to go, I'd want to take Snort with me. Aparicio, too. And I'd like to have Blas Villegas there to cook for the hands."

"Blas? The boys at the J Bar would kick like hell over losin' him. But all right, he's yours."

Something inside told Hewey to turn and run, but he stood his ground. "You sure you're ready to take a gamble on me?"

"If you're ready to take a gamble on yourself. Me; I think it's a cinch bet."

Hewey's hand trembled, for self-doubts remained strong, but he steadied it enough to hold it out and shake with Jenkins. "Deal."

Snort, Tommy and the Mexican hands had left their horses at the wagon yard. Hewey got the group together and started them walking in that direction, Tommy holding Snort's arm to keep him from weaving off into the street. A heavy figure moved ahead of them, also going toward the wagon yard. Fat Gervin was on his way to look at the horses he had bought, the ones he expected to turn a nice profit for him.

Jenkins climbed into his automobile while Peeler cranked the engine. Gervin turned to look as the car pulled away from the front of the saloon. He started to wave, but his hand froze in midair. Hewey wondered who he recognized first, Peeler or Jenkins, and how long it took him to realize they were working together.

Gervin staggered back a step. His body seemed to sag. He stared into the dust until the automobile passed out of sight around the livery barn. He slumped onto the edge of the wooden sidewalk, his arms hanging limp.

Most people called him Frank to his face. Only a few who had no tact or had nothing to lose called him Fat where he could hear it.

Walking by him, Hewey said, "It's been a pleasure to do business with you, Fat."

CHAPTER

14

Hewey had to pull his hat down tight to keep from losing it, for Alvin must have been driving all of twenty miles an hour. In an earlier time, Hewey might have suspected he had been drinking.

Alvin said, "It's been a good day." He knew Hewey had accepted Jenkins's offer. "I know you're anxious to tell Walter and Eve about it, but I need to go by my place first."

"The news'll keep, I guess." Hewey was still surprised at himself for accepting the job. Now he faced the awesome responsibility of living up to his promise.

Alvin said, "I suppose you've thought this all out and you're sure what you want to do?"

"Hell no, I ain't sure. The whole notion scares me plumb to death. The only thing I'm certain of is that I don't want to end up like Snort."

"Nobody ought to ever end up like Snort."

"I wonder what Spring . . . Miss Renfro'll think about me bucklin' down to be a foreman?"

"Only way to find out is to tell her."

Hewey chewed on his lip. "If all this had happened to me four years ago, things might've turned out different. I might not've gone off and left her."

"Maybe it's not too late."

"I'm afraid it may be. Farley Neal told me he was fixin' to ask her to marry him."

Alvin chewed on his thoughts for several silent moments. "How much money have you got, Hewey?"

"Mr. Jenkins gave me two hundred dollars. Except for what I had in my pocket, that's about it."

"Some people don't have near that much to start a new life on. Of course, a bachelor don't need much . . . a change of clothes now and again, a little tobacco and whiskey money." He gave Hewey a speculative look and nearly ran out of the road ruts. "A married man, now, that's different."

"It takes two to get married."

"And one of them has got to do the askin'." Alvin gave Hewey another long look and this time let the car run off into the pasture. He had to turn the wheel hard to pull back into the ruts. "The worst she can do is tell you no."

Hewey's mouth went dry, yet he felt cold sweat breaking on his face. "Farley Neal is the better man for her."

"I don't doubt that, but you'll never know for sure that he's her choice unless you ask her yourself."

"You think I've got a chance?"

"What would I know about women? I'm just an old horse and mule man."

Alvin scattered the peacocks as he drove into the yard. Old Lady Faversham sat in her wheelchair on the porch. She was shouting something at Alvin, but the engine noise drowned out the words, which Hewey considered a blessing. Dust drifted up onto the porch, and she raised a lace handkerchief to her face. Hewey looked for remorse in Alvin's pudgy face but saw no sign of it.

Cora came out onto the porch. Alvin said, "I'll bet Cora'll bake you a cake when she hears about your new job."

Hewey doubted he could eat it, as nervous as he felt. The sound of voices drew his attention toward the barn, where Farley Neal and Julio were hitching a raw team to a sledge for training to the harness. Hewey watched a minute, wondering if Farley had asked her yet. "That's a good man yonder."

"Yes, and so are you, Hewey. If you're goin' to ask her, be damned certain you mean it this time. Be sure you won't be changin' your mind again and ridin' away without her."

Hewey walked up the steps, taking off his hat for Cora and nodding a silent greeting to Mrs. Faversham. Cora responded with warmth, but her mother only stared. He asked, "Is Spring here?"

Cora said, "She's in the parlor, Hewey. I'll take you."

Alvin caught his wife's arm. "Hewey knows the way."

Hewey opened the screen door and walked into the hall. The parlor was to the right, but he hesitated, twisting his hat out of shape in an effort to calm his shaking hands. He swallowed hard and entered the room. Spring sat with hoop and needles, crocheting. She smiled. "Hello, Hewey. Did you accomplish what you set out to do?"

"Better than we had any reason to hope. I doubt that Fat Gervin gets any sleep tonight."

"Nothing can pay for the harm he's caused you."

"What's done can't be undone. I've made up my mind to live with it and do the best I can."

"You'll do fine. You always did, after your fashion."

"Gettin' hurt myself has made me realize the hurt I caused you a long time ago. I wish I could undo that."

"As you said, what's done can't be undone."

"Just the same, if we'd married like we planned, look where we'd be now. We'd have us a farm of our own. We'd be somebody."

"And you'd be miserable, trying to make a farmer of yourself. You were a cowboy. You still are."

"That black bronc fixed it to where I can't be the kind of cowboy I was. But I'm about to try my hand at bein' a foreman. It pays better, even if it ain't as much fun." He told her about accepting the offer from Morgan Jenkins.

She said, "You can do it if you set your mind on it."

"The Circle W's a pretty place, in a wide valley with mountains all around . . . about the smilin'est country I ever saw. I wish you could see it."

She put down the crochet work. "That sounds like an invitation."

Flustered, he said, "I guess it is." He searched her face for a sign of acceptance but did not see it. He felt as if the floor were sagging beneath his feet. His weakened leg must be giving way, he thought.

She said, "If I didn't know you better, I might even think it was a proposal."

He meant it to be, in his own awkward way. He waited for her to say more, but she did not. She turned her eyes away from him. Disheartened, he took that for an answer.

He said, "All the way from town I wondered how I could get up the nerve to ask you, and I've done a poor job of it. I'm just a stove-up cowpuncher workin' for wages. You'll be a lot better off with Farley Neal." Breath came hard, for his throat had tightened to the point of choking him. Turning, he walked out the door to the hallway, then onto the porch.

Alvin and Cora looked at him in surprise over his quick retreat. Twisting the hat in his hands again, Hewey said, "Alvin, if you don't mind, I wish you'd take me over to Walter's right now."

Disappointment came into Alvin's eyes. "Sure, if that's what you want." He turned to Cora. "I may be late for supper."

Hewey walked to the car, his head down. He heard Old Lady Faversham say with satisfaction, "Good riddance if you ask me." He felt his eyes burn.

Footsteps told him Alvin was coming, so he opened the car door and took his seat.

He was startled by Spring's voice. "You didn't give me time to answer." She was standing beside the automobile.

"You didn't have to say anything. I saw the answer in your eyes."

"If you thought you saw doubt there, you were right. I haven't forgotten how close we came once, and how hard it was to see you leave. I wouldn't want to go through that again."

"With Farley, you won't have to."

"He asked me, and I told him no. I like Farley very much, but I don't love him."

Hewey took a deep breath. "You don't?"

"I've loved only two men in my life. One went to the war in Cuba and died. The other . . . just went. How do I know you wouldn't go again, Hewey?"

"I'm four years older, and I hope I'm four years smarter. I went off the last time lookin' for somethin' . . . I didn't know what."

"But you didn't find it?"

"If it was ever there, it's gone."

"What if some morning you wake up and the wind calls you, and you decide to go again?"

"I'm not claimin' it'll be easy. There'll be times it'll be tough. I'm liable to need help."

"You'll have Snort Yarnell."

"Most of the time Snort doesn't even know how to help himself. If you'll go with me, Spring, I'll never leave you again. Never."

Eyes shining, she reached over and clasped her fingers around his hand. "Then tell me about that smiling country."

He got out of the car and took her in his arms.

On the porch Old Lady Faversham cried, "Cora, do somethin'. A fox is loose amongst the chickens!"

Preacher Averill closed the Bible and smiled. "What the Lord hath joined together, let no man put asunder. Now, Hewey, you may kiss the bride. And if you don't, I'm fixin' to."

The wedding ceremony was conducted on the big porch of the Lawdermilk house to accommodate as many as possible of the couple's family and friends. A considerable overflow watched from the yard. About the only person Hewey could think of who had not shown up for the event, other than Fat Gervin, was Old Lady Faversham. Alvin said she was in her room, down with the vapors.

Music from Cora's piano came through the open parlor windows, and a gentle south breeze brought the pleasant prospect of barbecue from an open pit which Julio Valdez tended past the yard fence.

Though it was custom and his right, Hewey was shy about kissing Spring in front of so many, so he gave her a quick peck and an unspoken promise of better when nobody was watching.

Alvin was first in line to kiss the bride and pump Hewey's hand. Walter and Eve were next. Eve hugged Spring, then Hewey. She said in a shaky voice, "I'd almost come to the givin'-up point. This goes to show the power of prayer." Tommy was behind his parents, followed by Blue Hannigan and his wife.

Snort Yarnell kept almost at arm's length from Spring, taking her hand cautiously as if it were an eggshell. Eyes sorrowful, he turned to Hewey. "I never thought you'd do it, old pardner. First Old Grady and now you."

"But I ain't dead."

Snort cast a furtive glance back at Spring. "You might as well be. Things ain't goin' to be the same."

"Everything changes. You know you've got a job with me out yonder in the mountains."

"I'll be there. Got to go get a little drunk first, and I sure do dread it."

C. C. Tarpley had a strong grip for a man so recently given up to die. "Hewey, I owe you more than I can ever pay, but I brought you a gift." He handed Hewey a pocket watch. "Bought it in Midland. Cost me three dollars."

"You're a way too generous, C.C. I don't know what to say."

"Ain't no need to say anything. I've carried it myself for the past year or so. It keeps good time."

Merchant Pierson Phelps and Dutch Schneider had come out from town together. Phelps gave Spring a bolt of fine cloth, enough to make several dresses. Schneider brought a bottle of champagne. "Save it for when it is just the two of you alone."

Sheriff Wes Wheeler did not kiss the bride, but he took off his hat and bowed as he squeezed her fingers. "I hope, ma'am, that you can keep him out of jail."

"I shall make every effort, Mr. Wheeler. Between Mr. Jenkins and myself, we'll try to keep him too busy to get into any trouble."

Morgan Jenkins and his driver came along in their turn. Jenkins said, "Sorry I can't stay for the barbecue and other doin's, Hewey, but me and Peeler have got to get started if we're to make Alpine by dark." He pointed toward a new black buggy beside the picket fence. "That's yours to use on the ranch, but don't feel like you've got to be in any hurry about gettin' there. The day after tomorrow would be soon enough." He reconsidered. "Aw, take a little longer if you want to. Them cattle won't be runnin' off."

Alvin Lawdermilk had given the couple a pair of matched grays for the buggy. They trotted westward along the wagon road at an easy pace. Hewey said, "I thought we'd make camp at the Pecos River tonight."

He and Spring had spent their wedding night at the Lawdermilks', a poor place for privacy, especially when it seemed half the men in Upton County showed up to steal the bride and then give the couple a joyous and noisy shivaree that lasted until almost daylight. There had seemed little point in going to bed, and Hewey had not.

He held the reins in his right hand and took Spring's hand in his left. "Every time I saw you, I wanted to ask you to take me back, but I was scared to death you'd turn me down. I was ready to promise you just about anything."

"And I was afraid you were going to ask me and I couldn't say no 'til you *did* promise me just about everything."

"We've got a lot of lost time to make up for."

"We have the rest of our lives to do it."

"I feel kind of bad about Farley Neal, though."

"He's a fine man. He'll find someone, or someone will find him."

Jenkins and Peeler had taken most of Spring's boxes and her trunk in their automobile, leaving only the immediate necessities to be carried in the buggy. Hewey glanced at a basket just behind the seat. "Cora put enough barbecue and fried chicken in there to last us a week if we decided to stretch the trip that long."

Spring leaned to kiss him, her lips soft and warm. She rested her head against his shoulder and said, "We've spent four years getting this far. I'm not in a hurry to reach the ranch."

He put his injured left arm around her. It did not even hurt. "I'm not either," he said, and pulled the team down to a walk.